The Count

A horror novel

David-Jack Fletcher

SLASHIC HORROR
PRESS

Other titles by David-Jack Fletcher

The Haunting of Harry Peck
PL8ES
Raven's Creek

SLASHIC HORROR
PRESS

Originally published in Australia by Slashic Horror Press in 2024.

ISBN-13: 978-0-6457638-8-1
Cover design by Greg Chapman
Interior design by David-Jack Fletcher
Edited by David-Jack Fletcher

For my beautiful Paul. My husband, my best friend. My love.

Prologue

The razor blade glinted under the glow of the moon. A shallow yellow light emanated across the living room as Kath pressed the metal into her skin. She paused, the blade firm on her wrist, and clenched her teeth. She stood leaning against a wall in her living room, keeping an eye on the space where it would appear. Where it always appeared.

Digging deep, Kath bit her tongue. *Up, not across. I can't afford to fuck this up.* She looked around, trembling, and shrugged off the eyes she felt on her.

Eyes she'd never seen.

Eyes that knew her better than she knew herself.

Eyes that would watch her take her own life.

Digging deeper still, Kath let out a scream and drew the blade up her forearm, severing veins and tendons as she went. The impulse to stop, to avoid the pain, was strong, and her survival instinct pounded against her brain. But she couldn't stop. Not now. Not with the eyes on her.

Her grip wavered under the pain, streams of crimson pouring to the floorboards beneath her. As the blood dripped to the floor with a dull slap, the house around her groaned. The ticking began. It drummed through her ears, drowning out all other sounds.

"Fuck you!" Kath screamed, and tightened her grip on the razor blade. She looked at her arm for a moment, a river of red pouring from her pale skin. "It's not enough."

Passing the blade to her other hand, it almost slipped. Her grip weak. She'd severed the connections that made her hand function. She thought fast, dropping backward to the floor. The upper inner thigh was a good place, too. She could get more blood that way.

Her good hand started to tremble, and Kath hovered the blade over her left thigh. The house groaned again and the door leading to the backyard began to slam over and over and over. No wind. No breeze. The house was doing it.

Kath smiled, despite the pain and the blood loss and the fact she was about to die. "Got you worried, huh?"

The door slammed again. Kath nodded to herself, the bang of wood against wood a clear enough answer for her. She was hurting the house. The more she destroyed herself, the more she destroyed *the house*.

Tick, tick, tick. The ticking emanated through the house, in sync with her failing heart.

Slashing at her thighs, Kath groaned. Not strong enough to scream. Blood spilled to the ground, a pool of hot red coalescing around her backside, drenching her clothes. She stabbed at herself again and again, each attack less vicious than the one before, but just as purposeful. Strength drained from her, but the need to destroy the house plunged her hand into repeated action. She stabbed and stabbed until she was sure the veins and arteries had been sliced open.

The razor clanked to the floor, and she rested against the wall. Her legs stretched out before her, her sliced arm lazing against the wooden floorboards. Kath's gaze shifted to her only working limb, blinking through a blood-induced haze to see the ticking hands of her watch.

23:57.

Three minutes, you motherfucker.

Her eyes shifted to the spot where it had first appeared. Where she knew it would appear now.

The door.

Tick. Tick. Tick. The noise, the pulsating rhythm from beyond the door, was deafening.

That fucking door. She wished she'd never opened it, never ventured inside. But it was phasing in again now. As the house groaned deeper, the foundations shifting in the earth below, a thought occurred to her.

Dying isn't enough. The house could find someone else. *But if I die inside the room...* The door might close forever. There would be nobody to take care of the house. The house will die, too.

She had three minutes before the door would disappear again.

Tick tick tick. It was inside her now.

Kath dragged herself across the floorboards, toward the door, smears of blood trailing across the wood. With the use of only one arm, her task was difficult. She pulled at her own weight, gritting her teeth to find the energy to move.

The door was fading from view. She knew reaching it was her only chance. She had to seal it forever. Make the house die with her.

Her eyelids fluttered for a moment too long, strength dwindling. Kath pushed through the exhaustion, clawing at the floorboards with all her might. She couldn't feel her legs, drained of all that gave them life. They were hollow stumps, dead weight. She fought the heaviness of her body, had to keep moving. Pulling along the floor, her sliced forearms and thighs continued to leak. Through her haze, Kath saw the blood sink into the floor, and grimaced.

Keep trying to eat me, you fucker. It won't buy much time.

Tick. She felt the rhythm of the *tick tick tick* moving through her emptying veins.

It had been a good idea at the time. Threaten the house by removing its only source of energy. Kath hadn't expected it to hurt so much.

Should have waited till I was in the room. Fucking idiot.

The door was just in reach. Kath breathed hard as she lifted her upper body onto her elbow. Sweat poured from her hairline. Her vision grew blurrier with each passing tick of the house. She didn't have long. Her life force was mostly on the floor behind her.

In one swift move, Kath fell to her belly and lifted her arm with all her might. Grabbed the door handle. Twisted. Her hand slipped, slick with red. She tried again, gritting her teeth. Twisted. Pushed it open. She exhaled what felt like the last breath in her body, and Kath rested for a moment.

The house groaned again, and the walls bent in on themselves, shuddering. Sagging at the cornices. Paint running down the walls. That was her evidence she was making the right choice.

Groaning once more, Kath dragged herself through the door, and into a long tunnel. The ticking stopped. The silence reminded Kath of the months of isolation she'd spent in there. But it also reminded her she was alive.

She lifted her arm to check her watch. 23:59. Less than a minute before the door would vanish, along with everything—*everyone*—in it. As the seconds passed, Kath maneuvered her elbow to the door and jabbed at it. The door swung closed with a creak. She didn't even take one last look at the outside world.

Kath closed her eyes, letting the last of her blood drizzle into the floor. Feeding the house one more time before they both exited the world.

Shelley grimaced at the smell. Not because she didn't like it, rather because she didn't hate it. Psychologists would have had a field day with her. Once, in her teens, her parents had ordered her to therapy after finding her squeezing blood from a used tampon, though her mother had a wistful expression at the time—they never did talk about that, but Shelley always remembered. That psychologist had used the phrase 'bloodlust'. It appealed to her, and the desire for the scent of blood—her own, other people's, whatever—had only deepened. That's what worried her.

Now, as she walked through the derelict house, the air was thick with blood. Kath had been a good tenant. It was a shame to see her go. A bigger shame was *how* she went.

Poor thing. Shelley frowned.

She wore thick rubber gloves, the only kind for the type of job required here. Cleaning supplies were on the bench for her already. Shelley had long ago stopped asking where the materials came from. Just accepted they were there when she needed them.

Like a miracle.

Deep down, Shelley knew what went on in this house was no miracle, but it helped to think of things in less terrifying ways than the reality.

Sizing up the damage, Shelley sighed and got to work. The bloodstains on the floor, that was where she'd start. Moving to the living room, the gallons of blood Kath had spilled were seeping through the floor into the basement.

Please don't tell me I have to go into the basement.

The last time she'd been down there, Shelley lost time. There was no other way to describe it. Something had happened down there, that much she knew. But her memory was gone from the time she stepped over the threshold and into the basement, to the time she woke up in the living room upstairs with cuts on her arms and face. She'd licked the blood from her own forearms only to realize she tasted different. Her blood wasn't as sweet as it should have been.

Shelley tried to forget the other thing she'd woken up with. Couldn't think about that now. Instead, she grabbed a mop and started cleaning. The memories of that day came flooding back. Each splash of the mop against wood sent shivers up her spine. Shelley breathed hard and centered herself, licking her lips.

Whenever her brain turned on her, as it was doing now, Shelley conjured a tune. Among her favorites was an old theme song from *The Munsters*. Recalling it now, she began to whistle, the sharp sound filling the room.

Blood was a funny thing to clean. It was gooey, but also seemed to want to move. A sickly-sweet scent wafted up, brushing against the thin strands of hair inside her nostrils. She sneezed at the tickle and sniffed again. Clearing her nose, Shelley stared into the blood, her skin crawling with goose-bumps at the tints and shades within. It was incredible how the same blood could hold different colors depending on how the light hit it. The blackened, congealed parts—like a scab over a wound—had the sweetest smell. She gripped some of the drying substance between her thumb and forefinger, and rubbed, letting out a soft, "Mmmm." She held her fingers to her nose and sniffed again, daring herself to taste.

Don't do it, Shelley.

Instead, she wiped at the blood with the mop. Smearing it among the soapy water, Shelley licked her lips again. Tasting through her nose—the only way allowed. A few more strokes with the mop and the blood would be just a memory.

Shelley squeezed the red and brown water into the bucket and slapped the mop against the floorboards again. Just as she heaved with her elbows and shoulders, the room darkened. She stopped whistling and looked around. Peered out the window to see if the sun had gone behind the clouds.

Seeing that the sun was loud and proud in the sky, not a cloud to be seen, Shelley dropped the mop.

It's starting.

Taking a deep breath, she whistled again, her lips dry once more. Licking over and over, they felt cracked and old. The room darkened, shrouding the mop and bucket—and blood stains—in a shadow of gray.

As the light continued to drain from the room, Shelley heard a creak from behind her. Spinning to face the sound, she saw it.

The door.

A fracture in reality, that's what she called it.

The last of the light was sucked from the room and Shelley put her hands to her ears. She knew what came next. Even with her hands pushing against her skull, the *tick tick tick* coming from beyond the door shook her to her core.

Tick.

Her breaths became slow, stagnant. She strained her eyes in the darkness to see the door. A tiny thing, impossibly tiny. The *tick* came again, calling to her.

Shelley walked toward the door as it opened wider, the high-pitched creak an invitation. She'd been here before, though. Knew the intoxicating call of the clock.

Tick.

Shaking her head, Shelley pressed her hands harder to her ears until the sounds were obscured.

Tick.

"No," she said to the empty room. "Not this time."

She stepped back and turned away from the door. Her body shook, wanting to go inside. Wanting to see the clock. But her mind knew it wasn't what it appeared. Through the darkness, Shelley peered through the living room.

The rug. It was always there, every time.

With her legs trembling under her, Shelley raced to the rug, her hands falling from her ears, and picked it up. The ticking flooded inside her, filling her ears so she could hear nothing else. Her heart beat fast and heavy, she felt it in her throat, but the pulsating rhythm was absent.

Flinging the rug over the blood stains, Shelley picked up the mop and bucket, letting water splash across the floorboards, and bolted for the front door. The bang of it slamming sent chills down Shelley's spine. She ran to her car, threw the cleaning supplies into the back seat, and raced to the driver's door.

The bucket tipped over, lines of water trickling down the rear windows onto the upholstery. Shelley climbed into the car, thankful for the smell of soap and suds and blood. Thankful for the uncontrollable trembling in her fingers as she gripped the steering wheel.

Thankful for the sound of her beating heart.

"I need to get a new job," she whispered, and the ticking faded to a dull memory.

Part One

Part One

Chapter 1

Its uneven foundations tilted at an odd angle—almost like it should collapse or sink into the foundations. Giant windows to either side of the front door were like eyes from a 70s horror flick. He wondered how many people had died inside. But circumstances being what they were, Sam had little choice. Rental prices were skyrocketing all over the country, and unless he wanted to share with strangers, this would have to do.

Walking up the stone driveway, shards of rock stabbing at the soles of his shoes, Sam eyed the property. The house was a traditional gun-barrel design, and he saw life in its bones. Like it was a giant monster, the front door its mouth, the belly somewhere deep inside. The gardens sitting below the windows were like eyeliner. Black, rotten plants withering in the afternoon breeze. A detached garage was to the left of the house, like an amputated limb, and he wanted to put it back together.

He stroked hair out of his face and took a deep breath, expecting to suck in mouthfuls of detritus and loose dirt. But the air was sweet and inviting, caressing his skin like an old lover. Despite the outward appearance, the online photos of the interior weren't half bad, and Sam had decided to apply. The rental cost was low compared to the daylight robbery of others in the area, and he'd seen enough horror movies to be suspicious.

Despite the chills, standing at the house now, Sam felt something. The depressing lean of the structure, the sad windows and dead plants, seemed to invite him in. Something about the house spoke to him. Like he was *supposed* to be here. Besides, the feeling of the place wasn't so bad, now that he was here. Sometimes when he walked into a friend's house, he'd be overcome with emotion, sensing the energy bouncing off the walls. He could tell if it was a happy home or not. He'd almost cried when stepping into his father's new house after his mother passed away. The bleak energy, the emptiness of the walls, the way their hollowed voices echoed off the white surfaces.

I miss you, Dad.

This house, though... He had a feeling the deteriorated building with a creep factor of a hundred would be good for him. Like he'd be comfortable here for a long time. This house was a home.

When he got to the front door, Sam peered into the adjacent window. The guttering bent down toward the slanted glass like a frowning eyebrow. Freckles of brown and black mold smattered the corners of the pane, and a stain in the center of the window reminded Sam of a cataract.

His heart caught in his throat for a moment as the window seemed to look back at him. The sadness. The loneliness. A reflection of himself.

He gripped the rusted, bronze door handle and jimmied the key in the lock. It turned like wheels over gravel, sending shivers up Sam's spine as he forced the door open. A gust of hot air blew through the entranceway.

It's saying hello. Sam smiled. "Hello," he whispered, and felt ridiculous for doing so.

As if in reply, the hallway floorboards shifted and creaked. He smiled again, feeling that this house was indeed a friend. Damaged and decrepit on the outside, but warm and inviting on the inside.

Like me.

The scar traveling the length of his left cheekbone had been a deterrent for his peers since he'd injured himself at age four. Thinking back on it, Sam wondered if it was the scar that put people off, or the stories he'd told his classmates in school.

Once, when I was a baby, a man with a hook for a hand tried to kill me. He got the hook into my cheek, right here, see it? But my mom fought him off. Chopped his head off with an ax. So she says...

A few months back, at summer camp, a spirit rose from the lake and went on a revenge spree. I escaped with this scar...

At my fifth birthday, the clown my parents hired went psycho. He ripped into my face with a meat cleaver...

He had a new story each time someone asked, because the truth was too embarrassing. The damage was done, though, both to his face and to his relationships.

The stories I could tell about this place.

Standing just inside the doorway, he remembered he really only had one friend. The one person Sam could always count on, unlike the other neighborhood kids, or "crews" as 90s lingo called them. Patrick was his crew. Always had been. Always would be.

Walking down the hallway, gliding his fingers along the dusty walls, and gazing into the main living area, Sam pictured where his furniture might go. Where Patrick might sit while they listened to music or watched movies. It was a ritual they'd had since forever. Except instead of trawling through the horror aisles in Blockbuster, they now just scrolled through streaming services, eating popcorn before they'd selected a movie. At least now he didn't have to pretend to shut his eyes at Bela Lugosi's vampire.

Patrick would be coming along soon to help with the move, and as Sam leaned against the kitchen counter, rotting at the corners, he was grateful for the help. The realtor, or the owner—or whoever—hadn't bothered with fresh paint or dusting. Or anything.

Even though the crevices were dripping with water from the attic and there were spots of red all over the floorboards, Sam could see the potential. A stream of light cast shadows across the rear wall, by the back door. There was a patch of grass out there, though the realtor had said not to walk on it. Hadn't said why. Sam didn't care—sunshine hurt his eyes, and fresh air sometimes felt toxic.

The house felt like an extension of himself already. The dank, damp smell of years-old wood and plasterboard. The spots of red looked thick, like paint dripped from a brush.

Was the previous tenant an artist?

He considered this thought while inspecting a trail of red leading to the living room. The sweet smell lingering on the air outside came again as Sam approached an old rug. He hadn't noticed it earlier, and frowned.

The rug was askew, a fold at one end as though someone had moved it in a hurry. Kneeling over, Sam lifted the rug. Smears of red, like broad brush strokes underneath. Some looked faded, others were darker and more recent.

Just as with his broken heart, he knew with some time and care the place would be perfect again. To him, the

17

red markings were a symptom of the house's pain. It had suffered, just like he had. Sam pressed his fingers into the reddened floorboards.

"We both have scars." His voice echoed through the emptiness. Not in the same way as in his father's house, where it was cold and hollow. Here, the emptiness was a sign of promise.

A soft whistle—from a crack in the roof—felt like the house communicating with him. He couldn't make out the message.

Checking his watch, he realized just how early he'd been. The moving van was due in an hour, and Patrick around the same time. So, he went back to his car and ruffled through the trunk for a box. Finding the one he wanted, Sam traipsed back to the house with a half smile and set the box on the kitchen bench.

Graphic novels.

Sam had once been deep into a subreddit about the differences between comics and graphic novels. He'd argued back and forth with *comics4life* for hours about the nuances of the graphic novel. Patrick reminded him it didn't matter and that *comics4life* was probably a pimply thirteen-year-old just discovering what penises can do.

Sifting through the volumes of graphic novels, Sam lifted out the latest *30 Days of Night* installment, flipping the pages with care. His rules with a graphic novel were to never bend the pages, never get oily finger smears on them, and never crease the spine. There was no interest in selling them later or anything, it was more just that Sam had been caught with a mild case of obsessive-compulsive disorder. Some with the affliction would say things five times, others repeat a process until it was perfect.

Patrick would line his socks according to size, color, *and* crease. So, the line would change depending on how many times a particular sock had been worn. This, to Sam, was nuts. In comparison, his little clean-freak demeanor was perfectly acceptable.

Just as blood-drenched teeth tore across the page, the creature biting down on another human victim, Sam's phone beeped. Another of his oddities, he always used the native ringtones on his iPhone. He felt a sense of loyalty toward the phone, almost like the sounds were part of its identity.

One beep meant a text message. Although it would wait inside his phone forever, until he deemed it necessary to be viewed, Sam checked his messages straight away. It was as though the fact that he knew he had a message meant the person sending it knew he'd seen the notification. Like he had a responsibility toward not just the sender, but to the message, as well.

Resurfacing into reality from the depths of his graphic novel, Sam looked at the screen. Taking a breath, he hoped it wasn't from his ex. Lighting the screen, Sam sighed.

PATRICK

Be there in ten xx

Further to his sock habits, Patrick was a stickler for time. So, ten minutes meant ten minutes. Give or take a set of red lights or two. Sam took another breath, tight in the chest. Looking around, he realized he'd been reading *30 Days of Night* at the kitchen bench, standing in the emptiness of the new house without a sense of time passing.

Sam flipped through another few pages before packing the issue away. Just as he closed the box, tires crunched against the gravel outside. The beep-beep of the horn informed Sam that Patrick had arrived.

This is it. A new beginning.

Patrick knocked on the front door. The sound echoed through Sam's realization that his new life was here. He took one more deep breath and clutched his chest. It was tight, like fingers squeezing his heart. Ignoring the anxiety, Sam walked to the door, opening it to the only person he trusted.

Patrick Woodrow Griffin. His name sort of said it all, the sock thing being secondary to his more obvious quirks. The pink-rimmed glasses, the bow tie, the incredible amount of orange freckles all over his face and arms. He loved overalls for some reason, perhaps even unknown to himself, and he wore them every day of his adult life. Patrick's teeth were a little bent inward and yellowed from a teen smoking habit, but he didn't let that stop him from beaming ear to ear. All day, every day.

He was perhaps the most secure person Sam had ever met. Except for the socks, which they didn't talk about. At least, if they could both help it. They had the sort of friendship where talking was optional. There was no obligatory, "Hello", no solemn goodbyes on departure, no awkward silences when there was nothing to be said. Observers had often paired them as lovers, which at times, made Patrick adjust his bow tie. To Sam, Patrick would have been the perfect partner, but the dynamic had never flowed that way. It was too soon, anyway. As Patrick entered the house, letting out an eager whistle and a nod as his eyes scanned the place, not a word was spoken.

Sam followed his friend down the hallway to the kitchen, where Patrick picked at the rotting bench. Even then, not a frown. He turned to Sam and spread his arms for a hug. Sam went to him, letting the warmth of Patrick's arms and chest envelop him.

"This place is *so* you." Patrick giggled after a moment.

"I know." Sam withdrew from Patrick's embrace and the pair stood facing each other. "It really suits me."

Nodding, Patrick's eyes scanned, and Sam knew he was plotting the furniture setting. Sam sighed, looking at his phone again. Time felt strange in this house, though he couldn't finger why. Patrick had arrived only minutes earlier, but it felt like half the day had passed.

"He's not going to text," Patrick said, nodding at the phone.

"What do you mean?" Sam shoved the device into his back pocket.

"I mean," Patrick replied, "you look at your phone every few minutes. Danny's gone. I'm sorry."

Sam bit his lip. "It's only been a week. He might still—"

"No, Sam." Patrick raised an eyebrow. "He won't."

"Do you know who…" Sam let the question disappear into the room, and Patrick shook his head.

"Sorry," he said. "I just know they've been seeing each other for ages. Danny was pretty clear on that when I blasted him down the phone yesterday."

Sam perked up with a half smile. "You did?"

Patrick ignored him and turned his attention to the box of graphic novels. "Of course this is the first thing you grab." His eyes shifted back to Sam. "Your dad coming?"

Sam frowned and rifled through the box. Patrick folded his arms and looked at the floor. "What is that?" He motioned to the red marks.

Shrugging, Sam pointed to the rug. "I *think* it's paint. There's some under there, too."

"It looks more like blood." Patrick inspected closer, his eternal smile flickering for just a moment.

"Why would it be blood?"

Patrick shrugged. "Murder house." He beamed, adjusting his bow tie. "Awesome." He continued peering around the house, grimacing and wiping his hands across the walls and the kitchen bench. The surface was sticky, grimy, patches of something dark melted to the counterfeit marble. Remnants of the last tenant. The grime was on the walls, too, near the floor. Like a mold, crawling from the crevices of the wood. When he looked harder, the mold took a new shape: tendrils, vines, creeping through the floorboards.

Patrick eyed Sam, siphoning through boxes and emptying their contents without anywhere to put the items. His lips were curled in a smile, but his eyes told a different story. Empty, hollow. The eyes of someone trying to be happy.

"Have you noticed these walls?" Patrick asked, pointing to the mold. "I feel like this is a health hazard."

Following Patrick's finger, Sam shook his head. "I don't see anything."

"Murder house," Patrick said again, swallowing hard. The mold climbed up the wall in his direction—just an inch—and a coldness washed over him. "Awesome."

Chapter 2

A slight breeze drifted across Sam's face as he stepped outside. A layer of clouds blanketed the sky, but as Sam peered into them, his heart clenched. The serenity of the clouds, like fluffy white rabbit tails, and the wind caressing his skin, felt like a veil. Like the calm before the storm. Sam couldn't breathe.

Patrick glanced at him and rested a gentle hand on Sam's back. "It's okay, Sammy. It's just the nerves."

Sam nodded, letting Patrick's circular back rubs sink into him. They continued in silence for a few moments until the moving truck chugged around the corner and reversed into the drive in a plume of black gas.

Coughing as one, Sam and Patrick covered their mouths. Sam waved with the other hand. The driver stuck an arm out the window and waved in response. Sam smiled and gave Patrick a side glance. The truck stopped with a squeak, the brakes in need of a service, and an older, gray-haired, bearded man jumped out.

"One of you fellas Sam?" His shirt was stained with sweat, despite the cool weather.

Sam gulped. "That's me."

A hand shot out—the fingers a little pruned and wrinkled—the driver winking a smile. "Pete. Good to meet you." They shook for a brief moment and Pete turned his attention from Sam's scar to the house. Wiping grayed hair from his sweaty face, he continued with a nod. "This the Amityville place or something?"

"What do you mean?" Sam asked, as Patrick giggled under his breath at the joke. "I know the movie, but why would you say that?"

Pete shrugged. "Just a joke, kid. Looks a bit...haunted is all."

Letting out a deep sigh, Sam managed a smile and nodded.

"Well, uh, Jimmy's still in the truck talking to this week's bang. I'll give her the hard word and we can get started moving you in." Pete disappeared around the passenger side of the truck, smacking it with an open palm on his way.

Sam turned to Patrick. "What did he mean about Amityville?"

Smiling, Patrick patted Sam's back once more. "Are you kidding? Look at this place. There's a reason the rent is so cheap. I mean, all that mold…"

"What mold?" A woman's voice.

Sam and Patrick turned to face her. Probably early-twenties, wearing the same shirt design as Pete. Short, curly brown hair to her shoulders and a mole taking pride of place on her chin.

"Uh." Sam blinked. "In the house…"

"Oh yeah." She smiled, an appreciation in her eyes. "Everyone knows this place is haunted." She looked at the men before her, both eyebrows raised in confusion. "Oh, shit. I'm Jimmy. What happened to your face, man?"

Patrick wiped a hand on his overalls, then held it out. Jimmy grabbed at it like it was going to run away. Shook it hard. Sam gave a shy wave, tracing the scar with his forefinger.

"Jimmy, quit fucking around." Pete opened the truck doors and climbed in. "We're here to work, not piss about."

Jimmy rolled her eyes and mimicked Pete as he spoke. Turned away from Sam and Patrick and got to work. The truck had been packed so that big items were first out—fridge, lounges, bedroom furniture—and the moving pair heaved down the living room couch to take inside.

The house felt cozier with Sam's belongings, even if most of them were still in boxes. He found a box marked "Kitchen" and started unpacking. As Pete and Jimmy argued over how to get something through the front door, Patrick sat cross-legged in the small dining area, looking through boxes to unpack. He took out his phone and launched the music app, selecting a playlist he'd curated for the occasion, titled "Moving Day Hits". A collection of theme songs from the greatest horror movies of all time.

Grabbing at a set of bubble-wrapped knives, Sam let the theme tune to *Psycho* settle in his ears and began picking at the tape with his fingernails. He breathed hard when he'd spun the roll around twice without finding the end. The irony was that he wished he had a knife to slice straight through. Wiping at his face, Sam calmed himself, and tried again, managing to unwind the packing tape. The thin, brown plastic—sticky and warm from the congested heat in the box—had been wound around the bubble wrap a few times for safety.

As the tape came away—the low, tearing sound pulling at his anxieties of the break-up—Sam noticed the glint in the knives. The blades, shining at him. *Psycho*'s high-pitched violin chords slashed through the kitchen and the blades glinted again.

Sam took one of the knives by the handle. A blunt butter knife. But the blade shone in his eyes. He couldn't look away.

Tick.

The music disappeared. The room around him vanished. All that remained was him and the knife. He stared

27

at the blade. It stared back. Wanting something from him. Inviting him to…

"Sammy," Patrick said, "are you okay?"

He startled and turned his gaze to Patrick, who held a stack of vinyl records in his hands. He stood facing Sam, eyes full of sorrow and something else Sam couldn't pick.

The music returned; the song had changed. Sam blinked, realizing he still held the knife. He blinked again, sensing he'd been enamored by the blade for some time.

"I'm fine," he replied. The theme to *Saw* blasted through Patrick's phone speakers. A repetitive D minor sending goosebumps down Sam's arm. "I just…"

"You were standing there for, like, minutes, staring into that knife." Patrick frowned.

Neither had anything else to say. Sam dismissed the concern with a small shrug and started pushing the knives into a wooden knife block. Patrick waited for a moment, his mouth poised to speak, but decided against it, instead placing the vinyls on the kitchen bench, and returning to his spot on the floor. Glimpsing at Sam, he turned the music down and changed the playlist.

Chill mix.

Jimmy and Pete fumbled through the house with a coffee table and planted it on top of the rug Sam had noticed earlier. The rug. The red stains. Pete motioned his chin toward the reddened floor and Jimmy nodded.

"Told you this place was fucked," Jimmy whispered as they headed down the hallway, back to the truck.

Letting out a sigh, Sam continued unpacking. The house was perfect. Beautiful. He didn't understand why Jimmy and Patrick couldn't see that. His head started to throb, but he ignored it. There was too much to do. A few boxes later, the kitchen was done. Sam looked around, evaluating their progress. The fridge, the kitchen table, the lounge, and the media cabinet were all positioned. Patrick was fiddling with cables from the television. He hadn't even noticed all the furniture coming in.

"Wow," he said, interlocking his fingers and stretching his arms in front of him. "This place is starting to look good."

Patrick mumbled something from behind the TV. The words were obscured, but the tone was classic Patrick. Sam moved to the lounge and sat, staring at the rug. The coffee table—a cheap piece of round plastic from a discount furniture store—sat dead center on the rug. Being quite small, the coffee table was a blip on the rug's surface, and as Sam stared at the carpet, a pattern began to emerge.

Faces.

Tiny faces with gaping, tortured mouths, screaming a silent scream that nobody would ever hear. Sam cringed, felt a spike of pain in his chest. *I hear you.*

"Well." Pete's voice drew Sam's attention. "We're all done." He stood by the kitchen island, looking uncomfort-

29

able and shifting weight from one foot to the other. His eyes darted around the house but kept coming back to the smears on the floor.

Sam jumped to his feet, hand outstretched. "Thank you so much for everything."

Pete shook the hand once and cleared his throat, wiping sweat from his face. "Listen, kid. Uh,"—he paused, and bit a lip—"you might wanna think twice about this place."

Looking into Pete's eyes, Sam frowned. It already felt like home. It had from the moment he stepped inside. Now that his belongings were here, too, it was perfect.

"It's just that this place has a"—Pete stumbled around for a word—"a history." Before Sam could respond, Pete smiled weakly and headed for the front door in a slight jog.

From beyond the front door, Jimmy waved a goodbye. "Catch ya later, scar face. Good luck with the shit show."

Sam waved back, unsure what else to do, and then held a hand to his scar. It felt different. Deeper. Itchy.

The truck chugged away from the house, leaving Sam and Patrick alone. It was the knowledge that Patrick was still there that gave Sam a sense of relief. Just knowing someone was around, someone who didn't require mental energy. An occasional gentle hand on the shoulder was all Sam wanted at the moment, and Patrick was the guy to do it. As they passed each other in the hallway, or exited the kitchen, Sam would feel his friend's hand on his shoulder.

What he was doing was hard. It was a big deal to up-root your life after six years with a person you thought was your "one". As clichéd as that sounded, Sam had believed it. But Danny was gone now, in someone else's bed. In someone else's heart.

The afternoon dragged on. Patrick offered to stay the night on the couch, but Sam waved off the proposal. "You've already been so much help," he said.

Patrick eyed him nervously and adjusted his weight from one foot to the other. "I don't mind staying, honestly."

Something hung in the air between them, cutting into the silence as Sam thought over the offer. He looked around the house, stopping at the rug and the paint—*Is it paint?*—stains. For a moment, he was dragged away from Patrick, the world around him vanishing as the faded-red blotches filled his vision.

"Sam?"

He cleared his throat and shot his eyes back to Patrick. "I'm fine," he said. "I'll call you in the morning."

Patrick lingered for a moment, shifting his weight once more, and adjusting his bow tie. His mouth hung open, thick red lips forming a word. Sam gazed at the strips of flesh and swallowed. Whatever words Patrick had spoken went unheard through the thumping in Sam's ears.

Those lips. He shook the thought and held a hand to his forehead as Patrick disappeared down the hallway.

Sam watched him escape through the front door, the final grips of daylight receding under the sunset. Across the sky, orange and pink hues scratched into the blue, bleeding into the clouds above. Patrick's car faded into the dying light, and Sam stared through the open front door until the sun had vanished entirely, ushering in the gray of dusk.

The night always brought calm for Sam. It wasn't the darkness, or the quiet. It was the sense that something was over and there was something else brewing. The night was a mystery, only solved by daylight. The repressed hope that vampires were somewhere around the neighborhood also appealed to him. Something to break his attention from the fact that his existence without Danny was so completely and utterly mundane.

The night rolled on and Sam continued emptying boxes, this time some old photo albums from his childhood, and he looked around for a space for them. Albums were an odd one; lock them in a drawer somewhere and they were neglected, abandoned. Keep them out for the world to see and they weren't memories but living remnants of a past he didn't want to leave behind. And as the photos faded, the memories would, too. How to preserve them without the neglect, that was his conundrum.

Thinking through his options, Sam heard a noise. Soft, subtle, but direct.

Tick.

Like a whisper, the same sound he'd heard earlier in the kitchen. It was softer this time, yet somehow more urgent. Not a whisper.

A whimper.

The *tick* came again. Followed by another. Sam hadn't packed a clock. Certainly not one that ticked. The sound was dull, as though it came from another room. He moved through the house, the *tick tick tick* becoming just a little louder. Stopping at the linen closet, Sam pressed his ear to the wall. Through the plasterboard and paint and dust, a steady *tick tick tick*.

It's in the walls.

His heart jumped. The hairs on his neck stood up, and Sam felt a pang in his stomach. An instinctual warning to walk away. He didn't understand why, but he listened to that warning. Pulling away from the wall, Sam returned to the photo albums in the living room. Being surrounded by memories—as fake as the smiles were—comforted him. Retreating to the boxes, Sam heard the ticking again. It grew louder, felt like it came from above him. Below him. Around him.

As quickly as it had begun, the ticking stopped. Its absence left a strange quiet in the house, Sam holding his breath in anticipation for the next *tick*. Instead, in the eeriness, a whisper. A soundless whisper, carried on the tips of his fingers and inside his head. He didn't so much *hear* the words, but he *felt* them. Like a deep, forgotten instinct resurfacing.

He spun from the wall, eyes dropping to the rug in the living room. He let out a deep breath and inhaled through his nose. A sweet scent wafted inside him, and despite himself, his eyelids fluttered in pleasure. The smell like a taste, invigorating every ounce of his being.

Stumbling to the rug, Sam smelled it again—a deep, metallic scent—and fell to his hands and knees. It felt as though the rug was calling to him. The faces in the pattern—tiny, gaping mouths. The stains.

It's just paint, Sam thought, and knew he was wrong. Knew paint could never give him the urges tingling inside his muscles.

His breaths quickened—in, out, in, out, in out in out in—until he'd thrown the rug back, revealing the floor beneath. The crimson stains, gelatinous, though his rational mind knew they shouldn't be. Sam crawled toward the stains, his nose low to the ground like a canine on the hunt.

As he panted and moaned, unwilling to resist the delicate stench before him, Sam rubbed his left hand through the stain. The coagulated red squelched under his touch, the jelly bubble popping in tiny, noiseless explosions of blackened liquid.

Blood.

Sam moaned again, his mind comprehending the unnatural lust spilling from his eyes, but unable to do anything. He leaned in to the blood, his tongue poking to the floor, aching for a taste. As his pink muscle scraped against the floor-boards, licking at the blood, Sam fell to his side and heaved. His stomach was empty, but the biological urge to vomit was strong. He heaved again—still, nothing came out. The scent of blood reached him again, and Sam opened his mouth to inhale the fumes. He felt his tongue reaching from the depths of his mouth, and clapped a hand over his lips.

He couldn't deny what had happened. He couldn't deny the intense, burning need for the blood on the floor. He couldn't deny his shame. All he could do was lie there, next to the blood and the upturned rug—the faces smiling now—clutching at his mouth in the fear that if he took his hand away, he'd go back for more.

Just a taste, he thought. His hand slipped from his mouth.

Chapter 3

Danny waved him over, but it wasn't the familiar wave between friends. It wasn't the wave full of lust or the one newfound lovers give to one another. It was the reluctant, "I'm here, but I don't want to be" kind, and Sam returned it with a sheepish grin.

He entered the coffeehouse, still shaking off the events of the previous night, and held the door open for an older couple as they left. They nodded their appreciation, but Sam was too concerned with Danny—texting someone while he waited—to pay any attention.

Moving through the coffeehouse—a small, modern café with laminate flooring and eggshell walls covered with knock-off Warhols—Sam approached Danny. He was sitting in a booth, which was classic Danny. He never liked the tables, because chairs always dragged and scraped against the floor. He had always said tables were too public, and always went for the booths. This one was a pale-green, and as Sam plopped into the booth across from his ex, the color reminded him of a stale avocado.

Better than stale blood, he found himself thinking, and shook the thought away.

"Hi," Danny said, shifting a bottle of table water to one side so they could see each other.

Sam looked at Danny and then looked away. To the Warhols, to the floor, anywhere. "Hey."

"Thanks for meeting me."

With a nod, Sam pressed his lips together and drew in a shaky breath. "Why *did* you want to meet me, Danny?"

Danny's back straightened, the way he used to when he was preparing an uncomfortable speech. "The way we left things, I...I feel terrible." His voice was low, and his hand reached across the table.

Sam didn't reach back. He saw Danny's fingers, lean and bony. His eyes moved to the back of his hand, wiry purple veins peeking through the supple skin. Sam gulped and looked up at Danny's face.

"Do you want a coffee?" Danny asked. "My shout."

"You know what I like," Sam replied, his mouth wet.

Danny shuffled from the booth and moved to the counter. Sam didn't watch him go, more out of protest than a lack of interest. After his—*What am I calling it? An episode?*—experience the previous night, he'd been shocked back to reality when his phone beeped. Danny requesting a coffee. He couldn't say no. Well, he didn't want to. Somewhere in the back of his mind, he'd wondered if Danny wanted to get back together. To apologize for the affair and grovel back to his good graces.

His eyes shifted to the bottle of water, condensation pooling at the base of the thick plastic. It looked cold and wet and completely uninviting. Wiping at the bottle, Sam recoiled at its coolness and the dull nature of the water. It was just hydrogen and oxygen. It didn't even smell. It was just...nothing. The absence of substance, or stickiness or... redness...angered him, and he didn't know why.

"Won't be long." Danny surprised Sam with his return. "Vanilla macchiato...I remember."

Sam raised an eyebrow and scowled. "Why wouldn't you? It's been, what, a week?"

Scoffing, Danny shifted in his seat. He bit his tongue, but his cheeks blushed a cool pink. Sam liked that color. Not quite red, but close. He felt his own cheeks blush, the veins in his throat and neck throbbing hard. "Look, Danny, what do you want?"

"I... We..." he stuttered.

The water sliding down the plastic bottle irked Sam. The endless rush of emptiness in the liquid. The nothingness of it, like the nothingness of his relationship with Danny. His heart raced and he heard his own loud nose-breathing.

"Sam, I know I hurt you," Danny said. "I fucked up really bad. I'm so sorry about that."

"Well, I guess there's nothing left to say." Sam eyed the bottle of water again, the pool of condensation growing and growing and gro—

"I want to be friends," Danny continued. "I know what I'm asking, I know it's totally fucked up to even suggest it. But we had some great times together. I don't want to lose that."

Is this guy for real? Toss me away like a piece of shit, but sure, let's be friends.

Sam just looked at his ex, whose eyes pleaded with him. In the corner of his eye, that fucking water. Drooling down the side of the bottle like spittle from a coma patient. Dead for all intents and purposes, but moving just because it could. That *fucking* water.

"Can we get rid of this stupid bottle of water, please?" Sam grabbed the bottle and smacked it down on the table between them. "It's driving me mad."

Danny nodded and waved a waitress over. He handed the bottle to her, saying something Sam couldn't hear. His ears were pounding, blood pulsing hard through him. The waitress smiled at him, but he couldn't react. He couldn't do anything except hold his breath.

A few moments later, she returned with two coffees. Danny was traditional, just a long black with some creamer. No sugar, because his body was a temple and blah blah blah…

The steam of his own vanilla macchiato reached his nose, and Sam found himself calming. Just enough for the blood to stop gushing in his ears. He tuned back in as Danny sipped at the long black, commenting how it was too hot.

"You want to be friends?" Sam asked. "You think you deserve a friendship? How long were you fucking…whoever it is that you're fucking?"

Danny frowned and examined the swirls in his coffee. "I love him."

Sam said nothing.

"I know how hard that is to hear. But I love you, too. Just…as a friend. I didn't know how to process what I was, or, wasn't feeling, and I made a terrible mistake. I should have broken it off with you, I should have—"

"But if you hadn't met this guy," Sam said slowly, "would we still be together?"

"Probably. But—"

Look at him, squirming like a child. It's fucking—

"Okay, Danny," Sam sighed, more to silence the hatred in his head than anything else. "I mean, it's not *okay*, obviously. I don't think we can be friends. Not yet. But I'll give you twenty minutes while I have this coffee"—he pointed down at his drink—"and a croissant."

"You didn't ask for a…" Danny cleared his throat and nodded, sliding away to order Sam a croissant. When he returned, he was smiling. "So, Patrick said you found a place to live."

Sam nodded, lifting his coffee to sip at the liquid. It was bitter and hot and tasted like coal. He spat it back into the mug and hocked in disgust. "Oh my god." He grimaced. "I think they messed up my order. This tastes like dishwater."

"I'm sorry, I asked for a vanilla macchiato," Danny said, his mouth hanging. "I'll go get another."

Shaking his head, Sam pushed the coffee aside. The bit he'd swallowed had unsettled his stomach, and the thought of another made him ache. "Don't worry about it," he said. "And yes, I found a lovely old house. It really suits me. I'm happy there…on my own."

He threw in that last part to see how hard Danny would wince. He didn't.

Fucking prick.

"What's it like?" he asked.

It's my home. It's my home. It's my home.

"It's old, but it has original features. It feels like home, you know?" Sam gave a half smile and shifted in his chair. His stomach churned again, and he wondered where his croissant was.

"Don't take this the wrong way," Danny said slowly, "and I know I don't have the right to say anything." He chewed the inside of his cheek. "But...you don't look so good. Are you sleeping?"

I licked blood off the floor last night. "I'm fine," Sam replied, thinking about the faces in the rug. How they changed, how they smiled at him. They sat in silence for a moment until the waitress dropped a toasted ham and cheese croissant on the table. "I'm happy in my new house."

"So you said." Danny sipped the last of his coffee.

Yeah, that's what I said, Danny. Unlike you, I'm not a lying sack of— "You don't believe me?" Sam asked. Before Danny could reply, Sam bit a chunk of croissant and continued, "You have no right to question *my* honesty."

The melted cheese and mushed ham squelched around his mouth as he chewed, and the cooked flesh of the pig tasted worse than the coffee. Old and dry. The cheese gave it some life, but the saltiness of the flesh had been burned away by heat and steam. Regardless, Sam chewed. He grabbed his coffee and gulped, wincing through the horrible flavor.

"I thought you didn't like it."

"I don't." Sam swallowed his mouthful and his stomach churned. These were some of his favorite things—vanilla macchiato and ham and cheese croissant—yet they tasted like shit. Without realizing it, Sam began to picture the blood stains under the rug.

The way it had smelled. The way it had called to him. The way it tasted as his tongue grazed against the floorboards.

He took another bite of croissant and as the meat and cheese swirled around his mouth, bits of pig between his teeth, his stomach hurled. He leaned forward and a gush of vomit splatted on the table.

"Shit, Sam." Danny slid from the booth, repulsed. "What the fuck?"

He couldn't respond. His stomach ached, purging the coffee and the food from his belly. Wiping at his mouth, Sam gazed into the vomit. There was something else in there. At first, he couldn't see it, just sensed it was there.

Smelled it.

The blood rushed through his ears again. His body tensed, chest heaved. And he saw it. The crimson, dark and delicious.

Not here. He felt his eyes well with tears. *Not now.*

But the desire was too strong. He leaned forward, the steam of his vomit soaking into the pores on his face. There was blood in there. Somewhere. Hiding inside the bile and the undigested croissant.

"Danny"—Sam managed—"help."

Danny rushed to Sam's side and pulled him from the booth. "Let's get you home."

In that moment, with his guts on the table and his emotions spilling from his weeping eyes, Sam clutched onto Danny, and his ex held him tight. "Take me home. I want to go home. To *our* home."

"Sam, I... *He's* there. I don't think it's a good idea."

Pushing away from Danny, Sam spat remnants of vomit to the floor, conscious that the waitress—that poor waitress—was already approaching with a yellow bucket of soapy water, and a mop. "I shouldn't have come here," Sam said. "Go home to your new boyfriend."

With that, Sam walked away, ignoring the many eyes of Warhol's Marilyn on the way out.

Trawling the streets on his way home—*My home*—Sam contemplated the identity of Danny's new boyfriend; who had it all. Who was better than him. Who was worthy of Danny throwing away their lives together.

"I'm going to find that son of a bitch," Sam said to himself, "and I'm going to fucking kill him."

That's when he realized he knew exactly where this mystery man would be. He stopped walking, pausing long enough to figure out where he was, and which direction he needed to go to make the acquaintance of his replacement. His stomach quivered—like something was moving inside him—and he grimaced, knowing full well it was hatred.

There was only one thing for it.

Chapter 4

Waking with a sharp intake of breath, Sam coughed hard, shaking away the terror of a dream he couldn't remember. Leaning on his left side, he gagged and retched, a rope of yellow gunk spewing to the floor. He coughed again and wiped at his mouth with the back of his hand. Drawing his hand back, Sam saw among the viscous yellow vomit, a splotch of red.

Moving his other hand to his face, Sam realized he was holding something.

A knife.

Looking at the sharp blade, Sam grimaced at the blood dripping toward the floor. The blood was fresh, still wet and glinting in the morning light. The splash of red against wood echoed in his ears. He dropped the knife and stood, fumbling to the bathroom. Standing before the sink, Sam hurled again, his guts rejecting whatever was floating around down there.

Retching one last time, Sam wiped away the vomit and peered at himself in the mirror. Confusion spread across his face as saw it. Around his mouth and chin. Blood. He thought back to the knife, firm in his hand when he'd woken.

What is happening?

Spinning the handle on the cold water tap, Sam held his hand under the steady flow, cupping water and splashing at his face. Wiping away the yellow and the red and the exhaustion from yesterday's long hours, Sam studied himself again.

The clothes he'd been wearing yesterday were stained in sweat, armpits heavy with wet patches. Not out of the ordinary, since he'd not had a peaceful nights sleep since Danny—

"Danny," Sam whispered, turning off the tap.

The haze of sleep clung to him, and Sam pushed through, grasping for remnants of a dream he wasn't sure he'd had. But he'd seen Danny last night, he was sure of it. They'd had an argument, though he couldn't recall what it was about.

Traipsing through the house, yawning away the sleep in his veins and pushing himself to life, Sam noticed the sun streaming through the window in the back door. Casting strips of light against the floorboards. Illuminating the rug. And the red stains. He stepped toward the blood stains, a deep shame burning in his stomach.

He didn't recall licking the blood, but the blood around his lips might have been evidence to the contrary. The fact was, he still didn't remember what he'd done the previous night. It was like his mind was a void; his tiny little brain floating among the nothingness of his memory.

With a sigh, he saw the red stains looked the same as they had before. Which meant two things: he hadn't licked the floor like a fucked-up druggie, and the blood had come from somewhere—*Someone?*—else.

The blood stains were a strange thing to find, though. In a rental, there were often little scuff marks and signs of previous occupancy, but the houses were always cleaned, given a fresh lick of paint.

So why the blood?

He hadn't even stopped to consider it the previous day with all the moving. He'd just accepted it was there, which—now that he thought about it—wasn't like him. The shame in his stomach grew until it was bile in his throat, and he wondered how much more he could throw up in one day. The pile of vomit was still on the floor by the kitchen, wafting through the house like a scented candle.

Kneeling before the blood stains, Sam pressed a single finger to the floor. Scraped at the blood with his fingernail. The sound sent chills down his spine. As red shavings dug under his nail, Sam remembered when the realtor—Shelley—had shown him the rental.

She'd stood awkwardly before the rug, drawing his attention to other features of the house, and giving a lame excuse that the previous tenant had left the rug and said they didn't really care for it.

"It's yours if you want it, don't you think it looks wonderful here? Imagine your furniture with it, it'll be just like home in no time," she'd said, and then ushered him away before he'd even had a chance to look at the damn thing.

She knew. Knew what, though? *Don't be dramatic, Sam. She probably just hadn't gotten it cleaned yet.* Except, she *never* got it cleaned. It peeled away under his fingers now, scraping off with his nails, which meant it could be removed and Shelley had left it there on purpose.

His stomach growled at him, the more blood he scratched away, and the smell of the vomit and the iron in the dark red shavings filled him. He didn't want to be attracted to such horrible smells—had never been before—yet the urge to shove fistfuls of his own regurgitated waste into his mouth surged through him. The urge to lick at the blood came next, and Sam thrust his body away from the stains.

"This isn't real," he whispered. "This is…"

He had nothing to end that sentence with, just the dread and disbelief that he could want something so much despite it being sick and vile. In that moment, he only wanted one thing with more intensity, but he knew Danny wasn't coming back to him. Not after the café the previous day.

He picked himself up from the floor, before the urge to feast on the waste grew too large. Stepped back from the blood stains. In the corner of his eye, seeping from the ceiling, he saw a translucent liquid. Just a patch from a crevice, like a wet spot. It looked like the wall was leaking, like a faulty pipe splashing water on the other side. He stared at it for a moment, assessing whether it grew or not.

Nothing.

He knew it hadn't been there when he'd inspected the place the previous week. And it hadn't been there the day before, he was sure of it. Turning from the translucent liquid back to the blood, Sam smiled, without knowing why.

The house was a mess, the blood and vomit and weird goo in the ceiling were all what some people might refer to as "red flags". Waking up with a bloody knife—that was a first—completed the "get the fuck out of there" vibe. But he liked it here anyway. Despite all those things, all the alarm bells clanging around in his head, Sam felt that he was supposed to be here. Like the stars were aligning. Yes, this was *his* space. *His* home. And nobody could take it away from him.

Breathing through the last vestiges of his cravings for all that lay smoldering on the floorboards, Sam looked around at the packing boxes. He'd really only unpacked a couple, and needed to get to work. Moving through the house to a stack of three boxes, he lifted one down and tore the packing tape from the edge of one of the cardboard flaps.

DAVID-JACK FLETCHER

The sun warmed his back as he pulled objects from the box. It hadn't been labelled for some reason, and as he dug into the contents, he realized it was full of Danny's things. It was like the man was a magnet; he couldn't stop thinking about him, and how the first box he opened was full of his things. He pulled a framed photograph from the box, and gave a sad smile.

He and Danny on their first anniversary.

Gliding a finger over Danny's face—his beautiful, beautiful face—the sun reflected against the glass. As he stroked Danny's hairline, a third face appeared in the image, and Sam dropped the frame. A reflection, from over his shoulder.

Twisting around, Sam scanned the area. A flash of movement from the back door. He scrambled through the house, pushed open the back door, and searched the yard. The sun was hot on his face, his chest heaving from the adrenaline, and as he spun around to view the surroundings, he saw it. A shock of black hair flicking over the rear fence. He chased after it, climbed the wood so his torso was above the fence line, and saw a small figure running out toward the street.

Whoever it was, they were too far away for Sam to notice any details, except the long, black hair. From the size, it was a kid, but that's all he could make out about the person. Why they'd been in his backyard was the least of his concerns at that moment, though it had given him a shock. His

50

still-beating heart, rapid thumps in his chest and ears, were testament to that.

Trudging through the dead grass and ignoring the decaying flowers lining each of the boundary fences, Sam slipped back into the house and locked the door behind him. He didn't notice the trail of blood through the grass, leading back to the house.

His heart slowed and his breathing soon followed, but he couldn't shake the fear he'd felt. The sense that someone— even a child—could make their way into his new home and defile it in some way.

I'll get a security system, Sam thought. *I need to protect this place.*

In the living room, Sam dropped onto the couch with a deep sigh, his eyes rolling across the room until they landed on the vomit he had no intention of cleaning up. A stack of graphic novels toppled beside him. Between lingering thoughts of last nights dream and the confusion of waking up with a bloody knife, Sam thought he heard the theme music of *Halloween*. His cell phone.

Wiping sleep from his eyes, he searched the pile of graphic novels for his phone. He found it hiding under a collector's edition of The Strain. Patrick's name and goofy profile photo lit the screen as the phone chimed. Before answering, Sam's bleary eyes wandered to the small digital clock on the left of it.

9:21 a.m.

A chill swept through his bones, though he didn't know why. The *Halloween* tune sounded again as the phone buzzed in his hand.

Sam answered the call, hands shaking, and held the phone to his ear. Before he could open his mouth to speak, Patrick cried down the phone. "He's dead," he sobbed. "Danny's dead."

Tick, tick, tick...

Sam dropped the phone, and clasped both hands over his still-damp mouth. The knife stared at him from the floor, the blade slick with red, glinting in the morning sun.

Patrick's voice, a tinny whimper from the other end of the line, grew faint. Danny. His Danny.

Dead.

The screen was static, like an old television signal. Patrick was gone. Disconnected.

Sam looked back at the knife, limp on the floor. As though entranced, the shiny red surface called to him. Lifting the blade to his mouth, Sam sniffed at the blood, and despite himself, licked.

Tick. Tick. Tick.

He licked and licked, greedily sopping up the blood with his tongue, letting the thick liquid slide down his throat. He felt its warmth inside him, giving him life, as the ticking filled his ears.

The ticking stopped. Sam was enveloped in silence.

Ping.

Sam picked up his phone, the ping drawing him out of his stupor. A message. Unknown sender.

A GPS pin.

He pulled clothes from a nearby box and slipped them on without much regard for what they were. Just so long as they weren't drenched in blood. Grabbing his car keys and heading for the front door, Sam didn't notice the pile of vomit sinking through the floorboards and didn't register the low grumble from beneath.

Chapter 5

The GPS coordinates turned out to be Danny's home address. Sam slammed the car door and rushed across the street to his ex-boyfriend's property. A yellow and black police tape hung loosely from Danny's letterbox, slung around a nearby tree, and looped back to a thin metal pole at the edge of the property line. Sealing the house from the public.

Sam grabbed at the police tape and ducked underneath, ignoring the faint sound of someone yelling just over his shoulder. His heart was pounding in his ears, every thud of his footsteps against the dewy grass beneath like an earthquake. Body on fire, pressure building behind his eyes, he raced to the front door, scanning the front yard. Cops everywhere. Paramedics. Sad eyes. Exhausted faces. Wordless sighs sending fogs of breath into the cold morning air.

"I said," a voice came from behind, "you can't be here." A firm hand grabbed his shoulder.

Turning around, Sam stared into the eyes of an older policeman, the bleak expression ripping at his soul. Brown eyes of despair gazed upon Sam, and released his shoulder.

"You knew him?" he asked.

"He was my...we used to be..." Sam trailed off. His eyes shifted back to the house, peered through a gap between the door and the inside. The movement beyond the threshold was silent and robotic, and Sam flinched as a gurney rolled past the door.

"Ex-boyfriend?" Sam nodded and the officer stepped closer. "Come on." He wrapped a thick arm around Sam's shoulders and guided him toward the road. To the other side of the tape. "Have a drink of water with me."

The officer had a presence about him. Calming. Nurturing. Sam felt warm in his embrace and walked willingly with the man. He looked over his shoulder, back to the scene, and then thought about the bloody knife.

He opened the back door of his police car and motioned for Sam to sit. He ignored the request. "What's your name?" The officer held out a bottle of water for Sam.

Taking the bottle, Sam met the officer's eyes again. They seemed to tell him everything would be okay. They seemed to say he was safe here and that nothing bad would ever happen again.

"Sam," he replied.

"Detective Corrigan." With a heavy sigh, the officer took a sip from his own water bottle and twisted the lid tight. They remained in silence for a few moments, and Sam's attention drifted back to the house. To the knife and the blood and the vomit.

To the ticking.

The GPS pin.

Who sent it to me? How did they know about Danny?

A tear streamed down Sam's cheek, and the officer leaned close to wipe it away. Sam recoiled, but let it happen. It was nice to have a comforting touch. "I know it doesn't mean much," he said. "But we will find the person who did this to your ex-boyfriend."

It occurred to Sam that he didn't even know what happened. Patrick was nowhere to be seen and nobody had told him how Danny had died. Turning the water bottle in his hands, Sam asked, "What *did* happen?"

Corrigan ran a finger across the stubble above his upper lip and cleared his throat. Sizing up the young man before him. "Danny was killed." He paused, watching Sam's reaction as he choked on tears.

"No," Sam whispered, the ground becoming unsteady under him. His knees felt weak, and he clutched onto the detective for support, who held him like a close friend. "It can't be… He can't…"

"Why don't you sit down?" Corrigan mumbled softly.

Sam didn't want to sit down. He didn't want his heart to be shattering. He didn't want to be here at all. Pushing away from the detective, his stare lingered on the house. He looked through the team of forensics officers rushing about in their white costumes, like half-finished carnival clowns. He looked to the open front door, hanging ajar on its hinges.

"He's not dead," Sam said to the detective.

"Sam, he—"

Sam raced to the police tape, flicking it up over his head as he went underneath. Rushed across the front lawn— the large detective surprisingly fast on his heels—and pushed through the front door, letting the heavy wood slam against the interior wall.

Searching the house, he moved from the front entrance to the living room, heart hammering at the anticipation of what he might find. The room was untouched, unblemished, just an ordinary room. A three-seater sofa with a throw rug all messed up—someone had been using it. *He's here*, Sam thought. The television hung from the wall, still switched on from Danny's viewing. *He has to be here.* Sam didn't register what was playing, didn't care. Didn't register the forensics officers placing yellow, numbered cards on the ground and photographing them.

He noticed a coffee mug on the coffee table, and smiled. "Danny!" Sam called. "Where are you?"

The detective was behind him now, panting a little, and reaching at Sam's back. Before his fingers could touch Sam's shoulder, he was gone, racing through the house, down the hallway, calling Danny's name. Pushing past another officer, whose eyes were pleading him to stop, whose hands had tried to block him from going any further. Ignored the detective calling after him, begging him to stop. Yelling at him that he didn't want to see it.

It's a mistake, Sam thought, his heart settling back into its cavity at a slow and steady rhythm. *Just a mistake. He's in his room, sleeping.*

He barged through Danny's bedroom door, slammed it behind him to keep the detective out. "Danny, I—"

The scene took a moment to register. Even in the seconds where the red smears and puddles looked like a child's artwork, Sam dropped to his knees. The walls were soaked and still dripping. Sprays of red smattered the bed and the lamp and the ceiling fan.

"No no no no no no…" Sam repeated as he stood, the detective's bangs on the door sounding distant and muffled.

Among the bed covers and the sheets, the black fabric soaked through and slick with blood, lay Danny, naked. His face was serene, like he was just sleeping, having a peaceful dream. *That's all he's doing.*

Despite the mess and the visible wounds all across his body—arms, chest, stomach—Sam wanted to believe the love of his life was just resting. The wounds didn't make sense, not with how relaxed Danny's face was. His intestines and other organs hanging out of him like cold spaghetti didn't register at that moment. The stench of liver and kidneys hacked up across the bed were immaterial to Sam.

Moving to Danny's side, stepping through wet puddles of blood, Sam caressed his cheeks. His pale, devoid of life cheeks.

"He's cold." Sam reached for the blankets. As he grabbed at the soaked fabric, his eyes caught sight of Danny's neck. He gasped and stepped back. "What happened to—"

Coming through the door, the detective rested a hand on Sam's shoulder. "You can't be here, Sam," he said softly. "You don't want to remember him this way."

Sam turned to face the detective. "What did they do to him?"

"We have to go," the detective insisted, guiding Sam back to the bedroom door.

As they walked, Sam on autopilot, processing the scene, he looked back at Danny on the bed. The tears came fast and heavy—he broke away from the detective once more.

Launching himself onto the bed, Sam wrapped his arms around Danny's body, pulling the dead man close and tight. He kissed Danny's cold cheeks and cried into his neck. The detective pulled at him hard, but Sam resisted, clutching onto Danny with all his strength.

"Wake up, Danny, please!" Sam wailed, grabbing fistfuls of Danny's organs and scooping them inside the body. They fell back to the sheets with a soppy splat, and Sam tried again. "I'll fix this, I promise."

The detective hurled behind him, then swore at the mess and the fact that the crime scene was completely destroyed. Sam didn't care. He scooped again and again, but the organs didn't stay, until Sam's fingers were so slick with blood and mucus that he couldn't grip anything to continue scooping. Still fighting off the detective, he embraced Danny tighter than he ever had before and whispered, "I'm sorry, Danny, I'm so sorry," over and over.

Wiping his own vomit away, the detective took Sam hard by the wrist and released his grip on Danny. "Sam," he said. "This is so wrong."

Sam didn't respond, the words not making sense. He heard them, but it was jumbled, distant.

"I know how hard this is, but you cannot be here. You can't be doing this."

"He's going to wake up," Sam said. "He's just cold, that's all."

"No, Sam," came the reply. "He's never waking up."

The words floated through the room, bounced off the bloodied walls and hit Sam in the face. "He's…" There was nothing left to be said, and Sam retreated into himself, unable to fathom that he had just climbed into his dead ex-boyfriend's blood-drenched bed and tried to hug him back to life. Unable to grasp that Danny was dead.

Unable to admit that he'd spoken the last words to Danny that he'd ever speak.

And that he'd woken up that same morning holding a knife wet with red.

The detective pulled Sam away from Danny, more forcefully this time, and led him out of the room. It registered with him as they walked that people were staring, and he realized it was because he was covered in Danny's remains. He wiped at his arms and face, looking at his red-stained hands, and cried again.

The smell of the blood made him hungry, despite the terrible, horrible feeling rushing through his body. He was hungry, and he knew it wasn't for a burger and fries. As the detective ushered him out of the house, past the police tape, Sam wondered about Danny's new boyfriend. They were living together, weren't they?

Where is he?

"Sam!" Across the front yard, Patrick waved. It wasn't a happy, "here I am" wave, it was a desperate hand high in the air, letting Sam know he wasn't alone. "Sam, I'm sorry. I'm just so sorry." Patrick appeared by the officer's side and crouched before Sam, taking in the scene before him—Sam covered in blood, trembling, and wiping his hands at his jeans. "What happened?"

The detective mumbled something and Patrick gave a "Tsk". It wasn't a sound of disapproval, though. More of a "poor bastard" kind of thing. Sam listened to them talk, like they were old friends, about the scene.

"Patty, he really fucked up in there," the detective muttered.

"What happened?"

"I can't even... I've never seen anything like it."

Sam ignored the continued conversation between Patrick and the detective, staring back at the house.

"Is he really..." Sam let the words trail away, and the two men before him fell into silence.

Patrick nodded and wiped at his own tears. Turning to the detective, Patrick said, "Can you give us a sec? I think he needs some space."

"He's going to need to come down to the station," the detective said. "Now that his prints are all... Everywhere."

Sam noticed Patrick's hand low on the detective's back, the way they stood so close. "Please, just a few minutes?"

The officer walked away with a subtle nod to Sam, and he found himself watching his steady gait. His round belly and graying hair. Something about him stayed with Sam as the man grew smaller in the distance. Rejoining the other police officers at the crime scene.

"Sam, I don't know what to say." Patrick kneeled before his friend.

Sam didn't take his eyes off the front door as he said, "He's not dead."

Taking a deep breath, Patrick sniffled, and wiped away his own tears. "I've spoken with the detective before you got here. He told me what he could… Sammy, someone stabbed him," Patrick said. "Something like over a hundred times. Well, you saw that, I guess. But that's not all."

Sam creased his forehead, lips trembling. He managed to peel his eyes from the door. He met Patrick's gaze, searching for meaning in his friend's words. "What do you mean?"

"Are you sure you want to hear this? Maybe you should—"

"Just fucking tell me," Sam spat. "Tell me!"

Patrick nodded, avoiding Sam's stare. "They found marks on his neck. Like…bite marks or something."

The knife. The blood.

As the words drifted into nothingness around him, all Sam wanted to do was go back to yesterday, to feel time collapse around him, and to see Danny's face one more time.

"But…he's not even dead."

Patrick stared at him, reached for Sam's bloodied hand, then thought better of it. "I'm sorry, Sammy. He is."

"No. I don't believe it," Sam insisted. "I saw him yesterday. We had lunch, and… This can't be real."

Patrick stretched, the crouching position causing his mid-thirties body to cramp. Between the cracking of joints, and Patrick's stifled groans, Sam heard the screech of wheels against pavement.

The gurney carrying Danny's corpse rolled toward an ambulance, the back doors open. Waiting. The somber paramedics guided the gurney in silence, the friendly officer watching on. Sam hurried toward them.

As they loaded his ex-boyfriend into the ambulance, Sam clutched the side of the gurney. "Can I…"

One of the paramedics, a woman with long dark hair and fire-red cheeks, narrowed her eyes at Sam. The other, a young man, frowned in sympathy, but his stare was vacant. Sam asked again, motioning to the body bag.

"No way," the woman said, shouldering Sam backward. "This ain't a private show."

"I just need to see him." Sam's voice shook and a flurry of tears came. He noticed Patrick by his side, holding out a hand for Sam to take. He intertwined his fingers with Patrick's, and let the paramedics do their job.

"You've seen enough, from what we heard," the other paramedic mumbled, and then pursed his lips. "Sorry."

The door slammed shut, sealing Danny inside. He and Patrick watched the ambulance drive away, bumping up and down against the uneven road. Turning back to the house, Sam saw Detective Corrigan watching him again. A sad smile warping his face.

Sam walked to him. "What about the…boyfriend?"

Corrigan raised an eyebrow. "What do you mean?"

"Danny had a new… He had a boyfriend," Sam said. "Did he do this? Where is he?"

Frowning, the officer shook his head. "Nobody else here, I'm afraid. Just the deceased." Sam stared past the officer for a moment as the word sunk in: deceased. That's what Danny was now. Deceased. Dead. Gone. Stabbed. Bitten. "What happened back there, Sam? Do you need some help?" The officer placed a hand on Sam's arm.

I didn't even get to say goodbye.

He blinked and refocused. Met the officer's eyes again. The brown pupils, deep and endless. Calling to Sam from some safe place he didn't recognize. "I'm fine. I just need to go home." He could feel the officer watching him as he went back to his car. Patrick offered a hug, but Sam shook it off. He couldn't be touched right now. He just needed to go home.

At his car, Sam rested his head on the driver's window, unable to find the energy to open the door. The oxygen around him seemed to vanish, leaving him with nothing but the hollow void of death. He tried to focus on breathing, but the stench of blood drifted from his clothes again—and his face and arms and hands—and he held back another wave of tears.

Taking a deep breath, he lifted his head from the window and turned to the side, catching a glance in the side mirror. Behind him, the shock of black hair again.

He spun fast. The hair zipped behind a telegraph pole. Sam raced toward it, gritting his teeth, anger seething through him. He reached the telegraph pole, but nobody was there.

"Where are you?" he called. *Maybe they saw something. Why are they following me?*

He scanned again. Down the street. A small figure running around the corner. He chased after them as they scrambled through another residential yard, climbed a fence. Sam wasn't giving up this time—he followed the figure, climbed the same fence, crunched down on a flower bed on the other side. Ignored the small dog yapping at him to fuck off out of its domain. The figure was fast, really fast. He lost sight of them, but ran anyway, hoping to catch another glimpse.

Out on the street, he saw them again, the black hair bouncing up and down as they ran. He still couldn't make out any other details, other than that they were pale and small. He ran faster, as fast as he could, his lungs gasping, his chest heaving, the wind burning at his face against the blood.

"Stop!" he called, crossing the street. A car swerved to avoid hitting him and honked. He didn't take his eyes off the figure, racing around another corner.

Sam dodged an elderly couple walking their dog— the woman tugging at her husband, who growled at Sam to stay away or they'd call the police—and kept after the figure. His legs were about to give out, but he was catching up. He couldn't stop now. *Keep going!*

But his legs were going too fast and his lungs couldn't grab the oxygen. His feet burned and as he chased the figure toward another front yard, he tripped on the edge of the sidewalk. He tumbled across the concrete, scraping his face and hands, and rolled across to the grass.

Breathing hard, he sat up fast. The figure was gone.

His face ached, but he didn't have the energy to cover the wound with a hand. He sat on the grass, legs sprawled, and then fell backward in a heap of blood and sweat.

"The fuck you doing, son?" a voice came from the house.

Sam tried to sit up again, but the adrenaline was dissipating fast, and all he could do was lie there, staring at marshmallow clouds and soaring birds.

Footsteps crunched on the grass toward him. "I said, what are you doing on my lawn?" A man came into view, his white hair and wrinkled skin looking half-dead already.

Sucking in more air, Sam was conscious that the old man stunk of soap and cigarettes. He grimaced, and found the energy to sit up. "I'm sorry, sir," he said. "I was chasing someone. They ran into your backyard."

As Sam lifted his upper body into a sitting position, resting on his elbows and calming his breathing, the old man took a step back. His dressing gown hung open to reveal a yellowing wife beater and satin boxer shorts. Sam looked at him in confusion.

"I don't want any trouble," the old man said, raising his hands. "Whatever is going on here, I don't need to know."

"What are you—"

"Sam, what are you doing?" Patrick's voice came from behind him. He stepped over, clutching at a stitch in his midriff, and waved at the old man. "Sorry, sir, it's really not what it looks like. We've just come from a crime scene."

The old man swallowed hard.

"...We're not the criminals, I assure you." Patrick continued. Looking down at Sam, he said, "He's had a rough morning. We'll get going, I'm really sorry for the disruption to your morning."

Sam looked up at Patrick, his freckled face redder than normal, his bow tie slightly askew from running after him. "I saw someone. I saw..."

"It's okay, Sammy. Let's just get you home."

Walking through the streets back to the car, Patrick held an arm around Sam's shoulders. It was nice to feel his warmth, even if the close proximity meant Sam could hear the blood pumping through his friends veins, and he smelled good enough to eat.

His stomach knotted, but Sam ignored it. Thought about the figure with black hair and pale skin, and their small frame. *It must be a child. But why would a kid be snooping on me?* He tried to speak to Patrick, tried to tell him what was going on—that his stomach felt weird, that he'd woken with a bloodied knife is his hands, there was weird mucus in his house and a kid was spying on him—but he just walked.

"Do you want me to drive you home?" Patrick asked as they approached Danny's house.

Sam shook his head. "I need to be alone."

Patrick forced Sam into a hug. "Please let me take you. I don't think you *should* be alone."

"Patrick..." Sam managed, slipping from the hug and walking to his car. "I know you love me, and we don't have the sort of friendship where that kind of thing is said. But I love you, too. And I know you want to help—"

"Then let me take care you."

"—but I *really* need to be alone right now." He shed another batch of tears, didn't bother wiping them away.

Patrick considered his friend for a moment, and then finally nodded, biting at his lower lip. "Go get some rest. Clean up, and please—*please*—answer when I call you later."

Nodding, Sam opened his car door and climbed inside.

As he turned the key in the ignition, Sam saw a police car's indicator blinking at a set of traffic lights, and had an idea. The paramedics. The ambulance. They had Danny. He just had to find them and they'd show him this was all a sick fucking joke and none of this was real.

He stared into the blinking orange glow of the indicator, images of the bloody knife flashing through his mind. His stomach lurched as he did so, and Sam swallowed the bile back down, remembering the taste on his tongue when he'd woken this morning. The red around his mouth. The dream he couldn't quite remember, but the feeling that he'd had a busy, busy night. Thought back to Danny, in his bed, naked and hollowed out and leaking like a chocolate lava cake.

Sam couldn't shake off the way he'd been lying there, his face calm and perfect. No, he couldn't be dead. He didn't care that Danny was cold and stiff, and that rigor mortis had started setting in, blood cells pooling and bruising his skin. He didn't care that someone had stabbed Danny until his organs had spilled across the bed.

No. Danny is alive. He has to be.

The indicator blinked again as the traffic lights turned green and the police car turned the corner.

Sam knew Patrick was right. He shouldn't be alone. He also knew he needed to go home. Needed to wash away Danny and the sweat and the tears. And he would. But first, he had something to do.

He pulled onto the road and headed for the local county morgue.

Chapter 6

With fresh memories and trauma cycling through his veins, and Danny's dried blood on his face, hands, and clothes, Sam was aware he looked like a crazed murderer. Driving through town with wide eyes and an unblinking stare was just the cherry on top of a dreadful, disgusting pie. The sweetness of the blood lingering on his upper lip wafted inside him, and Sam tightened his grip on the steering wheel.

"Don't do it," he told himself. "Don't *fucking* do it."

His knuckles went white as he squeezed the wheel, tightening his lips and pressing his tongue to the roof of his mouth. But as he breathed hard and fast through his nose, the scent of blood—sweet, iron, rich—coursed through him.

Sam started to tremble, the urge to lick, lick, lick bubbling inside him, becoming a tangible need. He parted his lips and, uttering a regretful groan, licked at the blood on his upper lip. His eyes rolled back a little and he let the car drift to the left as the taste travelled across his tongue, feeding an odd, intense pleasure Sam had only ever known from orgasms.

The car bumped the edge of the road and Sam swerved back to the lane, the last vestiges of his orgasm ebbing away in small waves. He wanted to lick again—plenty on his arms and hands, and as he looked at his shirt he saw flecks of what might have been muscle tissue or bits of organs—but Sam switched on the radio and focused on the voice coming through the car speakers.

He saw the morgue up ahead, and the knowledge of Danny being so close, with the distraction of the radio host, seemed enough to anchor him in humanity. For the moment.

The morgue was an old building, not connected to the local hospital at all. Sam had thought, from swaths of television shows like *Tru Calling*, *Grey's Anatomy*, and whatever else, that morgues were in hospital basements. As it turned out, that was not the case in Harker County. The ambulance carrying Danny's corpse traveled across town to what appeared to be a derelict building, just on the outskirts, but several blocks away from the main road. He realized he'd driven past the building countless times before, and had never noticed it.

He trotted to the front door to find it locked by a security door, a small camera eyeing him with caution, and a buzzer beckoning his thumb for a pressing. A voice had greeted him—male, older, gruff—and told him this wasn't a Visi-tor's Center, and he had to have an appointment, or a badge, to enter the building.

"I just want to see him," Sam begged at the front door. Silence.

"Please," Sam tried once more, spittle landing on the buzzer's speaker. "He was my—"

"Sorry, son." The man interrupted. "No exceptions."

His thumb fell from the buzzer, his arm slinking low, and his body exasperated. He tried the door handle, knowing it would be no good, and his lower lip trembled when it didn't budge.

"You're going to have leave, son. And clean yourself up...you look like Jeffrey Dahmer on date night."

Sam looked up at the camera watching him, and then dropped his eyes to the concrete beneath him. His heart be-gan to thump in his ears, his vision started to blur. An all too familiar feeling—from the café, from the scent of the blood in his new living room, from a few minutes earlier in the car—swept over him.

He leaned forward on the door and banged his head against the thick, reinforced glass. "I. Need. Him."

"You get outta here right now, or I'm calling the cops," the voice said. "I literally have them on speed dial."

Sam banged again, tears welling in his eyes, and slid down the door to the concrete beneath. He couldn't breathe

DAVID-JACK FLETCHER

and he couldn't move. Just shudder as tears rolled down his face, leaving trails in Danny's dried blood.

A man appeared on the other side of the door, a hand resting on a holster at his hip. Sam managed to look up at him, his eyes pleading for help or mercy or anything else that would let him inside. His chest heaved and his shoulders shook, but the man only grimaced.

"Seriously," the man said. "Get the fuck out of here. You can cry, you can moan, I don't care. Don't make me call the cops."

Sam pulled himself together, just for the few seconds it took for him to stand. "I'm sorry," he said through the door. The security guard nodded, his hand still on his holster. "I'm going."

Turning on his heel, Sam went back to his car. Speaking to himself, he muttered, "I will see you again, Danny. I will."

Stopped at a set of traffic lights, Sam stared into the red light, the intensity burning into his corneas. In that moment, with cars and cyclists buzzing around, he felt connected to that light. *No, not the light.* Connected to the red. Swelling in his eyes, pulsating through the windshield. He felt warmth. Heat.

Red.

Blood.

The light clicked to green, and in his rearview he saw the driver behind flipping him the bird, mouthing something unsavory with a crooked smile. Sam lifted his foot from the brake pedal and accelerated toward home.

He spied the driver behind turning right at the lights, heading in another direction, and his eyes flicked to the license plate. *R33 L2T.* Without understanding why, Sam committed it to memory. Committed the driver's weasel smile to his gray matter. He'd see him again.

Driving through his neighborhood—the same streets he and Danny had laughed and cried and kissed and held hands—frightened Sam. It was less the memory of those moments with his beloved, and more the fact that he'd never have them again. While Danny had been breathing, there was a chance they'd reconnect. A chance, no matter how slim. Now all the remained was Danny's crimson interior he'd be washing off in a few minutes.

That wasn't the only thing he was scared of, though. As Sam pulled up to his new home, his head ringing with tension and flashes of Danny's smile, he understood his true fear. The ticking. Driving into the garage, he could hear it already. A soft murmur drifting through the airwaves. Pulsing inside him. He was afraid of that *tick tick tick* because he liked it.

Wanted it.

Needed it.

When he entered the house, the tension headache vanished. Almost as if it had never existed in the first place. But the ticking was louder. Clearer. More meaningful.

He moved to the living room, ignoring the smears of blood under the rug, and dropped onto the couch. Listening. *Tick, tick, tick.*

Sam smiled.

Tick.

His lips parted into a wide grin, and he closed his eyes, leaning back on the couch. Letting the sound fill him. Part of him questioned what was happening, but the emotional pain ebbed away with each tick. With each second that passed, the sound became more a part of him. He could feel it.

He *wanted* it.

The sound reminded him of Danny, and he sank further into the couch. A phantom touch caressed his face, just as Danny used to do, and Sam shed another tear. The *tick tick tick* of the unseen clock was like the rhythm of Danny's heart, and he remembered listening to it beat through his chest as they lay in bed talking. Dreaming. Planning.

Danny is gone.

Like his headache, the ticking vanished, and Sam was drowned by the silence. There was a heaviness in his ears, like they were waiting, eager for the sound to return. But as he opened his eyes, scanning the living room, he realized he was completely and utterly alone. Staring down at the rug, the faces he'd seen had vanished. It was just old cloth now.

There was no more dreaming.

No more planning.

No future.

Not even the mysterious clock kept him company.

"It is here, though," he whispered to himself. "I heard something."

That settled it. He needed to search the house. The first time he'd heard the ticking, he'd thought it was somewhere in the walls. Thinking on it now, that didn't make sense. Unless, for some strange reason, someone had put a clock in the crawlspace on purpose.

Standing with his hands on his hips, Sam gazed around the room, toward the kitchen. That's where he'd been the first time, wasn't it? Looking at some graphic novels? He stood in the spot he remembered being when the ticking began, but this time, he searched the surrounding area. Feeling at the walls at random, every bump and bit of chipped paint reminding him of the curves and crevices of Danny's body.

His movements became more purposeful, softer, tracing the corners of the walls with a finger, his breath catching.

Tick.

"There you are," Sam exhaled hard, as though he'd never breathed before.

Tick, tick, tick.

The sound was close, but he still couldn't figure out its location. Moving past the kitchen, he stopped at the door to the basement. Leaned against the wooden barrier, pressed his ear on the cold surface. He felt compelled not to enter, as though he wasn't granted the privilege just yet. He knew it was ridiculous, it was just a door. A door in *his* house. He could open it if he wanted to. But with his ear pressed against it, a soothing, hollow sound came from beyond. A whooshing.

No ticking down there.

As the clock sounded again, Sam looked up. *Maybe the attic?*

He headed for the hallway, by the front door. The attic access was there somewhere, he was sure the realtor had told him that.

Tick, tick, tick.

The ticking grew faster. Louder. It was telling him he was close. *Warmer, warmer. Find me.* Sam smiled again and found the opening to the attic. A small manhole, just his size. Like it was built for him. Racing back to the kitchen, he grabbed a bar stool, and returned to the access point. Stepping up and grabbing at the manhole cover, he pushed it inward and let a hot gust of air pour onto his face.

He gripped the edges of the hole and climbed up, shimmying with his legs until he was sitting on the edge of the manhole. Sam peered into the attic—just a hollow void with insulation bats and wooden beams, and stray wires. The ticking was distant now, and Sam felt confused.

Why is the house telling me to come here if there is nothing to see? Then he realized. *It's a game.* He couldn't explain it, like so many other things lately, but the house was playing with him. Testing him. Assessing his worthiness to live there.

And he loved that.

Knowing the clock wasn't in the attic, Sam climbed deeper into the space anyway. His hands—against the wooden beams—stuck to something. He looked at his palm, bringing it close to his face. Translucent muck. Like an oil, but thicker. *Mucus.* He sniffed at his palm. Nothing. Looking back at the beams, there was no trace of any oil or muck or anything. He wasn't sure where it had come from, or what it meant. All he knew, in that moment, was that he needed to keep going.

At the edges of the attic walls, high in the roof, mucus began to drip to the beams. The further into the attic he crawled, the wetter the roof became. As though the house itself was salivating at his presence. Sam frowned at the thought, and for a moment wondered if he was food, but then, realizing how ridiculous that sounded, shrugged it off.

He began to think of the mucus as a quirk of the house, even though his rational mind was sighing and telling him to get the fuck out of there. The emotional part of him was intrigued, and it *felt* right. It *felt* like home, just as the sad front windows had reminded him of his own sad heart.

He wanted to feel the house, get to know it. Be part of it, like it was becoming part of him. The further he crawled, clinging to a wooden beam, the more he felt enveloped by the house. By the ticking that somehow felt so distant but so close.

He felt eyes on him, and the sensation sent goose-bumps down his arms. Despite this, the sense of being watched—of being *seen*—comforted him, and Sam took a deep breath. To suck in the stale air of the attic, but to also let the house fill his lungs. This was his home, after all. He belonged here.

Still, the source of the ticking needed to be found, so Sam turned back, careful to grip the wooden beams as tight as he could. Making his way back through the manhole, he climbed down the bar stool, and noticed he'd left a handprint on the wooden thing. The translucent mucus, again.

"What…"

Inspecting it further, now with more light, he saw it was thicker and darker than mud or oil. At least it wasn't blood. Not this time. A goo of some kind, stained to his hands as he looked at them now. Wiping them on his pants, Sam refocused on—

Tick, tick, tick.

—what mattered. The clock.

Just as he began to step through the hallway, back to the kitchen, Sam's phone vibrated in his pocket. Slipping it from his jeans and peering at the screen, he saw it was from his dad. He paused on the message, debating whether to open it or not. His need to know what his father wanted, after months of silence, won out.

DAD

Are you okay? Do you want some company?

Fuck off, Dad.
His phone buzzed again.

DAD

I know things have been weird between us, but I want to make things right.

Sam sighed and was just about to lock his phone when it buzzed again.

DAD

I'm sorry about Danny...

Sam threw his phone across the room, watched it clang and smack against the wall and the floorboards, and stormed into his bedroom, toward the ensuite. It was time to get the blood and the mucus off him, freshen up, and maybe, just maybe, sleep.

After he showered, Sam climbed into bed, not caring that the midday sun was still high in the sky, and buried his face in the pillow. He resisted the urge to cry again, knowing it wouldn't do any good. Knowing it wouldn't matter, because when he woke up, this would have all just been a horrible nightmare, some dream that he'd tell Patrick about in the morning. And they'd laugh and say he watched too many movies, and then he'd call Danny and they'd make up…

He awoke with a start, pushing the bed covers off his head and staring wide-eyed into the shadowed bedroom. His phone was buzzing from its place on the floorboards. From where he'd thrown it.

Probably Dad again.

He sunk further into his bed, feeling the warm sheets against him and imagining Danny snoring by his side. But it wasn't snoring he heard, it was the vibrations of his phone. Again and again and again, like a hammer to his head.

Slinking through the dark house, he picked up his phone and squinted at the screen. His eyes adjusted to the light, and he saw what was vibrating at him.

Another GPS ping, from UNKNOWN.

"Strange," he said, and swiped to unlock the phone. To make sure he wasn't seeing things. "Huh."

The coordinates were new, but just as before, he felt compelled to go there. He pressed the pin and Apple Maps opened to reveal the location. Harker Country Morgue.

Danny.

Sam let the ticking fade to the background as he gazed into his phone. Maybe whoever was sending the messages knew what had happened to Danny. Maybe they wanted to help him. Maybe…

Sam thew on fresh clothes and raced to his car. If he couldn't see Danny earlier, he *had* to see him now.

Whatever it took.

Chapter 7

The county morgue was nondescript from the outside. Almost unnoticeable, if you didn't know what to look for. Sam smiled at the memories of driving past on his way to and from the Mexican place he and Danny liked. He was reminded of Danny's habit of opening the takeaway bags to sniff at the food during the drive, the memory lingering, even as he pulled into the sparse parking lot of the morgue.

Just a plain concrete building with a tiled roof, it looked as though it had not received much care for some time. The outside walls were riddled with dirt and graffiti. Sam was caught off-guard by the "Die Faggots" and "#homos4aids" tags that nobody had cared to wash away.

Like the bodies inside the building, the patches of grass leading to the entrance were bruised and rotting, dwindling into nothingness. Sam stepped over the dry, crunching grass, and peered through the glass door. It was tinted and scratched from years of neglect and abuse, but he could still see shapes and shadows moving inside.

With the sun on his back and the stench of dying grass moving through him, Sam pushed away from the door. As if being brought to life from a coma, he stared at his hands.

What am I doing?

He remembered Danny's house and the policeman and Patrick and then an overwhelming need to follow that police car, to get inside the morgue. To find Danny. To...do what? Remembered being thrown from the property. Standing outside the morgue now, Sam felt distant from himself. Distant from his body, like he was watching himself on a screen without any capacity to intervene. And yet, there was a pull. A yearning to see Danny one last time.

Tick.

Sam pulled the door handle down. Locked.

Back door. There's gotta be a back door.

He moved through the shadows, around the side of the building, until he was standing at the rear. It connected to a lane way, looked to be no cameras, which Sam thought was odd. He smiled anyway, sure that he could do this without being caught, and approached the building.

The back door was just a garage door, like at a private residence. It didn't quite make sense, with the front of the building being so heavy on security. Especially with the rear connected to an alley, where crimes were known to happen.

Sam approached the door, tried to slide it up. It clicked, releasing a high-pitched creak as it opened. He held his breath as the stink of bleach and chemicals washed over him and he walked inside. Careful not to make a sound, his footsteps were soft and purposeful. Someone was in there.

He moved from the garage into the morgue, passing benches of chemicals and bottles and implements used to cut people open. The bleach made him dry reach, and he craved the scent of blood once more. Anything, really, to get rid of the inhuman smell of chemicals.

Why did I think of blood as the first option?

He heard movement ahead. and he ducked behind a bench. The coroner—a woman dressed in a white coat, hair pulled in a tight bun—walked around an embalming table, high heels clicking against the linoleum floor. Sam watched her movements, the sway of her hips and the fluid motions of her arms as she approached the body on the table.

Her back to him now, he stood and continued forward. A sharp tool glinted in the corner of his eye, and Sam looked at the implement. He didn't know what it was, but it was heavy and bulky, and he imagined whacking the coroner over the head with it.

Shaking off the fantasy, he held his breath and moved forward again. The coroner, just ahead, back facing him, leaned over the body on the table, muttering to herself. As Sam approached, he was less and less sure of what he was going to do when he reached her.

I should go back. Wait until she's gone. What the fuck am I doing?

He was enamored by the body on the table, though. It wasn't Danny—*Of course not, he's not dead*—but they had the same expression as he'd had when Sam saw him in his bed earlier that day. Serene.

A white sheet draped over the person's dignity but couldn't hide their expression. *Not serene. Why had I thought that?* Empty. Eyes open, mouth agape in fear. A hand jutted out from under the sheet, fingers clenched with rigor, as though scratching at something.

At someone.

He wanted to turn back. Before the coroner looked up and saw him. She was youngish, maybe his age. She was confident, he could tell by the way she carried herself. Straight shoulders, inquisitive gaze on the corpse. She caressed the body with gloved fingertips, as though she knew the person.

Sam crept on, unsure why he couldn't turn back, and suddenly he was outside his body again. Watching himself through TV static. The woman looked up, her eyes searching the area. Searching Sam to figure out if he was a threat.

His body tensed. He raised his hands. "I know I'm not supposed to be here," he said. The woman lifted an eyebrow, then folded her arms. "My friend...my ex, actually. He...he..."

"He died." She finished the sentence for him with a nod and a sympathetic smile. Sam swallowed hard and lowered his hands. "The stabbing?" she asked.

Sam nodded.

"Looks like you got stabbed, too," she said.

"Huh?"

"Your scar," she continued. "That's definitely from a stabbing. Who did that to you?"

Sam looked away and gulped.

"They dropped your ex off this afternoon." She shrugged off her earlier question and walked to the back wall. To the corpse storage boxes, whatever they were called. Body fridges? "You want to see him." It was a statement.

"I just..." Sam said, pausing to find the words. "I need to say goodbye."

The woman scoffed, but opened one of the drawers, anyway. "That's what funerals are for." Sam's lip trembled at that, and she lowered her eyes. "Sorry. I work in the morgue for a reason."

"Can I?" Sam asked.

She looked him up and down, assessing the threat once more. Sam was a typical nerdy guy—no gym, no exercise, no muscle—and she pursed her lips at his form. Giving a sigh, she looked across the room to a wall-mounted phone.

"I really shouldn't," she said. "Plus, you broke in. You're a criminal."

"I'm not, I promise."

"You look familiar," she muttered, thinking. Snapping her fingers, she pointed at him and stepped back. "You're the guy! Gary showed me the footage from earlier, the crazy dude covered in blood. He said you might show up again. We filled out a police report, you know."

Sam stumbled on a series of umms and ahhs coming before he found his tongue. "I'm not dangerous. This morning, I had a bit of a... I had an incident. With Danny."

The coroner stepped back again, her brow furrowed, but a familiar expression in her eyes. She was scared, but also something else. Pity. Sam could see it, he knew it. And he'd take advantage of it.

Stepping toward her, he said, "I can't leave without seeing him. Without knowing for sure that he's dead."

"Your boyfriend is dead, I can assure you." Her voice was firm and sharp, just a hint of a tremble.

He stepped closer. It felt like he was outside himself again. Watching his body do these things when his mind was screaming to run away and never look back. To go home and crawl into bed, and stay there until the end of the world.

Another step.

"Please. I need to see him."

The coroner gulped, and eyed a drawer. "If it'll get you to leave, I will show you."

Sam smiled, only with his mouth, though. His eyes still pleaded. "Thank you."

She walked a few steps to a drawer and pulled it open. "Here he is."

Sam approached, still watching from outside himself. Part of him wanted to close his eyes, part of him wanted to apologize and head for the rear exit. Part of him wanted to curl up next to Danny and die with him in that drawer. But he kept walking, despite himself. And his heart pounded.

Tick. Tick. Tick.

All the way out here, away from the house, the ticking was still with him. Guiding him forward. Goading him.

"I wouldn't normally do this," she said, "and you are forcing my hand."

"I know, I'm sorry," Sam said, though it was robotic and sounded unnatural.

"You look pretty messed up already. It's not pretty, are you sure you want to do this?"

"I don't care," Sam replied, and stood over Danny. "I need to see him."

The coroner nodded, looking him up and down again. "I shouldn't show you this..." She stepped aside and invited Sam to see.

He lay naked, his skin bluing a little, but mostly just pale. Devoid of color. His face was peaceful, like he was having the most beautiful dream. *No, empty. Hollow. Dead.* Sam expected to see the rise and fall of Danny's chest and had to remind himself it wasn't coming. The coroner watched him and then pointed to the exposed abdomen.

"Tell me what happened."

The coroner began to shake her head, and Sam shot her a look that mad her stop. She breathed long and hard out of her mouth, and then nodded.

"See the bruising around this wound?" She traced a finger along a section of sliced flesh. "The stabber was forceful. And see the tearing at the neck? The sick fucker took a real good bite."

Sam held back tears.

Tick.

"He was stabbed over a hundred times." She looked at him as she spoke, gauging his reaction to the news. Sensing something in the way he held a hand to his mouth, she continued. "His torso was essentially stabbed so many times it came off. That's why the guts are all...messy."

Looking down at the organs, packed inside Danny like teddy bear stuffing after its fallen out. He scrunched up his face and muttered, "Fuck."

The coroner was calmer now, realizing he wasn't a threat, just some traumatized guy who didn't understand boundaries, and maybe had a bit of trouble with the law. She licked her lips. "Once the organs have come out, it's really hard to put them back in place. I mean, you *can* do it with some, but the intestines here"—she pointed with her index finger—"will never be able to be put back properly."

"Who would do this?" Sam whispered through a heavy breath, the stench of the organs settling into his skin. His own stomach craving the decaying intestines.

"Don't know much else." She shrugged. "Not until the autopsy." Gazing down at Danny like he was a prize, she sucked in deep breaths above his face and neck. Smelling him.

"Is that a technique you get taught?" Sam asked.

She smiled. "No, I just like the smell of freshly dead people. What about you?" Blinking at her, Sam stepped back. She shrugged and pushed the drawer back in, closing the door. "You should go now. You've seen what you came to see."

He wanted to go, but his body wouldn't move. He tried to lift a foot, tried to turn, and run out of there. He couldn't. He and the coroner stared at each other in silence for a few seconds until the buzz of Sam's phone echoed through the morgue.

Digging it from his pocket, Sam saw it was another GPS pin. His eyes flicked from phone to the coroner and back again as he clicked on the pin. Apple Maps zoomed into the red marker and a location appeared.

"Harker County Morgue," Sam said, confused.

The coroner craned her neck to see what was on Sam's phone screen. "That's us," she said.

Tick.

"I know...but I'm already here."

She turned away from Sam, heading back to the corpse on the table, and mumbled that Sam should be on his way. That she wasn't sure why she'd let him see his dead friend and to please keep it quiet, because she didn't want either of them getting in trouble.

As she spoke, Sam remembered the knife. Waking up with blood in his mouth, and the taste of something he hadn't recognized at the time. He recognized it now, though. He had tasted it and loved it and wanted more.

Suddenly, he understood why the coroner had smelled Danny's dead body. She could smell it, too. The scent of death lingering in the air between him and the coroner. It was rich and sweet and beautiful. He opened his mouth to ask her, to see if she knew what was happening to him when—

Tick, tick, tick.

—he heard the ticking clear as day. He knew that the clock—here and now, in this room—moved for him. Spoke to him. His phone buzzed again. The same GPS coordinates. Again. Someone wanted him here. Someone wanted him to do something. And he knew just what it was.

Before he could stop himself, Sam stepped toward the coroner, fingers clenched tighter than he knew was possible.

Chapter 8

"Lunch is ready," Shelley called through the kitchen toward the living room. The television blared over her voice, the screen cast dim lights across the child sitting in front of it. Moving to the living room entrance, Shelley leaned against the doorframe and folded her arms. "Turn it off and come eat."

Two little eyes flicked toward her and then back to the television. An old cartoon about a half-dog half-cat. Shelley hated that fucking show. For one thing, the creature had no arsehole. For another, every episode was like a fever dream, very inappropriate for children. Especially hers.

She cleared her throat as loud as she could, invoking the age-old, "If you don't do what I want right now, you will regret it" grumble.

The child slumped for a moment before reaching for the remote. Holding it up to the screen, she glared at Shelley, and then switched off the television. "That was my favorite episode," the child mumbled.

"After what you did last night, I don't care," Shelley said, swallowing hard. She hoped the kid didn't hear it. Hoped she didn't see the thinly-veiled fear behind her eyes. "Come eat, pumpkin."

Shelley should have aborted, that much she knew. As soon as the first bump appeared, she should have gone to the doctor. Or grabbed a fucking coat hanger and ended it. She'd tried once, but her hand had shaken so terribly she'd scratched at the vulva and not much else. Every time she made an appointment with Family Planning, something had gotten in the way. Like divine intervention or something. At one point, about six months into the pregnancy, she considered approaching the media. She could even see the headlines: *Virgin mother pregnant with savior.* Except she knew what grew inside her was nothing of a savior. Not even close.

"Don't call me *pumpkin*." The child climbed into a seat at the kitchen table, rubbing at a fresh cigarette burn, and picked at her food. Salad sandwich. No meat.

Shelley smiled at the grimace on the child's face. *Bitch.* She took her pleasures where she could; stubbing out her butts and depriving the child of meat was about as good as it got for her.

The child grumbled as she picked at tomato and lettuce and carrot. They both knew this game, and Shelley was convinced the kid would play. Eat the food, go back to the television. Don't eat the food and go to *the room*. Shelley always hoped the kid would choose the room. At least that way she'd get a few days of peace and quiet.

"Eat up, honey." Shelley sat opposite the kid, her words drenched in sarcasm. "It's good for you."

"You know what else is good for me?" the kid asked.

Shelley shrugged. "Why don't you tell me?"

"Meat." The eyes lit up. "Delicious, raw flesh. All that strawberry topping. That's my favorite."

Strawberry topping... A lie she'd told the girl as a smaller child, when she'd first tasted blood. "I know it is, honey." Shelley reached across the table and patted the child's forearm. Tried not to grimace as their skin touched. "But you aren't getting any meat today. You had your fill already."

The child stared at Shelley for what felt like forever, both of them engaged in a contest of power and will. When Shelley didn't break, the child grabbed her lunch plate and threw it across the kitchen. The tomato leaked over the tiled floor, lumps of lettuce and carrot scattered around the place.

"That's it." Shelley smiled and pointed a sharp finger out of the kitchen. "Down to the room. Now."

"No, I'm sorry," the child replied, falling to the floor and grabbing handfuls of salad. "I'll eat it."

"Too late." Shelley leaped at the child, grabbing at her torso and upper body. The kid screamed that high-pitch wail she always did, kicked and struggled, and Shelley smacked her in the mouth. For a second she thought the kid would spit out a tooth, and she got excited. Dazed, the kid quietened down, and Shelley hoisted her over a shoulder.

"Please," the kid cried, settling down at the realization her attempts were futile.

Alligator tears. Ignoring the plea, Shelley waltzed through the house toward the basement, a concrete box sealed up tight underneath the main bedroom. Kicking open the wooden door, Shelley walked into the dark room and lowered the kid onto a blackened mattress on the floor, stained with dirt and grime and piss.

The kid tried to run, but Shelley grabbed her by the hair and threw her back to the mattress. Yanking her by the ankle, Shelley clasped an iron buckle around the kid, chaining her to a wall.

"You stay down here until you can behave."

The child glared at her mother for a few beats and then said, "Can I at least have my teddy?" Squinted into the dark room for her toy.

Shelley looked around. By the far wall, a teddy bear. The once-brown toy was now a deep black, unwashed for eight years. The stitching had come apart on the arms and one of the legs, stuffing leaking like blood.

"Here you are, pumpkin." Shelley passed the teddy, and the kid snatched it, holding it tight to her chest.

Standing in the doorway, Shelley gazed down at the child. She'd stopped yanking at the chain years ago, accepting it the way dogs accept the leash. As she moved to close the door, the child said, "When are you going to give me a name?"

Thinking it over, Shelley twisted her face in disgust. "When you deserve one." She slammed the door and headed upstairs, leaving her daughter to ponder in the dark. As echoes of the kid's pleas drifted up the stairs, Shelley thought back to the house where it all started. She wished she could remember what that house had done to her. And why it had cursed her with this fucking child.

Eight years of torture and all she knew was where it happened. No other question had been answered. She pondered at the last eight years of her life as she returned to the kitchen. Kicking the lettuce and salad around the floor, Shelley moved to the kettle and switched it on. As the water began to boil, she imagined all the things she could do to that kid with the steam.

Smiling to herself, she poured hot water over a tea bag in a mug and watched the brown water swirl.

Staring at the basement wall, the girl waited, and tried to shed a tear. She'd seen this in films and cartoons. When people did something bad and got caught, they cried. Or when someone died, or they injured themselves. She did love it when they spilled strawberry topping everywhere. She also knew people cried when they were alone in a pitch-black basement, being punished for not eating salad—again. She strained her eyes, squinted, and poked at them.

Nothing.

Well, except for her eyes being sore from the poking. She scowled at herself for her stupidity. It wasn't sore exactly, not pain in the way people on TV showed it. She poked harder. She'd tried this exact same thing many, many times before, and each time the same response.

What am I missing? she wondered. *Why can't I just be a good girl and cry for Mommy?*

Sighing in the dark, she waited. He'd be back soon, and then she could ask him what was going on. And this time, she'd make him answer. Until then, she had teddy. Placing him down, she began digging into the moldy fabric of the mattress with her nails. She loved to dig and had no idea why.

"Teddy, my love?" the girl asked the rotting bear after a while.

In a voice she liked to think was the doll's, she replied to herself, "Yes, my beautiful girl?"

The girl smiled. "Why does Mommy hate me?"

"It's because you don't cry." The doll told her.

It wasn't that. Not *just* that. She knew it was something more, but it eluded her grasp. Footsteps above didn't elude her, though. Her mother upstairs, rushing about, doing whatever it was that she did while she was trapped down here.

Not exactly *trapped*, but without his help, she couldn't sneak out again. So she waited.

She held the doll to her face, squinting at it in the dark. It's little glass eyes glinted somehow, and the girl always wondered how that was possible.

Then she realized.

Behind the teddy bear. The wall.

Pulsing slowly, back and forth. It was coming alive again, just like last time, a dull gray glow emanating from the surface.

The girl smiled and hugged the teddy bear close to her chest. Waited for the wall to light up and show her how it breathed. She liked to sync her own breathing to the wall's. Since her teddy didn't have lungs and she liked the sensation of being in rhythm with someone else. Even if they didn't have a face.

It glowed brighter.

"Hello," she said. "I was waiting for you. Will you help me get out again?"

The words came into her head. Soundless, but overpowering. *Why didn't you eat the salad?*

She sighed hard and thrust her teddy to the dirty mattress. "I didn't *want* the salad. It doesn't taste good. I wanted to eat some meat." She looked away from the wall, ashamed. "I had the...hunger...again."

Your hunger is your gift.

"A gift?" The girl straightened, narrowing her eyes. "Then why does she hate me for it? Mommy, I mean."

The wall stopped pulsing, the glow dimming a little, casting shadows across the girl's face. She repeated the question and waited. All she did was wait, it wasn't fun anymore.

"Hello? Are you still there?"

She hates you for lots of reasons. The pulsing resumed. The gray glow of cement as it expanded and contracted.

The girl picked her teddy up again and hugged it tight, frowning. "What did I do? I'm a good girl, aren't I?"

A deep, hollow sound came from the wall. She recognized it as laughter, a slow, steady beat. *You aren't a girl.*

The girl stood up, angry. "Excuse me! Yes I am. I don't have a penis, and that makes me a girl!"

More laughter, the pulsing getting faster. *The sex organ doesn't define you, child.*

"Well then, what—"

You're not any gender. You aren't human.

This was news to the girl. She looked human. She had two arms, two legs, ten fingers and toes. She had all the correct parts for a human, she looked just like people on television.

If she wasn't human, was she like CatDog? Some half-half beast? No, she was just like all the real people she saw in her movies. Except—

"This is because I don't cry?" she asked, stepping closer to the wall. She poked her eyes again until they stung. "I try, but nothing happens."

What else can't you do?

The girl thought for a moment, coming up blank.

Bleed for me, child.

"What?"

Bleed for me. Pulsing, pulsing, pulsing.

Expand, contract.

"I don't know—"

Bite your arm. Break the skin. Bleed for me. Now.

She licked at her lips and considered the request. Sure, it was odd, but she was intrigued. Plus, she did like the taste of strawberry topping. It had never occurred to her to drink her own. *Silly,* she thought. *Such a silly billy. Why didn't I ever think of that?*

Setting her teddy on the mattress once more, the girl took a breath. "I'll just take a little bite," she said.

Bleed for me.

She sniffed at her arm and found a spot she liked. Salty and warm, but not the same as that guy she—

Biting down, she felt the skin break open, her teeth sinking into flesh. She'd gone deeper than she thought. This wasn't the same as the last guy she'd done this to, though. She expected red liquid to flow from the wound, pour into her mouth and drip to the ground.

She took her teeth out of her arm. "Huh. No strawberry?"

You can't bleed. You aren't human.

"But…if I'm not a human, then…what am I?"

I'll tell you everything.

"Am I like my teddy bear? He doesn't bleed either." She thought about this, noticing that the gaping wound in her arm didn't hurt. "But he doesn't talk or move."

I'll tell you everything. But first, you need to do something for me.

The girl opened her mouth to speak, to say she'd do anything to know what she was and why she can't bleed or cry or feel pain. She took a step toward the wall—pulsating hard with excitement now—and felt the chain around her ankle.

"Hey," she said. "Aren't you going to help me get out again?"

The wall stopped moving.

"Where'd you go?" she asked, waited. Then: "Hey!"

Nothing.

"Pfft. You're just like Mommy."

She figured that would work, and it did. The wall pulsated again, slow and rhythmic, and she synchronized her own breaths with it. Relishing in not being alone.

Not today. The voice came again. *You need to do something for me.*

The girl shook her head. "No. I just did do something for you"—she held out the wound on her arm and pointed—"so now, you have to do something for me." Folding her arms, she pursed her lips. "That's how it works."

The wall stopped glowing. Stopped pulsating. And the girl was thrust into darkness once more.

"You should have just done what he wanted." The teddy's voice came.

"Shut up, teddy." The girl dropped to the mattress with a thud and resumed digging.

Chapter 9

The coroner scratched at Sam's face, a futile attempt to defend herself. In the end, he'd pushed her against the gurney. She and the corpse tumbled to the floor as Sam's hand locked around a scalpel.

The inside of his brain screamed and begged and screamed again, fighting with all its strength to stop his body. He watched through eyes that, in that moment, did not belong to him. He felt the scalpel sink into the flesh, splitting it apart under the force of the blade. The coroner stared up at him as her guts fell to the floor beside her, snatching at her own intestines and liver to put them back in. Her insides hemorrhaged and she coughed a stream of blood.

Sam watched from outside himself as he slashed at her face and arms. He fell to his knees, though not from any sense of willpower. Whatever will he once had was gone, and he watched on through the prison of his eyes.

It was the smell that repulsed him the most. Even as he leaned in to the coroner, watching the skin on her neck pulsing up and down, it was the smell. Her intestines and whatever else, messing up the white tiles beneath them, sent an acrid stench through the morgue.

Yet somehow, the pulsing of her neck was hypnotic. Everything else disappeared and for a moment Sam wasn't just a visitor in his own body. For a moment he was there, present and in control. Staring at the neck of this young, confident woman.

Wanting to taste her.

"I can't," he whispered.

Tick.

She looked at him again, her eyes begging for this to please be a dream. Sam swiped away a strand of hair sticking to her forehead. Kissed it. Beads of perspiration coalesced around his lips, and he licked them into his mouth.

I can't do this.

Tick, tick.

The pulsing of her neck slowed, and the smell came again. Sam fluttered his eyelids, hungry for the red inside her veins. As much as he wanted to push away, as much as he wanted to leave this place and never look back, he caressed his nose against the skin on her neck.

And bit into her.

Tick, tick, tick.

She was too weak to scream or beg or defend herself. She just lay there, letting Sam gulp her blood like water from a fountain. And drink he did, swallowing her blood with a vigor he didn't know he had. His stomach churned as the liquid settled inside him, devouring the sweetness like candy.

When he was done, Sam sat back on his haunches, wiping at his mouth and chin. He looked at the coroner, her skin pale and tinged with blue, and stood. Turning back to the drawer holding Danny, he opened the door and pulled out his ex-boyfriend.

He wanted to taste him one more time. Bent over the corpse of his once beloved, he opened his mouth. Sam's phone buzzed again. The GPS pin for "Home". That's when he realized Danny wasn't his anymore. Whatever was left of the coroner wasn't his, either.

He spent the next twenty minutes dragging their bodies to his car, folding their limbs in strange directions to fit them both into the trunk. As he drove away from the morgue, blood still staining his chin and his clothes, Sam looked at himself in the rear view mirror.

"What have you done?" he asked.

For a moment, it seemed as though his reflection moved on its own. For a moment it felt that he was, again, watching himself from a distance. Yet something inside him knew a truth he didn't want to admit. A truth he couldn't hide from, no matter how far he drove.

I enjoyed it.

When he arrived home, the car's headlights shining against the brick façade of the house, Sam's heart clenched. The way it does when someone runs into an ex-lover or an old friend. He missed the sight of this place, even though he'd only lived there for one day.

The window sills glowed in the dim yellow lights from Sam's car, casting shadows like eyebrows along the brick. It was as if the bricks of its forehead moved into an expression of sharp, twisted satisfaction.

Sam felt it, too. The satisfaction. Pawing at the drying blood on his mouth and chin, he licked at the red stains like an addict. Tasting the sweetness of the coroner once more. The garage door rolled up on its own, without Sam even pressing the button on the automatic door.

"I'm home," Sam whispered.

He knew the house heard him. As the door rolled back down with the car safely inside the garage, the metal churned, as if to say, *Welcome home.*

The car idled for a moment, black fumes filling the tight space of the garage, until Sam turned the ignition off. He sat in silence for a moment, searching for the *tick tick tick* that he was longing for.

Nothing.

He opened the trunk to see the bodies of Danny and the coroner, faces still mangled in fear. The bite marks in the coroner's neck leaked fluid onto the carpet. Sam didn't care. They were here. With him.

Home.

Looking upon Danny, the paleness of his skin and the bruising from rigor, Sam felt a pang of guilt. He searched his memory, but still couldn't remember where he'd been the previous night. If he'd woken up with Danny's blood all over him.

Surely not. I would never.

He repeated the mantra as he pulled Danny's corpse from the car, grimacing at the smack of dead flesh against concrete. He noticed the blood seeping out of the car onto the garage floor. The *drip drip drip* catching his ear.

What am I doing?

Dragging Danny's naked body through the garage, he pushed open the door leading to the inside of the house. Heaving, he lost his footing on the floorboards, and slipped. Danny's upper body slapped against the floor, face first, as Sam fell backward into the opposite wall.

Tick.

The sound comforted him as it came again and again, the clock sensing its meal time was near. The comfort of the *tick tick tick* waned as Sam realized what he'd done. What his body had done as he watched from inside his own mind. Powerless.

Tick tick tick.

"Stop it," Sam said, staring at Danny's corpse. "Just stop it. Don't make me do anything else."

Beneath the ticking, Sam recognized another sound. It wasn't that he heard it, rather he sensed it. Words, creaking up at him from the flooring and from cracks in the house's frame.

"What are you saying?" Sam asked, covering his ears to hide from the ticking. "I brought them here for you. What else do you want?"

He wasn't sure who he was speaking to, and didn't expect an answer. Yet he waited in the silence, anyway. Gave the house a chance to speak to him. Keeping his eyes and ear peeled for sound or movement, Sam got to his feet.

As he stood, his eyes began to water and he drew in a horrible stench. Rot. Decay. Looking down at Danny, he saw the skin harden and crack. Shriveling like an old prune around Danny's bones. He reached a hand to his ex-boyfriend, stopping only when the skin burst open, spitting blood and mucus across the tiled floor.

Sam watched, hands over his mouth, eyes wide with a mixture of fear and excitement. His stomach churned for a reason he couldn't yet identify. A deep sense of hunger washed over him and it made him sick.

Danny's body continued to decay before his eyes, the blood melting into the floor. Like the floorboards were eating him. The house groaned as Danny sank further into its grasp, and Sam shed a tear.

"Danny. I'm sorry."

It was all he could muster, despite the years of love and pain and laughter they'd shared. The nights of sleeplessness, talking in sweet whispers across the bed. The mornings of complete inanity, making toast and scrambled eggs while Danny hummed a stupid tune to some musical they'd seen years earlier. It was all there, in Sam's head. In his heart.

As Danny sank through the floor out of existence, Sam's heart sank, too.

Tick.

It was as though the house was eating the memories. Eating the love they shared. Eating it all. Body and soul.

Tick.

Sam collapsed to the floor, grabbing at the wooden flooring for remnants of Danny. Remnants of his blood and bones. A spot of red caught his eye and Sam moved toward it, leaning in to smell it. Smell his ex-boyfriend, one last time. It vanished into the tile, eaten like everything else.

His stomach churned again, and Sam realized he hadn't eaten human food since the previous day. The grum-

bling and churning didn't feel like hunger, though. It reminded him the coroner was still in his car, staining the upholstery.
Reminded him of the enjoyment he'd felt at watching her
body fall apart, feeling his teeth penetrate her skin.

*I didn't enjoy it. I can't enjoy that. What's happening
to me?*

Standing on trembling legs, he looked into the garage.
The coroner was there, lifeless. Staring at him.

Tick.

His breath caught in his chest and Sam started to cry.
He'd killed her. He'd bitten into her neck and torn flesh from
her body. Drank her blood like a savage. He'd watched Danny be eaten into nothingness by a house, and the pains in his
stomach told him it wasn't over. It was just the beginning.
The house groaned again, wanting more. Wanting the dead
woman in the car.

"No," Sam said through tears. "I can't do this." He
wasn't sure how he'd done it in the first place. What had come
over him or why.

Tick. Tick.

He raced deeper into the house. To the living room,
surrounded by boxes and memories and a life he didn't know
anymore. Picked up a photo album, to grab onto who he
thought he once was, and who he wanted to be again.

Tick.

In the corner of his eye, something appeared.

Tick.

From his place in the living room, standing by a box of old photos, Sam cast his eye past the kitchen to what he had earlier thought was just a wall. But as he looked closer, there was an old lock—one of those barrel bolts that slid across over the back of the door—painted to match the wall color. It was strange because that wall was attached to the hallway linen press. The linen press was two feet deep—a generous size—so the smaller door that had just appeared here couldn't be attached to that.

It shouldn't exist.

Sam abandoned the album to the living room floorboards, and made his way to the door. Darkness had set in now, casting shadows across the house. He switched on the nearest light—the one in the hallway—and tapped on the door with a knuckle. Hollow. It was small, like Frodo's front door. Not a perfect rectangle.

How did I miss this before?

A soft ticking came from beyond the door. As he stepped closer, the ticking started again. He swung around to face the kitchen, but the sound shifted. It was around him. Encompassing him. Something was in the house. He could feel it.

Whatever it was had taken Danny.

He shook the feeling and continued to the door. His hands slick with sweat, he rubbed them against his jeans, conscious of a line of perspiration dripping down his nape. Something was behind the door. He breathed through a chill. The house felt so much like home already. For a reason he didn't understand, Sam felt compelled to keep walking.

It needs me. His thought came in the rhythm of the *tick tick tick.* Sam gave a half smile at the ridiculousness of the words. *It needs me.*

The ticking grew louder with each step. Sam let the sound fill him, comforted yet disoriented by it.

Kneeling once more, so his eyes were level with the top of the door, he saw a dim yellow light emanate from the gaps between the old wood. Sliding the bolt, Sam opened the door. Jerked back an inch as a musty stench washed over him. Coughing through the warm, dry air, Sam peered inside. It was a tunnel, the walls appeared to be stone. At the end of the tunnel, a larger room, and the source of the light.

The yellow glow belonged to an old light. The kind that hung down from the ceiling by a cord. It was so faint that Sam couldn't be sure it was there at all. The ticking was deafening now, echoing against the walls of the room. Peering into the tunnel, it seemed the room at the end should have been in the garage.

This doesn't make sense. The door is in a wall that connects to the closet. Then leads to a tunnel that realistically should be where the garage is. How is this possible? The garage...the coroner.

Crawling on his hands and knees, Sam squeezed into the tunnel. The ground was hard on his kneecaps, and his movement lifted dust into the air. He barely fit, the tunnel walls just wide enough for his shoulders, though he had to shimmy forward with force. The rock walls smelled damp and moldy, and as Sam continued toward the room at the end, he felt the walls closing in on him, his knees beginning to ache and his fingers turning blue from the cold, wet rock. Keeping a steady eye on the dim yellow glow, he pushed through what felt like a hundred yards—*Definitely should be in the garage now*—and emerged into the room at the end.

The space was bigger than he would have thought, like an old storage space under a staircase. He couldn't stand without hitting his head, so Sam kneeled on his knees, ignoring the ache. He cupped his hands by his mouth and breathed into them, warming his fingers only slightly.

He looked around the room, his eyes focusing on the weak light. Like the tunnel, the room was made of rock, cobwebs strewn from the crevices in the low ceiling. The light dangled by a single chord. Sam couldn't see a light switch, and scanned the room again. Scratch marks in the rock on the far side of the room—five feet away. He estimated the room was square, the walls appearing to be of a similar length. Sam narrowed his eyes, sensing he was somewhere he didn't belong.

The room appeared empty, but just as Sam motioned to turn away from the yellow light, something gleamed in the corner of his eye. From a dark corner in the room, as though whatever was there didn't want to be revealed.

A clock.

The clock. "Is that you I heard?" Sam felt odd saying it out loud, though he was sure the clock heard him.

Just a normal old clock, like the ones they had in school. Plain white, black numbers and a red second hand. He moved forward, sniffing hard against the stale air, to get a closer look at the timepiece.

The hands didn't move. The tick grew louder. Thumping in time with his heart. Each tick felt like a punch to his chest as he drew closer to the clock. It called to him, the clock. Almost like it was his. It belonged to him, always had.

It's ticking for me.

The static hands caught his attention, growing a deep black he couldn't look away from. The yellow light faded, yet the clock hands were as visible as in the midday sun. The long, thin minute hand stuck between ten and eleven. It felt like the time was telling him something. The ticking—like an echo—continued.

He crouched before the clock and caressed its face. Despite the darkness, the clock face shone against his hands. Another gentle finger on its face, and the hands remained inactive. As though they had never known movement at all.

Tick.

Straining to check his own wristwatch, Sam noted the times were different.

It's telling me something, Sam thought. *Talking to me.*
8:52.

Sam's chest grew heavy, his breathing stifled. As he gazed upon the clock face, something inside him stirred. Something he did not recognize. He drew breath after deep breath, reaching for the clock. Yet just as his fingers caressed its surface, Sam pulled away. It seemed odd to him that he should want to touch this clock.

He stayed there, time fading into a memory, unable to look away. The outside world meant nothing, the last vestiges of a life he didn't want. Danny, Patrick, all of it. Memories, just lingering at the edges of his consciousness.

Danny...

A smile grabbed at the corners of his mouth. He remembered Danny's face, the way he smelled, the way he joked. His laugh. The way he sipped his coffee and blew on it, even when it was lukewarm.

My Danny...

Sam backed away on his hands and knees, toward the tunnel, squeezing into the tight space once more. The door was ahead of him—too far. Memories of Danny clouded his mind, he squeezed farther down the tunnel. Back to the door. Back to the real world. Pushing himself along the tunnel, it felt as though the rock walls closed in around him. Shrinking in on him until the tunnel was nothing more than a cavity.

A coffin.

Chest heaving and clenching around his heart, he crawled. Despite the claustrophobia, the dust, and the staleness of the room, Sam knew he'd discovered something of great importance. He wasn't sure what to do. Leave the room and do…what? Unpack boxes? It seemed so trivial with the clock face staring back at him.

I should go back. But he stopped. Couldn't move.

It was as though time, just as his body, stood still in this room.

Sam blinked, wondering how long he'd been staring at the display. The tunnel felt even smaller now, and he gasped for air that was damp and foul. The walls closed in, no longer a rigid surface, but fleshy and organic. Bending and writhing like skin, pressing against his body. He could barely move, and as he pulled himself closer to the door—the handle just beyond his outstretched fingertips—the tunnel walls settled onto his skin. The fibrous flesh of the walls was warm, unlike the rockiness he'd traveled through earlier.

The space was changing, turning into something else. As the fleshy walls pushed into him, Sam breathed out hard. Despite no air left in his lungs, despite the tightness of the space, he felt warm and cared for. He stopped trying to move. Stopped fighting against the walls and the dust and the darkness enveloping him. In that moment, he understood that the tunnel and all that made it was part of a larger structure, inviting him to become part of it.

A womb.

Snug around his body, the walls seemed to expand and contract, breathing around him. Despite the comfort and safety offered by the darkness, Sam thought of Danny. And Patrick. And, for some reason, his father. Unfinished business, all of them.

He attempted to move to the exit. As he neared the door—fighting against the flesh walls that seemed to suck him backward—it felt as though he was being birthed. Squeezing headfirst out of the tunnel, away from the room, back to the real world. Leaving the clock, and its unmoving hands, on the other side.

The clock.

The clock that defied time. Sam checked his wristwatch. The hands ticked normally, as though nothing had happened at all. 1:59 a.m. He collapsed against the wall, next to the tiny door, staring but not seeing anything. Unable to comprehend what he'd just experienced.

Closing his arms around his chest, he sucked in the air, fresh but sickly. Through the sound of his breathing, the ticking returned, and his breaths slowly began to move in the same rhythm as the *tick tick tick*. His own heart mirroring the heartbeat of the house.

Sam didn't know how many minutes had ticked past, only that when he was ready to move. The faded glow of the moon kept his new house from complete darkness.

He couldn't spend all night sitting in the hallway. He stood, reaching for the light switch on the wall. The light flickered to life a second later, revealing the living room once more. By now he had forgotten all about the photo albums and the memories contained within. He continued his work, emptying box after box, it was as though he was on autopilot. Every few seconds, he would peer back at the impossible door in the wall, listening for the heartbeat of the house.

The rhythm of the *tick tick tick* entered Sam as though it was part of him. Thumping inside him. Inside his heart. Until it overpowered everything he was. His eyes grew heavy. Sam sat on the lounge the movers had clumsily placed over the stained rug. A stack of vampire graphic novels toppled next to him. Looking at the front covers, Sam smiled at the fangs and the bats and the obligatory woman screaming for safety, like the coroner had.

Tick.

The coroner. She was still in the car, rotting away and leaking onto the carpet in the trunk. The ticking came again, just as the thought entered his mind. He turned away from the graphic novels, and faced the living room. Among the boxes and memories, something older stared out at him.

The rug.

The faces.

Sam swallowed hard, and stepped toward the rug, his eyes wide and unblinking. The faces appeared in the rug, mouths hanging, hungry. Starving. His stomach knotted, and his breath caught. The faces began to change, eyes opening like black holes in the fabric. Dead, dark eyes, staring into Sam's very essence.

He knew what needed to be done.

And he would do it.

The last vestiges of the coroner sank into the flooring around him, and he watched with disbelief. Not only for the fact that a house had swallowed a human being, but that he didn't hate the sight of it. Disbelief that somewhere inside him, he was glad. Satisfied.

Sam rested his forehead against the wall, felt the plaster turn into wood. A small doorknob sprouted by his hand and Sam turned it, falling into the tunnel. As he hit the floor, Sam felt at ease. Inside this space, with the walls pulsating like lungs around him, he felt safe. Like Danny and the coroner and the death and blood were all just bad dreams. Like he belonged here.

Shutting the door, Sam locked the world away. He crawled through the tunnel to the room, each movement feeling fluid and natural, his body at ease. He gazed across the dimly lit room at the clock.

My clock.

The ticking stopped again. He moved toward it and took note of the time. It didn't matter, though. Time didn't exist here.

And he liked it that way.

Sam closed his eyes, exhaustion washing through him, and he clutched at the graphic novels, unsure why they suddenly felt so important. With a first edition of *American Vampire*, tight in its original wrapping, firm in his hand, Sam gave into the beckoning sleep.

Part Two

Chapter 10

Jimmy sucked down the pot smoke in a heavy breath, feeling it cloud her lungs and spread, like piss through a swimming pool. Sinking low into Pete's lounge with a stretch and a yawn, she let the fabric consume her. She loved that sensation and since she was four joints in, she felt like she and the couch were one and the same.

Pot was the only thing that had kept her going until Pete came along. She never did learn Pete's deadname, and never asked. Hell, she didn't want anyone to ask about her boy name, either. She made it complicated by shortening a girl's name—Jemima—back to a traditionally boys name. Why? Because fuck society's rules, that's why.

Fuck society and fuck everyone. Abandoned by a family that didn't understand the difference between sex and gender. Abandoned by friends who couldn't hack having a trans friend. Abandoned by everyone, really.

Except Pete. He'd given her a place to stay after she'd shown up to group that first time. A transgender support group, the only one in a fifty mile radius.

Shifting deeper into a groove in his lounge, Jimmy breathed the pot out. The plume of smoke drifted to the ceiling and she felt her whole body relax into the fabric of the lounge. Like she was melting into nothingness. She fucking loved that feeling.

Sinking further into the abyss of her own mind, Jimmy didn't notice Pete walk into the room. Freshly showered, a towel round his waist and another scratching at his hair. She saw his mouth moving, but the words were a blur. Like reality. Just one mess of a blur.

"You hearing me?" Pete walked over and tapped Jimmy on the side of the head.

Jimmy laughed, the sound whistling off her teeth.

"I'm serious," Pete said. "We should warn that guy."

Warn, she thought. *Warn? Warn who? Warn, that's a funny word. Warm. Swarm.* Jimmy giggled as the words cycled through her mind, barely noticing Pete leave the room. *Swarm. Swarmer. Kormer...Korma?* "I could go for some korma, sure."

Pete retuned, dressed in cargoes and a polo. "What are you talking about korma for?" He shook his head and snatched the joint from Jimmy. He snapped his fingers in front of her eyes and she blinked to focus. "Jimmy, I had a real bad feeling today in that house."

Nodding, Jimmy licked her lips. She could also smell that korma already. Pulling her mind back to reality, she said, "Yeah, man. I know what you mean." She had no idea what was going on. *Where's my korma?*

Pete sighed and shook his head. The beginnings of a double chin wobbled just a little as he did so. Jimmy grinned, hypnotized by the movement. She followed his eyes and settled on the sadness she saw there. She sat up straight, abandoning the comfort of the lounge and mentally slapped herself.

"Pete?" she asked, wiping the drug haze from her face. "What's up, man?"

He sighed again and cleared his throat. "That house today. I've never had such a bad feeling before, right here in my chest." He placed hands over his heart. "It's a bad place. I think we should head over there and warn that guy before anything—"

"Before what?" Jimmy slurred, giving in to the effects of the pot once more. "What do you think is going to happen? The house is gonna, like, what? Eat him up? It's a house."

"It's more than that," Pete muttered. "I know it." Moving past Jimmy to the kitchen counter, he grabbed his car keys and headed for the front door.

"Where you going, Petey Pete-Pete?" Jimmy broke into laughter again, writhing on the lounge at some unfathomable joke.

She heard the door slam and raced toward it. Pulling it open to expose the fresh night air, she saw Pete driving away in his white station wagon. As the car got smaller, Jimmy called with all her might, "Hey Petey, get me some chicken korma!"

Pete watched from his car as Sam pulled into the driveway of the rental house. He wondered how the young man hadn't noticed the way the house moved. Like a face, reacting to the life suffering inside it. The panes at the front windows—its eyes—were thick and dark, like dark circles of exhaustion. Yet, as Sam drove into the garage, the house seemed to inhale and smile. A twisted, sharp smile.

It's alive.

He clutched the door handle and as the door clicked open, he paused. Watched. Sam peered into the darkness beyond the dim yellow glow of the garage, looked in Pete's direction. Pete lowered in his seat and held his breath. He was safe. Sam hadn't seen him, had he?

Sneaking a look out the car window, Pete watched Sam close the garage door. The look on his face was a mix of terror and delight. Spots of red scattered across Sam's skin and clothes.

Blood. It's blood. It has to be.

Pete swallowed hard as the garage door sealed tight, locking Sam inside. The scraping of metal against metal rang into the night air, and Pete broke into goosebumps. He shivered, a cold sweat lacquering his arms and neck. The pit of his stomach lurched and he shivered again.

He'd had this feeling only once before in his life. The afternoon before his mother died and a hummingbird had pecked at his kitchen window. He'd not seen or spoken to his mother in fifteen years—the day he'd come out as trans and was subsequently disowned—yet somehow, the hummingbird's *peck peck peck* told him only one thing. His stomach had lurched then, too, and his skin had broken out the way it was now. A layer of cold sweat dripping to the ground, as it dripped now onto the old carpet of his car floor. The phone had rang then, the speaker carrying the bad news, and Pete half expected his cell to ring now.

Nothing. Silence.

But that feeling remained.

Taking a deep breath, Pete gripped the car door again and pushed it open, letting the warm night air wash over him. Against the sweat and the goosebumps, his head whirled. The dizziness made him bend over and hold his knees. His throat, dry and scratchy, closed up, denying oxygen for a moment.

He focused on breathing, sucking air into his nostrils until he was able to intake oxygen through this mouth again. Finally, Pete stood straight and gazed at the house once more. He could hear sounds from the garage, but couldn't identify them. It just sounded like someone shifting around in there. Moving things.

Crossing the road, Pete stepped onto Sam's lawn. The grass seemed to bend around his footfalls, avoiding his weight rather than being crushed by it. Walking to the front door, he poised a fist to knock, but stopped.

"I can't do this." Sam's words breached the wooden door as a whisper.

Do what?

Pete put an ear to the door and listened. For what, he didn't know. No more words were uttered and the house fell into a deep silence. Pushing away from the door, Pete lifted his hand once more and curled it into a fist.

He knocked once before the door opened, creaking to a stop to reveal an empty house.

"Sam?" Pete called. His heart stopped in his chest, his ears honed to the sound of the young man's voice. He listened hard, but Sam didn't reply. "Sam, are you home?"

A light flickered beyond the cannon-style hallway. In the kitchen. Pete stepped inside the house. Moving past the front door, Pete's skin broke into goosebumps once more. His stomach thrashed inside him—instinctual warnings to get the fuck out of there. He ignored the danger he felt writhing in the walls and floor of the house. He ignored his better judgment. Kept walking.

"Sam," Pete called again, louder this time.

Still nothing.

He reached the kitchen and saw the light above the counter flickering again. Staring into the yellow glow, Pete remembered the noises in the garage, and turned to trace his steps back down the hall to the interior garage door.

It looked like any other disorganized garage, made worse by the fact that Sam had only just moved in, and Pete did a lap of the space before shaking his head. *What am I doing?*

He walked back to the door, ashamed of his actions and smirking at his own overreactions. As he reached the garage exit, a glimmer of red from under Sam's car caught his eye. Approaching the car, the red stain underneath the trunk got brighter. It was shrinking, though, and Pete rubbed his eyes.

As though the blood smears were sinking into the concrete, the red was vanishing. Pete reached into his pocket for his cellphone and launched the camera. He switched to video and filmed the disappearance of the blood.

"Oh my god." He crouched low to get a better look.

Blotches of thick, coagulated blood in the shape of finger prints lined the trunk of the car. Pete reached for the lever to open the trunk, unsure if it was locked or not.

I have to try. I have to know.

As his fingers felt for the lever, the garage door slammed behind him. The phone slipped from Pete's hand as he jumped and spun to face the wooden barrier. The door opened again—*Nobody there*—and slammed, sending a chilled echo through Pete's spine.

His stomach thrashed again and Pete raced for the door, abandoning his phone under the car. He had to get out of there and find Sam. The house was…alive…no. The house was…something. As Pete stumbled through the interior garage door, slamming into the hallway, his mind spiraled into the unknown.

The house. The house. Something is inside this house.

The kid was in danger. From what, he had no idea. The garage door squealed shut behind him and Pete toppled to the floor, scraping his chin against the floorboards. A pinch of blood oozed from his split skin and Pete watched in horror as the liquid was sucked into the floor. He jumped to his feet and headed for the front door.

The kid. He's in danger.

His insides screamed and pleaded and screamed again, but Pete knew he couldn't leave. Not while the kid was in the house. Something was going on, every molecule in his body felt it. And just the same, every molecule told him to stay. To find the kid and then get the fuck out of there.

Spinning around to face the guts of the house, Pete stepped back toward the kitchen. The light still flickered, like a heartbeat, soft and steady.

"Sam?" Pete called again. "Please, kid, it's Pete. The mover. I think you're in danger." His words disappeared into the warm glow of the kitchen lights. Scanning the area, Pete saw a small door.

Walked toward it.

He gripped its tiny handle. Locked. The veins in his fingers burned at the touch of the metal handle and he shot back with a wince. Rubbing his fingers, Pete heard a noise. Not a noise.

A scream.

From the basement.

"Sam!" Pete launched to the basement door at the back of the kitchen, kicking it open. The stairs leading into the belly of the basement were shrouded in shadow and a smell Pete didn't recognize. Like rotting meat, but sweet. The stench washed over him like cool air on a hot day. Inviting him inside.

He moved to the first step, squinting through the darkness and gripping his palm against the stair rail. No light. No sounds. No scream.

Nothing.

Pete drew a heavy, sharp breath, and took another step. "Sam? Is that you I heard down here?"

As Pete continued down the steps, the darkness enveloping him like a cocoon, he noticed the door closing behind him. It was as though he watched it through a screen, like a dream or a movie. The thin strip of light under the basement door disappeared, leaving Pete to call for Sam once more in the pitch black, as the time on his watch rolled over to 8:52 p.m.

Chapter 11

The child peered through the pitch black, teddy bear snug in her arms, trying to make shapes out of the darkness. It was a game she played, ever since the first time her mother had chained her down here. Kneeling on the mattress now, her eyes started to see things.

Being immersed in complete black was both strange and exhilarating. She didn't know where she ended and the darkness began. They were one. It took some time for her to really understand that, but once the knowledge crept into her brain, she couldn't think of it any other way.

It was the three of them down there: her, teddy, and the dark. Each one a unique individual, yet somehow—impossibly—the same person. It didn't matter, then, that she didn't have a name. Because in here, in this place, she was known. She was truly seen, and the darkness didn't mind her habits. It *liked* them.

She supposed there was the fourth one, but he came and went, and he was mean to her last time, so she wasn't counting him this time. No, just the three of them.

The dark moved around her, swirling with a gentle breeze, and she twisted on her mattress, squinting to what she suspected was the back wall of her dungeon. Her mother tried to convince her it was her room. But she knew. She knew it was a prison.

Why didn't I just eat the salad?

Teddy knew why. The limp old doll had all the answers, and pretending to speak for it now, the child said, "It's not about the salad."

Sighing, she nodded. "I know, teddy. I know." She thought back to how her hunger had gotten the better of her. How that guy had been in the wrong place at the wrong time. How there was a whole house cordoned off with yellow tape because of her.

The back wall of the dungeon seemed to glow in the darkness. Only sometimes. The occasional visitor. As she stared at the wall, the concrete around her began to shimmer, the gray cement breaching the pitch-black darkness, offering a glimmer of light.

"You're back." She smiled, though she was still annoyed.

Her teddy stared, too. Its glass eyes watching the concrete pulse and contract.

The child shimmied on her knees to the wall. The chain around her ankle tightened—she couldn't move any closer. "I'm sorry I got pushy about you letting me out again."

The concrete pulsed again, expanding and contracting like lungs. She wished she could touch it. Find out who she was speaking with. Instead, she clutched her teddy tight in her arms and closed her eyes.

The voice came back, forcing its way into her head.

"Fine. I'm listening," she said. "What do you want?"

A silence filled the room. Even the sound of her own breathing disappeared, and she was left with nothing but the glowing concrete wall. It communicated with her, sharing its hopes and dreams. Its desires. Its needs.

The child sighed, though the sound was sucked away by the wall. "I'd like to do that," she said. Her words absorbed into the air without a sound. Yet, she knew she'd spoken them. "If you just take the chain off again—"

The wall heaved, cutting the child off.

"If you can't do that again, then... Oh... She does?"

A burst of light came from behind her, yellow and bright. The child grimaced as she spun to face it. The door was open, a silhouette filling the space.

"Who are you talking to?" Shelley asked from the doorway.

The girl eyed the wall behind her—the concrete had reverted back to the regular, non-breathing variety—and shrugged. "Do you see anyone down here?"

"I heard you talking. Having a conversation."

Again, the girl shrugged. "I'll eat the salad now. If you want."

Drawing a deep breath, Shelley sat at the steps by the door. The stairs leading up to the house, where she was sometimes allowed to go. "We need to talk about the other thing."

"Oh." The girl frowned. "That."

"I know you like it," Shelley paused, "but you can't go around eating people. That young man had a life."

"It wasn't my fault," the girl said, folding her arms. Teddy hung from her inner elbow, glaring at Shelley, whose silhouette didn't move.

"Whose fault is it, then?" she asked.

The girl thought for a moment and unfolded her arms, cuddling her teddy to her chest. "I'll tell you if you give me a hug…and some ice cream with strawberry topping."

Shelley stood and moved to her daughter, flicking on the light. Towering over her as she approached, Shelley's face was blank. No hatred today. No love, either. Never love.

Whatever that looks like.

"One hug," Shelley said, "and you tell me what's going on."

"And the ice cream?"

Shelley shook her head.

The girl sighed hard. "You're mad at me for eating that guy," she said, reading the sadness in her mother's eyes.

Shelley shook her head. "I have the thirst, too."

"You do?" The girl got to her feet. "Then why are you punishing me?"

Another silence filled the room, though different to the last one. Sound wasn't sucked into nothingness this time. This silence was heavy with unease.

"You want to know why I'm punishing you?" Shelley finally asked, and kneeled before her daughter. Looking her dead in the eyes, she said, "Because you're a *fucking* monster."

The girl dropped her teddy and looked at the ground. The darkness never called her a monster. Her teddy never recoiled from her touch. Nothing down here made her feel ashamed, except when her mother came to visit. Looking over her shoulder, to the back wall, the girl smiled. She'd do what it asked of her, from now until the end of time.

"A hug?" She held her arms out to Shelley, frowning.

"You'll tell me who you were talking to?"

The girl nodded. Her mother wrapped loose arms around the girl and patted her back. The girl tightened her own grip and Shelley writhed to move away.

"Get off me," she cried.

The girl squeezed as hard as she could until Shelley started to cough. She beat at the girl's back, but she kept

DAVID-JACK FLETCHER

squeezing, surprised at her own strength. Shelley spluttered and moaned for air, but the girl's grip was too tight, and after a few more moments there was no more fighting or moaning or coughing.

"Go to sleep, Mommy," the girl said, and her mother dropped to the concrete floor, her head smacking hard against the cold, hard surface.

Reaching to Shelley's left foot, the girl slid off her mother's shoe and tipped it upside down. A small metal key clanged to the concrete. She picked it up with a smile and turned to the back wall.

"You were right," she said. "How'd you know it was there?" The wall began to glow again, pulsing and pulsing and pulsing—the steady rhythm like a song—and the girl unlocked her chain. Looking down at her mother again, the girl took a breath. "Why couldn't you just love me, Mommy?"

The wall expanded and contracted again in a slow, steady rhythm. It calmed her, and she walked to the wall, finally able to touch it. To connect with something that loved her. And it did love her, she sensed that.

Placing a hand on the wall, it didn't feel like concrete. It was softer, but still coarse. Like wounded flesh. Her hand wasn't enough. She needed more of the wall against her skin. Spreading her arms wide, she latched on to the wall in a hug, pressing her face hard onto the fleshy wall, and sound vanished once more.

140

"Of course," the girl said into the silence. "I will do whatever you ask." She listened a moment longer and moved away from the wall, gazing into the deep gray. Searching. "Are you my father?"

The wall expanded and contracted again.

The girl hugged the concrete again. "Will you give me a name, Daddy?"

Expand. Contract.

"Ooooh I like that," she said. "Thank you, Daddy."

"Who..." Shelley groaned from the floor.

"Mommy, you've been a bad girl," the child said, moving to her and reaching for the chain. "You don't deserve Daddy's present."

"Present?"

"You're memories."

As the words spilled into existence, Shelley's head throbbed and ached, right behind her eyes. She squeezed them shut, and rubbed at her temples.

"You need to stay down here a while and think about what you've done." Teddy scowled.

Shelley blinked, barely conscious. "No, don't. Please."

"Your begging means nothing to us." The girl clasped the chain around Shelley's ankle. She waved to the wall and headed for the door. Headed for upstairs. She had so much to do.

"Get back here, you little bitch!"

"Teddy," the girl said. "My name is Teddy. And I'm going to get my ice cream!" She slammed the door, skipping up the stairs, Shelley's screams trailing behind her.

Eight Years Earlier
The way the letter had been sitting on her kitchen bench was strange. She lived alone and her neighbors were assholes, nobody could have collected her mail for her. Yet, there it was. A yellowing envelope, frayed at the edges with small snail bites taken from one of the bottom corners.

The way it gleamed in the afternoon sunlight sent shivers up Shelley's spine, though she couldn't pinpoint why. It was just an envelope.

Setting her work bag down, Shelley took off her business jacket and undid one of the buttons on her blouse. She couldn't wait to get out of her pantsuit and settle in for the night. But first, there was the matter of the mail.

She moved to the kitchen bench, and held the envelope up, staring at the smudged ink on the front that spelled her name. She tore it open, and slipped out the paper—a ratty note written on lined A4 paper with nothing but an address on it.

"Tsk." Shelley sighed. "Another one."

This one didn't feel like the others, which had started appearing in her mailbox when she'd inherited this house from her mother's estate. That, in itself, had been strange, but then letters started showing up, giving her an address to go to. They were always creepy old houses with weird stories—even a lighthouse—with fresh-faced families looking to start over for one reason or another.

She'd been curious—*Who wouldn't be?*—and found the address a few towns over. So began her entrance to the weird and wonderful world of real estate. Or, as she called it, the cleaning business. That's what she did. Cleaned up the mess after the families had either killed themselves, each other, or some other unseen force had taken their lives.

Though she despised what she had somehow been pulled into, she mostly despised that she enjoyed it. Not the dead families or hacking up kids and mashing the bodies into pulp. She enjoyed the work itself. Real estate.

Now, she held the latest in a series of what she'd come to believe were demonic letters, perhaps from the Lord of Darkness himself, and she found she couldn't resist. Even after the last cleanup, which she'd been scraping out of her hair for a week.

It was the blood she couldn't resist.

The day was getting on, though, so Shelley put the letter back on the bench and went to the fridge for a bottle of yesterday's crimson rewards. Her needs repulsed her, but she also loved being different from everyone else. As she pulled the door open, she stepped back with a sharp breath. "Fuck."

The letter was inside the fridge.

"How do you even do that?" She never knew who she was speaking to.

The letter seemed to stare at her. The piece of paper taking a life of its own. Shelley picked it up again and slammed the fridge door shut.

"Not. Tonight," she said. "I've had a shit of a day and I just want to drink some blood, watch my programs, and rest."

A *whoosh* came from the front of the house, sending a shockwave of cold air through the kitchen. Shelley rushed out to the hall and saw the front door was open, crunchy autumn leaves smattering the entranceway.

The message was clear. *Now. Now. Now.*

Dropping her shoulders and looking up at the ceiling, Shelley let out a long, sharp, "Uuughhhh."

Without another word, Shelley felt in her pocket for her car keys, and plucked them out. She didn't close the front door when she left, telling herself it was out of protest, but knowing the entity living within would never let anything happen to the house.

The address was just across town, and Shelley pulled up to the old place with a yawn. Even though it was only 6:53 p.m., she'd been up since the crack of dawn. She went to the house, unsurprised to see keys in the lock of the front door—they always were—and pulled them out. Stepping inside, something felt different about this place.

All the houses had a strange vibe, but they all felt the same. A heavy presence sort of weighing her down, pushing against her temples. This house, though, felt warm and inviting. The hairs on her arms felt a slight breeze, despite the fact she'd closed the door and no windows were open. She knew it was the house saying hello. Sometimes they did that.

"Yes, hello." Shelley was short, still unsure why coming here tonight was so urgent.

Moving through the house, it was nothing special. It was just an ordinary haunted house. *No. Not haunted. That's a common mistake.* She reminded herself the house had nothing to do with it. The trouble began with what was under the house. Under all the houses. It still amazed her that nobody really knew about these gaping holes in the ground, wounds in the planet that led to something beyond comprehension.

"What am I doing here?" Shelley asked as she stepped into the living room. "I don't see any bodies to clean up." She sighed. "And I'm still thirsty, thanks to you."

It appeared to her from across the room. Little smudges at first, but then, seeping from the floorboards, more of it came. Shelley walked to it, a translucent gooey liquid, and kneeled down. Pressing into it, her hands slick with the muck, she grimaced.

"You're disgusting." The grimace flipped into a smile, and Shelley somehow felt at ease there. The gooey muck wasn't anything new. It was the house's way of saying it was hungry. *Salivating.*

A trail of saliva moved through the house. Getting to her feet, Shelley followed it, and found herself at the basement door. Pushing it open, she headed down the stairs, unbothered by the deep, deep darkness that greeted her.

She stepped further down the stairs, the soft creaks of the wooden steps guiding her careful movements. Without knowing where she was going, Shelley trusted that the house needed her. Her shoe touched dirt, and she stopped.

Odd.

It felt like dirt was a message, though Shelley shrugged that off, and took a deep breath. Tried to look through the darkness to see why she was here. A light above her began to flicker, just enough of a dim white glow for her to see it.

The hole.

Despite her sense that the house needed her, and that she should trust what was happening here, her heart clenched and her breath caught. She knew where that hole led, and was hesitant to step too close, lest she fell.

Tick.

The abruptness of the sound shocked her, and she twisted around to see where the tick had come from.

Tick, tick, tick.

146

She got the message. *Time is running out.* She still wasn't sure what she needed to do, but the ticking sounded again and a trail of translucent muck bubbled from the dirt toward the hole. With a low, shallow breath, Shelley stepped forward.

Trust the house. Trust the house.

The only thing running through her head at that moment was how she, in fact, did not trust the house. Despite the warm feeling and the breeze through her hair upstairs, something was off about this place. The tick came again, ushering her closer.

"I'm going," she whispered, and she knew the house was listening. More gooey muck oozed from the dirt, the house telling her it was starving. *I'm not it's next meal, I'm not it's next meal.*

The basement door slammed shut behind her as Shelley stood now at the edge of the hole. She stiffened, waiting for something—anything—to happen, but just that incessant *tick tick tick*. The flickering light above became more solid, and Shelley used the glow to gaze down into the hole.

Two yellow dots were down there. Far down. She squinted to get a better look. Whatever it was, it was coming up to meet her. She knew what wasn't protocol. Something was seriously wrong here. Those holes seemed to stretch right into the molten rivers of Hell—they were deep, unforgiving—nothing was climbing out of there.

Yet, the yellow dots grew brighter. Closer.

"Nope," Shelley said. "I can't do this. Not this one."

She turned to the stairs, intent on climbing to the main house, when something grabbed at her arm. She looked to the pressure on her skin, saw nothing. Searching the basement with her eyes, she was alone. Yet, something had touched her.

On the stairs now, she felt it again. A force gripping at her arm. She pulled away, but it grabbed her tight. She flung her other arm around, swiping at the invisible threat, and felt nothing but air.

Tick tick tick.

"Fuck off!" Shelley yelled, swiping again.

Whatever had grabbed her let go. She stood on the stairs for a moment, holding her breath and straining her ears to listen for any movements or sounds that weren't hers.

Nothing.

Releasing a heavy breath, she started up the stairs again. One step up and she felt a sharp pain on her arm. Not a grip this time.

Looking down, she'd been scratched, thin lines of red seeping from a shallow wound. Breathing fast now, she started to run up the stairs, stopped again by a grip on both arms.

"Let me go!" she screamed.

Whatever held her arms pulled hard and she fell backward down the stairs, fumbling over herself until her head slammed against the dirt with a thud. Vision blurry, just for a second, she thought she saw a shape. A shadow.

She maneuvered to lean on her elbows, to get a better look. Something scratched at her face and Shelley winced from the abrupt pain. This one was deeper, the blood leaking thicker and faster.

Crawling backward, she tried again for the stairs, went to turn—

"No!"

Pressure around her ankle. It had her. Whatever *it* was, it wasn't letting go. With incredible force and speed, it pulled her across the basement floor, Shelley scraping at the dirt for anything to hold on to, and finding nothing.

She disappeared into the hole, her scream vanishing into the pitch black.

The falling sensation stopped—she floated among the nothingness engulfing her. That feeling of warmth came again. The feeling that comes on Christmas morning when the snow is falling, the fire is roaring, and the tree is shining. Hot cocoa in hand, heart beating slow, cheeks flushed with that sensation that everything is going to be okay. That you're surrounded by the people who love you most in the world, and you feel like that moment will last forever.

Until it doesn't.

Tendrils in the darkness—*No, they are the darkness*—snaked toward her in the void, lapping at her skin and caressing the wounds on her face and arms. Shelley fought the urge to scream, unwilling to give in to the fear coursing through her veins. The tendrils snaked lower, across her breast, down past her belly button. Flicked at her clothes, gripping at her blouse and her pants. In a swift motion, it tore them from her body.

Still unwilling to scream, Shelley closed her eyes and pressed her thighs together. She knew it wouldn't matter, and when the dark tendrils proved her right, she had no choice but to let them sink into her, letting them—

Now

Shelley screamed in the basement—her basement—as she remembered what happened to her in that dark, endless hole all those years ago. How the darkness defiled her, inside and out, and how it had spat her back from the void to bear a child.

She'd always suspected, but had never had proof, or the memories. As they rushed back to her—a gift, Teddy had said—she curled up on the filthy mattress and wailed. Her tears, thick and fast, pooled on the mattress beneath her, and Shelley pressed her face into the stained fabric and screamed again.

Screamed at herself for daring to forget.

Screamed at the house for raping her.

Screamed at Teddy for existing.

Screamed because it was the only thing she could do in this dungeon, locked away in the dark with nobody to help her.

Finally, she collected herself, and sat upright, breathing hard.

Never again, she thought. *I will never again be your dutiful fucking slave.*

Chapter 12

He didn't know when the idea came to him, but at some point, sitting in the dark, in the silence, clutching at his graphic novel and staring at the unmoving clock, Sam decided to re-enter the world. Something inside him pulled at the seams of his mind, like he needed to be there. For something.

Some*one*.

And so he made his way back to the real world, still grappling with the notion that this door to nowhere existed. And that he'd found it. Or, rather—and he didn't know how he knew this, either—the house had let him find it. Had opened up to him, invited him into its heart.

Exiting the tunnel and pushing himself back into regular space and time, the ticking began again. He'd forgotten what time the clock said, but it didn't matter. It wasn't his responsibility. Whatever would be would be, right?

He cracked his neck and stretched, feeling so at ease and relaxed despite Danny and the coroner and the bodies being sucked into the floor. Despite it all, he had never been so relaxed. The ticking vibrated through him, and Sam stretched again, releasing a deep yawn. His phone vibrated, and for a moment—a small, imperceptible span of time—Sam worried it would be another GPS ping. Worried what that would mean, what, or who, he'd find there.

The fear vanished, and he looked at his phone. He had four missed calls and two texts.

The missed called were from his dad, and he furrowed his brow in confusion and anger. After radio silence for seven months, he'd tried to call four times—once an hour from 5 p.m. to 10 p.m. the previous night—and left a text:

DAD

I heard what happened. I'm sorry, Sammy. I'm really sorry. Can we chat? Please?

Sam paused on the message, his finger hovering above the text box to type a reply. Instead, he deleted the message and checked the other one. A smiled tugged at his lips.

PATRICK

We need to talk. I'm worried about you. Lunch? My shout.

Sam replied with a thumbs up emoji and suggested they meet at 12:20 p.m., at the café he and Danny liked. A heart reaction came through a moment later, and Sam checked the time. It was already 11:45 a.m., so he rushed to the shower.

The sensation of water on his skin reminded Sam of Danny. The way his fingers would trace his body, ever-so-softly, almost the way a breeze moves through the hairs on an arm. A whisper of a touch that would send warmth through Sam's entire being. The shower was like that, despite the water cascading over his body with force. For Sam, it was gentle, and he stood under the water for a while, letting the steam envelop him. Until the smell of the water made his stomach ache.

When he emerged, the bathroom mirror had steamed up. Sam wiped at it to reveal his reflection, and stopped. His face. Something about his face was different. His gaze drifted across his lips to his nose, to his eyes and eyebrows. Falling on his scar, he grimaced.

It had changed color.

Scars, with age, tend to dull and fade, which Sam's had done some years earlier. Now, as he stood naked and vulnerable before his own reflection, it was a deep black. He leaned closer to the mirror, touching at his scar with his fingers, and noticed something else, too.

Veins.

He pressed at the skin, expecting it to be hard and scabby, but it was soft and pliable. Softer than he was used to, like he could almost poke a hole right into his skin. Yet it wasn't dead skin; it didn't appear to sagging or brittle or dry. It was fresh.

He smiled.

Time was getting on, and Patrick was always early, so Sam got dressed in fresh clothes, and headed to the café. As he'd suspected, Patrick was there when he arrived—a full twenty minutes ahead of schedule—fumbling with a menu and gazing out the café window. A water jug sat in the middle of the table, he'd poured himself a glass already.

Patrick waved when he saw Sam, and Sam nodded in return. Sitting opposite his friend, they looked at one another for a few moments, in silence. This was a normal thing for them, their friendship transcending the typical social scripts. Patrick poured Sam a glass of water, and Sam did his best to ignore the sweat on the bottle. His stomach knotted in disgust, but he was more interested in his friend.

"How are you feeling?" Patrick asked, then shook his head. "Sorry, that's an awful question. I mean, Danny is... You must be devastated."

Sam looked from the sweating water jug to Patrick, feeling a tight pull in his chest. Realizing Patrick was waiting for a reply, that worried expression peering at him through the freckles, he said, "I don't know what I feel."

It was true. He couldn't think about Danny without remembering his smile and his scent and the way he looked on that morgue table. A statuesque version of what used to be Danny, but was now just a mockery. And the way he tasted, god that had been good. Sucking the blood from him and the coroner—

"I just miss him." He continued, sniffing away phantom remnants of death and decay.

Patrick nodded, and wiped at his eyes. "I know what happened with you two was rough, but I also know you still loved him."

Sam's eyes flicked to the water jug, droplets seeping to the table. He grimaced and looked away. He was confused, because the shower had been so inviting. The only difference between the water here and the water there was where it came from. The water here was pure, natural. He could smell the rich oxygen. He retched, and covered it with a cough.

"…the cops think it was foul play, but they aren't saying what happened." Sam realized Patrick had been speaking and he'd not heard a word. Tuning in, he caught the last few words, and nodded.

Danny. It's always Danny. "I went to the morgue," he said, and wished he hadn't.

"You did? They let you in?" Patrick's eyes were wide.

Sam bit at his lower lip, and averted Patrick's eyes. "No, they sent me home. I just wanted to see him." Not a

lie, just not the whole truth. It was the most he could ever do
without Patrick seeing right through him. Even now, as Sam
met Patrick's gaze, he could see the gears turning.

"I just hope they find whoever did it." Patrick changed
the subject.

"What do you mean?" Sam asked.

"Well, they said 'foul play', so I'm guessing it wasn't an
argument. Someone did this to them, Sam."

"Wait..." Sam trailed off, rubbing at his temples,
trying not to vomit at the stench of the water. "Did you
say *them*?"

"Yeah. I mean, they don't think it was Danny's boyfriend, even though they can't find him. They said there was
another set of prints."

Sam pushed the jug away, a streak of water messy
on the table. "Who is telling you this? Aren't these details,
like, confidential?"

Patrick adjusted his bow tie, and blushed. "I, uh,
yeah. Well..."

"Spit it out, Pat." Sam's stare was as dead as Danny.
He smiled, but his eyes betrayed the frustration he tried to
hide. Patrick ignored it, knowing full well that Sam was suffering. He opted for "good friend", as he always did.

"I've been meaning to tell you, but with the breakup
and the move and everything, I didn't feel right about it."

Sam stared.

"That detective—Corrigan—he and I have been dating." Patrick blushed again, his orange freckles red like the hunter's moon. "For a while now."

Fuck you, Patrick. Fuck you, fuck you, fuck you. "Really?" He really wanted to drink something, but his stomach was knotted and twisted. The café—airy and bright—felt tight and dark, and the oxygen had left the room. He coughed and rubbed at his neck.

"It was pure coincidence that he got the case." Patrick continued. "Last night, after we… Well, he told me a few things. Please keep it quiet, he's really not supposed to—"

"Do you love him?"

Patrick swallowed hard and smiled. "We haven't said it yet, but…I really do. He wants to solve this case so much, he's working really hard at it. For me. And for you, obviously."

His face started to burn, and he squeezed his eyes shut. The smell of the water was mixing with the scent of food at the other tables. A couple at the table over had spring rolls, and Sam choked at the smell of the old meat wrapped inside.

"Are you okay?" Patrick asked.

Sam nodded and motioned to stand. "Mmhmm. It's…um…great news, Pat. Really great. Congratulations. I should get going, though, I have unpacking to do."

"Wait." Patrick countered. "You aren't leaving yet. We're having lunch. And before you cut me off and run away, I'm not taking no for an answer."

Despite himself, Sam smiled. This was Patrick to the core. He knew what Sam needed, and he knew just how to say it. Sam plopped back down, his temples starting to ache. His brain was on fire, his guts quivering inside him, though he didn't know what for.

"Okay," he said. "I won't eat anything, but I'll have something to drink." Patrick pushed the water jug in his direction and Sam retched again. "No, I'll have something harder."

They called a waitress over, and Patrick ordered shellfish. Sam ordered Kraken with coke and lime. "And keep them coming, please."

The waitress laughed. "We're not a bar, mister. You can order one at a time like everyone else."

Sam watched as she waddled away, her hips swinging side to side. He'd remember her, too.

"How's the new place?" Patrick asked, cupping his glass of water and sipping. The sound his tight lips made as they sucked on the glass made Sam weak at the knees. Just the way he'd done it to the coroner, when he'd been slurping the life out of her neck.

"There's a constant ticking sound," Sam said. He'd had no intention of saying anything to Patrick about the house. Not the clock, the tunnel, the room. The way it sucked bodies into the floor. None of it. The words had slipped out, and he cussed himself for it.

"You mean like a water meter or something?"

159

"No." Sam shook his head. "I mean, like a ticking." He could see the worry etched into Patrick's face, the frown lines around his mouth, and decided to talk to his best friend. "Okay, look. There's something weird about the house."

Patrick nodded with a knowing smile. "It is a murder house."

"It's not that," Sam replied, though he thought that was quite plausible. "It's like...it...it *wants* me there. Like, I feel so safe there, so at home. But there's this ticking, and when I leave the house I just feel like"—he gestured to his chest—"I don't know."

"It sounds like anxiety to me," Patrick said. "Which would be totally normal, like, with Danny and all."

Now he'd started, Sam wasn't sure he could stop. He tried to keep his mouth closed, but the words kept coming. "It feels like my chest is tight and my brain is about to explode. It's on fire and I have these terrible headaches. And look, my scar is changing. It's black now, and it feels weird. And I keep thinking it's connected, you know, like something's happening, and I'm getting these weird GPS pings from an unknown number, and—"

"Slow down, Sam."

"—now after months my dad is, like, calling me non-stop and he wants to chat, like what the fuck is that about? And when I'm at home, I just feel—"

"Sam." Patrick pressed. "Take a breath."

He did, but the inhale just brought more stench from the food in the café. He coughed again, and put his head in his hands.

"It's going to be okay, Sam. You're in shock and you're grieving."

"I need to go home."

"I think you should call your dad back," Patrick said.

It caught Sam off guard. He looked across the table as the waitress brought Sam's Kraken and Patrick's bowl of seafood whatever-the-fuck it was. The saltiness of the fish and the creaminess of the sauce was like a wave of detritus. He held a hand over his mouth.

"I called him." Patrick continued. "I'm sorry, I know I shouldn't have. But I think if you talk to him and work through some things, it could help you deal with Danny."

He stared at Patrick, whose eyes were red and watery, and shook his head. Removing the hand from his mouth, he said, "I can't believe you. You, of all people." He stood and thrust his chair backward, tipping it over. "I can't do this."

Storming from the table, he barged through the café door, and into the street. The stench of seafood and water and spiced rum was replaced with cement and dirt and sweat and car fumes. His head ached, and as he walked down the street toward his car, Sam fought the urge to be sick.

When he reached his car, he kneeled down, hands on his knees, in the gutter, breathing hard. Breathing through the fact that Patrick, of all people, had called his father. The man who'd abandoned him after his mother passed away. The man who—

He looked up, blinking through his rage, when he saw it. The license plate. That *fucking* license plate.

R33 L2T.

Sam straightened, and got into the car.

Chapter 13

He knew it was crazy.

He knew the thrumming in his ears wasn't right, nor the breathing coming in unsteady waves. Yet, his foot wouldn't budge from the accelerator, instead applying more pressure.

He followed two cars behind. His mind raced, he told himself it was a bad idea.

Go home.

The car ahead turned a corner. He followed.

Go. Home.

He felt a tingling in his chest and arms and fingers, and the soft *tick tick tick* vibrating through his entire body. His stomach quivered, aching for blood, and Sam thrust his foot on the brake. The car behind honked long and hard, and Sam focused on breathing. Drowning out the high-pitched beep and ignoring the desires swelling in his body.

"What the fuck is wrong with me?" His lips trembled and a tear escaped his eye. The same eyes that were now scanning the road for *R33 L2T*. The same eyes that were desperate to find that car, and the man within.

He knew it would silence the ticking, and he told himself he had followed the man to satisfy the strange desires lingering inside him. Desires from the house.

The car behind honked again, and Sam watched in his rearview as the driver exited the car. With his heart thumping in his ears, another headache thrashing through his brain, Sam pressed his foot against the accelerator. Intent on leaving, but somehow his foot didn't move. Hovered instead on the pedal. A smile tugged at his mouth and he shook it off, the movement of his head sending a wave of nausea of over him.

"The fuck you doing, man?" Came the voice of the driver, followed by a sharp tap on Sam's window.

He narrowed his eyes and stared at the man, despite himself. This wasn't like with the coroner, where he felt outside his body. This wasn't like watching from beyond. His movements were his own, and it terrified and exhilarated him.

"I'm having a rest," Sam replied, his voice low.

The man, a thick, tanned, muscle-bound jock of a person with a flat nose and sharp jowls, slapped the window. "This ain't a rest stop, pal. Get moving."

Sam winced at the movement, his mind racing. *Go home. Kill him. Go home. Kill the fucking asshole. GO HOME.*

Another knock at the window, harder this time. "You alive in there, bro?"

That was it.

Tick tick tick.

His body made the decision, his rational brain caught somewhere between thoughts, and the familiar feeling washed over him. Being outside his body. The ticking overtook whatever it was the man was yelling at him. Pumping through him like blood and oxygen.

Foot on the accelerator, he pulled over to the side of the road, giving a friendly wave as the jock went back to his car, revved a few times for good measure, and sped past.

Go home, Sam.

He followed the driver, and this time, there was no conscience to stop him from what would come next.

The jock had a keen interest in driving without purpose, from what Sam could tell. His muscle car—a red two-door sports coupé with an awful, black stripe down the hood—drove up and down street after street, trawling the neighborhood for who knew what. Sam heard techno music blaring from his speakers, this time following right behind, rather than two cars away. This guy was too much in his own zone to notice Sam, he was sure of it.

The only other thing Sam knew for certain was that he had a tire iron in the trunk and when this guy pulled up, his skull was going to taste metal.

As the jock turned down a side road, Sam thinking how perfect that was, his head throbbed again with the *tick tick tick.*

He could feel the house inside him—*How is that even possible?*—influencing him. Following the jock down the side road, he was powerless to disobey what the house wanted. The house. His home. His perfect refuge—

No. It can't be.

His blood ran hot at the dissent, as though the house knew what he was thinking. Just as he, inexplicably, knew what the house wanted.

The jock's car had stopped, the engine idling. Scanning the area, Sam saw they were alone. Isolated.

Turn around, Sam, go—

Perfect.

He turned his own ignition off, climbed out of the car, and opened his trunk. A spare tire, the tire iron, and his "bag of bags"—a large duffel that contained all his smaller enviro shopping bags—were all that were contained within. He grabbed the tire iron, slammed the trunk shut, and walked to the jock's car.

While his mind raced and his body trembled, his steps were slow and purposeful.

Tick.

Calm. Confident.

Tick tick tick.

His hand wrapped around the tire iron, squeezing the metal hard, and it was his turn to tap on a window.

The jock wound his window down. "Why are you following me?"

"Oh." Sam was impressed. "You noticed that, huh?" He felt his mouth moving, heard his own voice, but it wasn't him. He was back in the car somewhere, trapped. Watching himself become...whatever this was.

"Yeah I fucking saw ya. I ain't an idiot," he spat.

"You *ain't*? Huh. Well, did you see this?" Sam held up the tire iron with a smirk.

The jock scowled, rested a confident, muscly arm over the door. "What do you think you're going to do with that?"

Sam considered this for a moment. *Go home, it's not too—*

He lifted the tire iron and brought it down on the jock's side mirror, watched it crumble to the road beneath. He swung again, but was thrown by the car door slamming against him as the jock burst from his car.

"YOU MOTHERFUCKA!"

Laughing, Sam steadied himself. Squeezing the tire iron again, he swung hard and fast. The jock blocked with a forearm and countered, landing a hard punch in Sam's face. He fumbled backward, but swung the metal again. As he fell to the road, the tire iron landed against the jock's midriff. He fell to the left, clutching at his side.

"The fuck is wrong with you, bro?" he asked through gritted teeth.

Sam was on his feet, tearing across the tarmac to the jock, who still fumbled. He swung the tire iron again, relishing in the dull thud of metal against skin. He smiled when he saw blood leaking from the jock's cheek, just below his already-swelling eye. A hand clamped to his face, he stumbled backward with a confused, pained "Oomph." He took longer to recover than Sam expected.

Jumping at the chance, he body-slammed the jock to keep him unsteady, and swung again, this time at the back of the head. With a pop, the jock was down, a pained groan escaping his lips. His hand moved to the open wound on his head, his brown hair matted with blood, and Sam stomped hard on the man's ear.

"What's wrong with me?" He huffed. "I'm hungry."

He couldn't see if the jock responded—his face pressed against the road—but he imagined a twisted expression of confusion and fear, and felt the blood rush through his body. Even though Sam watched his body do these things, unable to stop the attack, he couldn't deny the excitement bubbling inside him.

Tick tick tick. Tick tick tick.

Mounting the jock's back, each knee firm against his arms to keep him in place, Sam leaned to the man's head. The stench of fresh blood filled him and despite himself—all dignity gone—his eyes rolled back. It was sweet and warm and he wanted it.

"Please," the jock mumbled, barely conscious. "Please don't hurt me."

Sam spat a laugh, the irony not lost on him. This man, a muscle-bound jock, should have been able to take Sam out with no trouble. Yet, here they were, Sam straddling his back as he sucked in the scent of jock blood.

It's not me, he reminded himself. *It's not—*

But it was his mouth on the back of the man's head, lapping at the blood. It was his fingers digging into the wound to see if he could find brain matter. It was his stomach untangling—*Finally*—as the blood found its way inside him.

His phone buzzed in his pocket, and Sam's fingers, bloodied and trembling with excitement, slipped it free. A GPS ping. He pressed the red pin and was somehow not surprised to see it gave his exact location.

"I'll be home soon," Sam said, placing his phone back in his pocket. "Then we can both feed."

He moved to his car, opened the trunk, and threw the tire iron in. Sizing up the jock, he sighed hard, knowing this was the real test. He was somehow strong enough to beat the guy to a pulp, but he wasn't sure he could drag him across the road and get him into the trunk.

One way to find out, he thought, *and began pulling on the jock's arm.*

It was easy. Too easy. Like the jock weighed nothing.

With his belly satiated for the time being, and the jock bumping back and forth in the trunk, Sam began to re-enter his body. The *tick tick tick* still plagued him—it was forever inside him—but at least his actions here his own now.

He swallowed hard, knowing what was going to happen when he got home. Knowing the house was going to eat the jock, swallow him into the floorboards like Danny and the coroner.

It's going to be me soon.

The thought popped out of nowhere, and it sank into his bones. How did he know it wouldn't be him next? How did he know the house wouldn't come for him? That the next GPS ping was for him.

Pulling into his driveway, he left the jock to rot in the trunk, and ran inside. The impossible door was there, glimmering, waiting for him. He crawled inside, pushing through the space until he was eye to eye with the clock.

2:02.

The time, according to his phone, was 1:55 p.m. Something was about to happen. Someone was going to die. He could feel it in the air, like an ongoing storm.

Unless... Sam thought. Unless *I stay here. Time stops in this room, right? If I stay here, nobody will get hurt again.*

It was like the room knew his thoughts, the walls beginning to heave back and forth, like lungs. Like he gave life to the space. His body began to relax and the while there was no sound, a heaviness in the room filled him. Sam shook it off, and headed back to the tunnel. The walls there, too, heaved and groaned, calling for him to stay.

He pushed through the door into the house, and the *tick tick tick* filled his ears. As he stood, the seconds began to feel like hours, as if his body was pushing through an invisible, thick, mucus. His mind raced, but he was trapped in slow motion, struggling to acclimatize to this reality. He felt his blood pulsing through him, squeezing its way through his veins like poison, itching and hot.

My...body...isn't...mine. His thoughts were slowing down, too. Forcing himself to finish the thought was exhausting, he prayed he could collapse. Prayed he could end whatever this was. The house had him in its grip, and whatever it used as fingers was tightening.

"Let me go," he said, and his words came out at normal speed. Nothing made sense. He tried to move again, taking a step, and felt a weight against his leg, pushing him down. "I said, let me GO!"

His foot punched hard to the ground, a spike of pain shooting from Sam's heel up through his leg. He cried out, but was glad for the speed of the pain. Like lightning, as it should be. He could move again, yet still stood, unmoving.

At least it's my choice.

As if another lightning strike came through his head, interrupting the *tick tick tick*, Sam reached for his phone. The clock had read 2:02. It was analogue, so it could have been 2:02 a.m. or p.m. Either way, it was now 1:57 p.m., and his heart was sinking.

Moving to the front door, intent on getting the jock inside before the early afternoon heat stunk out his trunk, Sam heard a noise. A dull thud.

Is that…the basement?

His eyes flicked to the basement entrance, the door he wasn't allowed to go through. It was ajar, a crack of shadow streaming into the house. Like the darkness inside had tendrils, reaching into the daylight.

Another thud.

"Hello?" Sam called from the door, still unwilling to move beyond the threshold.

His ear to the door, eyes narrowed to focus, Sam heard it again. Someone was down there. In his house. In his home. Hiding. Waiting. Waiting to hurt him. Or worse, waiting to hurt the house.

"Who's down there?" he called again.

"Sam?" A hand grabbed at his shoulder, and Sam spun around, tripping into the basement door.

172

It flew open and the hand—warm and familiar—grabbed Sam's to steady him.

"Dad?" Sam stared at his father. "What the fuck? You scared the shit out of me."

His dad smiled. "Sorry. I called out from the front door, but you didn't answer. Then I heard you talking. Are you okay?"

"What are you doing here?" Sam asked, ignoring his father's question. His eyes drifted to the basement, the door now wide open. The thud hadn't come again, but Sam listened for it anyway.

"We need to talk," his dad said.

"I'm kind of in the middle of something." Sam waved him off.

His dad looked from Sam to the basement and back again. "What's up, Sam?"

Avoiding his dad's eyes, he replied, "You need to leave."

1:58.

Tick, tick, tick.

The thud came again, and the ticking pressed into Sam's brain like an icepick. He doubled over, palms at his temples, and screamed. Sam's dad leaned in, patted his back, mouthing something. Sam could hear nothing but the ticking. It had never been this loud, almost like it came from right inside his head, vibrating into existence from his gray matter.

Sam's dad was yelling now, the sound like a tiny echo, and he grabbed at Sam's shoulders, shaking him. He wanted to tell him to stop, that the pressure in his head was too much, that he was about to explode into pieces, but all he could do was scream until his father's shaking sent him beyond the basement threshold.

Silence.

His own breathing.

His father's voice, soft now. Asking if he was okay. Begging Sam for a response, asking what was happening, firing questions the way he did without waiting for a response.

Sam gasped and heaved, the pressure in his head gone, just the quiet thrum of the *tick tick tick* that somehow comforted him. "I'm okay," he said through deep breaths. "I'm okay."

1:59.

Except now that he was past the threshold to the basement, Sam felt more than okay. Like with the jock, he felt strong. Powerful. Like nothing in this world, or the next, could hold him down.

The thud sounded again, and both he and his father turned toward it.

"What was that?" his dad asked.

The power rippled through him, and he smiled. It was different than with the coroner. It was different than with the jock, too. More intense. He wasn't hungry, he didn't feel the need for blood. He just wanted to go into the basement. He was allowed in, now.

Invited.

"Go home, Dad," Sam whispered, and began the downward descent into the dark.

The stairs creaked as he stepped down, and it was like coming home. The creaks were reminders that the house was damaged and weary and pained. Like his heart. He quickened his pace, eager to get to the bottom. The darkness enveloped him as he went, yet Sam had never felt so seen. Not since the first time Danny had looked at him and somehow seen into his soul.

Danny…Danny's gone.

Or the way his smile melted Sam's worst nightmares into distant memories.

He's gone.

Or the way—

He's not coming back.

At the bottom of the stairs, Sam saw—through the dark and the shadow—that the ground was dirt. Basements were usually cemented, so he found this odd, and smiled. Dirty and dusty and unfinished.

The thud came again. Somewhere in a distant corner of the room. Sam couldn't see anything there. He stepped further into the darkness, feeling an incredible pull, like an umbilical cord guiding him through the space.

He took another few steps, ignoring the *thud thud thud*, though it sounded like a warning. A desperate plea for him to stop. He couldn't.

A light came from above and Sam shielded his eyes, taking another step.

"Sam, stop!" his father called from the top of the stairs, hand poised over a light switch. The desperation in his voice was alien to Sam, he hadn't heard it for years.

He resisted the urge to keep walking, straining against the invisible umbilical connecting him to the basement, and took his hands down from this face.

His father rushed to him. "Step away from it, Sam."

As though in a trance, the *tick tick tick* thumping away through his body, Sam looked down. The thud came again, and Sam tilted his head.

"Sam, please," his father said. "It looks really deep."

He stood in front of a hole in the ground. In the Earth. A gaping void three feet in diameter. He gazed down into it, the sensation of falling gripping him. Like being on the edge of a cliff, afraid if you get too close you will fall. Except he wasn't afraid, not with the umbilical guiding him to this exact spot.

Taking another step, his shoe scraping against the dirt at the edge of the hole, his father pulled him back hard. Sam fell to his ass, and he looked up.

"Dad?" he asked, blinking.

"Sam, what the fuck is going on?" his dad kneeled beside him, concern oozing from his eyes.

"I..." he trailed off, looking back to the hole. "It needs me."

His dad shook his head, searching Sam's eyes for reason and logic. His lips parted to speak, but Sam slipped free from his father's grasp, was up and on his feet, rushing back to the edge of the hole.

"It needs me, Dad."

He spread his arms wide, ready to jump. His father tackled him to the ground, away from the hole, and held him down. "Sam, something is *very, very* wrong here. We need to leave."

Sam pushed his father away, scowling. "How dare you."

"What—"

"How *fucking* dare you. You pretend I don't exist for months, then suddenly you show up acting all fatherly." Sam spat, getting back to his feet.

He pushed his dad in the chest, mostly to get him to move away and leave him alone. When his dad came back, arms wide for a hug, saying something about being sorry and that he was here now, Sam pushed again.

"Sam, stop this. This isn't you," his dad said.

"How would you even know?"

He pushed again.

His dad fell backward, his eyes wide in confusion. His mouth formed an "O", and he disappeared into the hole.

The time ticked over to 2:02.

Sam moved to the edge, searching for his father. He was gone. Staring hard, Sam began to see shapes and shadows moving in the dark down there, but they were nonsensical blobs of matter. Just his imagination.

The umbilical loosened, and Sam, without knowing why, turned around and went upstairs.

Back to the room.

Back to his clock.

Chapter 14

Patrick let Corrigan's arms wrap around him, and he pushed his head into the detective's chest. Soft graying hairs tickled at his cheek, and he breathed in the man's scent. A tear streamed down his face, and Corrigan wiped at it, forever observant and gentle.

"What can we do?" Patrick asked, his voice low and trembling.

Corrigan sighed, his hefty chest sinking back into the bed. He shifted a little, ushering Patrick's gaze to his own with a hand under the man's chin. As they lay there, naked and enveloped in each other's bodies, the detective wiped again at Patrick's tears. "I have to find Danny's killer," he said.

"You should have seen him." Patrick continued. "He was so different at lunch. Running out of there like that…"

"Death hits people hard. Especially this kind of death."

Patrick rolled over to become the little spoon, and pulled Corrigan's burly arm around him. Kissing the back of the detective's hand, he cuddled into the man, hoping he was right. Something niggled at him, though. The sense that something was wrong with his best friend.

"Was he like this when his mother died?"

Shaking his head, Patrick said, "Not really. He was quiet and cried a lot. Today was different. Like he was someone else. He's been weird since he moved into that house."

The murder house. Patrick creased his brow and reached to the bedside table for his phone.

"What are you doing?" Corrigan asked.

"Googling. I know that place has a reputation, but what if it's true? What if it is haunted?"

Corrigan breathed into Patrick's neck, stifling his disbelief. "I really don't think that's the case."

"I know, I know. You aren't a believer, and I've seen too many movies. But the fact is, Sam is acting really weird, and it only started when he moved."

"Bub, didn't Danny die the day after he moved in?"

Patrick ignored him, and kept scrolling Google search results about the house. A few news stories from years earlier. People had died there, it was true, but that was true for lots of rentals. Especially houses that were so old. If there was something wrong with that house, it wasn't going to be discovered in a feeble Google search. He needed—

"Corry, I need a favor," Patrick said, invoking the pet name he had for the bearish detective.

"I can run a check on the address," he replied.

"How did you know what I was going to ask?"

Corrigan kissed the back of Patrick's head and squeezed him in a firm hug. "Because I know you, bub. And I will help you wherever I can."

Patrick rolled back around, tracing the curves of Corrigan's naked body, and then resting a hand on his soft belly. "Thank you. I'm going to keep searching, but I want to go to the library archives. Drop me off on your way back to work?"

Checking his wristwatch, Corrigan nodded. "My break is just about over. Lots to do, killers to find."

Patrick smiled, but it was filled with sadness.

"I wish there was time for a round two." Corrigan gave a deep purr, and kissed Patrick on the neck. "I need my hunky redhead to get me through the afternoon."

Smiling for real this time, Patrick pushed the man away. "Go get dressed." He got out of the bed, flinging the sheets back as he did so. Corrigan slapped Patrick's butt and gave a woof noise, before groaning in discontent and then heaving himself out of the bed.

"Fine, but you owe me," he said, almost blushing. "Let's get you to the library."

The library was part of the city's future-planning strategy, building a brighter tomorrow and investing in education. It was filled with state-of-the-art technology, soundproof meeting rooms, and an archive section with what Patrick liked to think was a near-complete history of the world in microfiche.

As he scanned files in the library database, sifting through meaningless records of murders and suicides in the general area, he stumbled on an old listing from when the town was first being built. He paused for a moment, then decided to request the microfiche from the librarian.

She was a young woman, which surprised Patrick, though he didn't know why. He'd assumed librarians were all older, thin-lipped from saying, "Shhhh" too many times, with pink-rimmed glasses and beehive hair. Her name was Lizzy, though, and she looked to be around thirty.

"Ooooh, microfiche," she said, after Patrick requested the record. "Hardly anyone asks for those anymore."

Patrick nodded and adjusted his bowtie. "Just doing some research."

She smiled appreciatively. "Follow me." Motioning to Patrick, she led him into a small room at the back of the library, and rummaged through some drawers. "Here we are."

"Thank you so much," Patrick said, eyeing the roll of microfiche.

"What are you researching?"

This was the trouble with people his age. Nosy. The beehive-haired version of the librarian in his head would have been better, Patrick imagined.

"This old house, on the other side of town."

"Ah, the murder house," Lizzy replied with a wistful smile. "I've heard of it. So creepy. Why are you researching that?"

Patrick sized her up, growing more impatient, and decided to tell her the truth. "My best friend lives there, and I think the house is haunted. Or, like, changing him in some way." He gauged her disbelief. "I just need to understand that house."

Lizzy didn't even bat an eyelid. She just handed the roll to Patrick. "Fine, don't tell me. Do you know how to use the machine?"

"I'll be fine," Patrick replied, watching her leave the room. She switched off the lights, as was needed for his viewing, and left him to it.

The record was old, from 1913, when the town was being built. It was an article from the now-defunct *Harker Daily*, detailing the difficulties building on the land. Dirt wouldn't move. Frames wouldn't stand. Metal had bent and ripped apart. After some of the builders reported hearing strange voices and sounds, they'd begged the Catholic Church for help, and a priest was brought to the site to cleanse the land.

According to the record, the priest—Father Curtis Campbell—had told the *Harker Daily* he'd never encountered anything like it. He'd sprayed the land with holy water, recited prayers and rituals.

"It's not an entity," Campbell had told the reporter. "It's the land. The land is evil. There's nothing I—or anyone—can do about that."

Patrick swallowed hard as he read the next quote from the peace. "Abandon this town. Or abandon all hope."

Something interesting happened then. Another small article, in the next issue of the *Harker Daily*. After the builders and contractors had left, heeding Father Campbell's advice, a land investor—Morris Hart—had taken interest. He'd travelled up from the south to see if he could make a deal for the supposed "cursed land".

"I made the discovery only because I almost fell into it," Hart reported.

A three-foot, circular hole in the earth. He'd teetered at the edge, rocking back and forth, until he felt a force push him away on his ass. Crawling back to the edge, he'd stared into the abyss, into the darkness that stretched into forever.

"I can see why it would deter the ordinary citizen. However, I knew what had to be done."

The report continued to detail how Hart had built a house over the hole. He'd encountered no issues—no bending metal or frames coming down without reason. The dirt moved easily, like sand, he'd said. The only thing was that the hole refused to be covered. No amount of concrete would fill it in. No wooden beams would stay put. It wanted to exist, and Hart had decided to let it.

"Something is here on this land," he told the reporter. "But it's not evil. My house will never come down, and I encourage everyone who can to build here. It will be a beautiful town one day."

From then on, the town filled with houses, and nothing strange ever happened again. Except a few deaths in the house, which Patrick already knew about.

"It's the land that's haunted," Patrick said.

Looking into the history of the land, though, he found no trace of any reason why it should be haunted. Or cursed. Or whatever. It was just ordinary land. He flicked the lights on and removed the microfiche, knowing what he had to do next.

Another internet search through public archives revealed that Morris Hart had lived in that house until his death in 1999, which made him 102 years old. There was no marriage record, but he did have one daughter, Alice. His search turned to her, in the hope that she'd have some answers. Although, she was born in 1948, and would be quite old herself.

Searching for Alice, he found she died not long after her father, in 2005. No children.

A dead end.

"Fuck." Patrick huffed, and ran a frustrated hand through his hair.

Lizzy appeared at his side from nowhere. "How's the research? You understand the house yet?"

"Not really," Patrick said.

She leaned forward to peer at the computer screen, sucking on her lower lip. "Well, this is your problem. You're looking at the people. You *should* be looking at the land."

"I did a land search." Patrick shrugged. "All I found was a giant hole. Literally."

"No," Lizzy giggled. "I mean, if you want to understand the house, you need to understand the land it's built on." She paused. "The hole in the earth—what's that about? That's where you need to start."

"Huh." Patrick nodded. "That's a good idea."

Lizzy waved off the compliment and walked away, a spring in her step. Patrick turned back to the computer screen and Googled, "Hole in the Earth".

The first few results were about music and movies and other useless junk. As he continued to scroll, though, he stumbled upon a website titled "Strange natural phenomenon". The entry description mentioned a conspiracy theory about a series of holes around the world. Patrick clicked it.

According to the site, researchers as far back as the 1600s had been discovering holes around the globe, all of them three feet in diameter. There was no explanation for these holes, some of them appearing overnight. Patrick furrowed his brow as he looked at old photographs of the same location, taken one day apart. The first had a man and his wife, baby in arm, standing on a patch of land. The second, taken the day after if the caption was to be believed, showed the same man and his wife pointing at the hole in the Earth.

The website linked to articles from public archives, digitized copies of newspaper articles. The earliest one was from 1633. The report indicated colonists in Missouri had set up camp, only for part of the site to be swallowed into the ground overnight. The first reported three-foot hole. Since then, they popped up everywhere. Researchers had explored these holes, dropping lanterns to see how deep they stretched, only for the light to be swallowed, too. Eventually, in the 1800s, scientists began sending people into these holes, though after an unrecorded amount of them never came back, the experiment was stopped.

It wasn't official, but conspiracy theorists suggested the Russian attempts to dig the deepest hole in the ground during the 1970s—the Kola Well—was a response to this natural phenomenon. Nobody had ever been inside one of these holes and made it out.

Except one.

Morris Hart. The land developer.

Patrick clicked a linked article about the Kola Well and the team leading the experiment, certain there was a mistake. It couldn't be Morris Hart. Not the *same* Morris Hart. The article loaded, and Patrick shot up from his chair.

What was he doing in Russia in the 1970s? How does he look exactly the same as he did in 1913?

The picture in the article was Morris Hart, but Patrick knew it couldn't be. Even if it was the same man, he'd have aged somewhat. Yet in the image, he wasn't a day older.

Patrick sat back down, heart racing, and read the article. Hart Industries, an American company specializing in earthmoving, had popped up in 1969 in Russia. Morris Hart was leading the expedition into the holes, to see what was down there. After losing numbers of explorers—again, unspecified—Hart took the plunge himself in 1979.

The report stated that Hart, attached to a harness, had been lowered into the hole until the light on his hardhat had vanished, and his calls of "Lower, lower" could not be heard. Even then, his team had continued until there was no rope left to lower. Approx. 23,000 feet. The deepest into the Earth any human had ever been.

His team waited for the signal—a sharp tug at the rope—to bring Hart back up. They'd been under strict instruction not to bring him up without that signal. So they waited.

For four days.

Sure he was dead, or dying, after such a lengthy period of time down there, the second in charge gave the order to hoist him back up. The ordeal took another fifteen hours, moving slow to ensure the integrity of the rope wasn't impeded. When Hart finally emerged, he was unconscious, covered in translucent mucus, with a smile etched onto his face.

He woke another three days later in a hospital in Murmansk, refusing to speak. Instead, he returned to the US. Hart Industries shut down, and there were no further records until his death in 1999.

"What the hell is down there?" Patrick muttered to himself. "And how is this connected to Sam?"

Chapter 15

Teddy had watched from the street as Sam attacked that man. She was impressed, though had no real point of comparison. The fights she'd seen had all been on television, and she was smart enough to realize Hollywood and the production studios didn't mimic reality. They certainly didn't capture real-life sounds very well, not the sound of bones cracking or the thud of skin suits dropping to the ground.

Skin suits. That's what her daddy called them. She called them *skinnies*.

Sam dragged the dead skinnie into his trunk, and slammed the door, resting his hands against the hot metal for a moment before looking around to make sure he hadn't been seen. Teddy smirked when he nodded to himself.

Idiot. I'm standing right here, he didn't even see me.

She watched him from behind a telephone pole, her black hair hanging to one side as she tilted her head for a better angle. Squinting, she stared at his face. Tears. So…human. She didn't get it. What did the release of liquid from an eye achieve? It seemed an inconvenience, proven by the fact that Sam wiped hard at his face to rid his eyes of the infection. He leaned against the car for a moment, holding his head in his hands, and then clutched at his heart.

Her smile faded, and she looked down at the grass.

She pressed a hand to her own chest, where she knew her heart was, but could never feel it. It never pumped, yet here she stood. Walking and talking and breathing, like any other skinnie. Looking at her hands—pale, milky skin, blue, blue veins—she was reminded once more that she'd never feel the sensation of hot blood rushing through her own body.

She sighed.

As Sam got into his car and sped away, Teddy wiped at her own face. No tears, but she sometimes pretended she could cry. Like Hollywood, she was good at faking. Not perfect, but good enough.

Daddy had told her to find the red-headed freckled guy. The one named after a saint, whatever that meant. She'd pressed him for the actual name, and where to find him, and the information appeared in her brain, like it always did.

Yet, she had found herself here instead. Pulled to Sam again, felt the need to help him, though she didn't know why.

Now he was gone and her father's words—his mission for her—came flooding back.

Patrick. Find him. Do the deed. Go home.

Looking up the street, she saw traffic and heard people yelling at each other. Down the street, the same thing. She supposed it didn't matter which way she went, so long as she ended up at the library. Often, she'd wondered how her daddy knew all these things about these people, but she'd never asked. He was a beautiful thing, and he loved her, but she knew—she could tell—he was angry.

Like me.

Walking wherever her feet took her, which she knew would inevitably lead her to the library, and her next offering for Daddy, she kicked at the ground with her bare feet. Listened to the slap of her heel against the sidewalk. Passersby gave her the side eye, and she gave it right back, narrowing her eyelids just a touch to indicate her discontent for their actions.

The library wasn't far, as it turned out. She stood at the edge of the parking lot—just a small thing with four spaces—and peered through the windows at the front. They were tinted, so she couldn't see much of anything inside. But she knew he was in there.

"Get some shoes, white trash!" a guy in a passing car yelled at her.

Teddy twisted around to face the traffic.

"Daddy liiiiike!" another guy called, followed by a wolf whistle and some lude movements out the window. A group of his friends in the car guffawed like morons.

"I'm eight, you fuckin' pedo!" She smiled, despite the sickness of the moment. Engaging with the skinnies was always fun.

Turning back to the library, she stepped forward, only to stop again when Patrick emerged. Teddy had seen enough movies and TV to recognize the look on his face. Fear. He rushed in her direction, reaching into his pocket. Pulling out his phone, he began touching the screen.

She walked closer, her breath catching. *Could I just do it right here? Could I jump on him and take his heart?*

Patrick looked up, noticing her. Waved with his free hand.

Teddy stopped. Waved back.

"Are you okay?" he asked. "Do you need help?"

Teddy frowned. He was being nice to her. He wasn't like the other one. Danny. "Um, I..." For once, she didn't know what to say. She'd expected him to be like the other skinnies, like the pedo who'd cat-called her a few seconds earlier. Not this. His face now read: concern.

She sat on the grass by the parking lot, and started digging, scraping away the surface of the dirt.

Crouching down, Patrick motioned to his phone. "Do you need me to call someone?"

Shaking her head, Teddy bit at her lip. "Do I look like I need…help?"

Patrick considered this for a moment, and Teddy saw his eyes taking her in. Her bare feet, her dirty face and arms, greasy hair. The cigarette burns. Her torn and unwashed dress. He gave a slight nod. "No offense, but yeah. Is your mom or dad around?"

Teddy giggled. "Do you like to dig?"

"Uh, sure," Patrick replied. "You mean, like, at the beach? Everyone does that."

Looking into Patrick's eyes, Teddy squinted. "What's at the bottom?" She tilted her head. "Where does the hole go?"

Patrick shrugged. "It just…keeps going, I guess." He paused, confused, and thought about the Kola Well. About Morris Hart. "Listen, are your parents around?"

Teddy giggled. "My daddy is around. I never really know where, but he's just, like, there, you know?"

Standing, Patrick sighed. "I know what you mean, trust me. But, uh, is he close by? Can I take you to him?"

He had that look again. Teddy was confused, and kept digging. He was a genuine, nice skinnie. She'd seen them on TV, but hadn't met one. Not as far as she knew, anyway. She was used to the people like her mommy. The ones who hated her, just because they could.

I can't hurt him.

Patrick noticed her thinking, the way she shifted her weight from foot to foot, and chewed at her nails. He lifted his phone again and started pressing the screen. How those things worked, she'd never know.

"I like to dig, but I never get to the bottom." Teddy sighed.

Ignoring her comment, Patrick said, "You know, I have a friend. His name's Corrigan. He's a policeman, very friendly. I'm going to give him a call, and we can get you home. Okay?" His voice was weird, like a few octaves too low. She knew he was trying to sound friendly and inviting, but it came out condescending.

Awww. That's adorable. I really don't want to hurt him.

She knew her daddy would be mad, though, and looked at him once more. Sizing up how she might do it, she stopped when Patrick's eyes lit up.

"Hey, Corry, I need a favor." He winked at her and smiled, as if to say, You're going to be okay. After a pause, he continued. "A little girl here at the library needs our help. I think she's lost, maybe. Can you come by, and help me get her home? I'm worried about her, she's only young and the city is...the city."

Another pause. Teddy stepped away from Patrick. *I can't do this. Why does Daddy want me to hurt this one?*

"Right, we'll just wait here," Patrick said, and then: "I love you, Corry."

It both disgusted her and made up her mind. "I have to go."

"My policeman friend is coming, he'll take you home."

Teddy shook her head and stepped away. "No, I should go, before it's too late."

"Why?"

"Because you're a *nice* skinnie." Teddy smiled, and walked back to the road. Over her shoulder, she said, "Nice to meet you, Patrick."

She heard a few footsteps behind her, and then nothing. Like he'd tried to follow her and decided against it. She was glad he chose to stay put, her hands were wrangling for a neck to choke, and she didn't know if she could suppress the urge for much longer. Only one thing could cure that desire.

Ice cream.

She'd checked the freezer for ice cream, and the fridge for strawberry topping. Her mommy hadn't been shopping, it seemed. No matter, she could go shopping herself.

Scraping her feet against the sidewalk again, letting the spikes of pain remind her she was alive—at least in some capacity—she headed out on her new mission. To find some cold, wet, melting, ice cream. And maybe, just maybe, some runny, runny strawberry topping.

A few blocks from the library, she found it. The large ice cream cone revolving above the door kind of gave it away. Licking her lips, Teddy entered, and widened her eyes at all the choices. Tubs of different-colored ice cream stashed away behind counters, a mild fog crisp against the glass barricade. Her stomach flipped.

How many types of vanilla are there?

A lady behind the counter, wearing a plastic-rimmed hat and a name tag that Teddy ignored on purpose, greeted her. "Hello there, young lady. What can I do for you?"

Teddy put her elbows on the counter and brushed hair off her face. "Why do you have so many colors for vanilla ice cream?"

The lady smiled, but her eyes were filled with disdain. "Take a look, honey. We have way more than just vanilla."

"But...vanilla is all there is. There's only one type of ice cream, everyone knows that."

Now her face read: amused. "No, darling"—the way she said "darling" angered Teddy, whose face flushed—"have a look. We have different kinds of chocolate, we have hazelnut, cookies and cream, pistachio… Heaps of flavors."

It didn't make sense. Teddy's mommy had always said there was only one kind of ice cream. *Why had I believed that? She's always lying to me.* "You mean, I can have any of these?"

"That's right, hon." The lady smiled again, this time with a genuine pleasantness. "As long as you can pay for it."

Skinnies are so weird.

She assured the lady she had money, and that her daddy would be in any moment now to fix her right up. Picked out a brown one, the color of days-old blood. The lady said it was Belgian Chocolate Ripple or something. Great. It looked like she could grind her teeth against it, rather than lick it. Either way, it did look tasty.

"Can I have strawberry topping?" Teddy asked.

"With chocolate? Are you sure?"

"It's my favorite."

The lady grimaced. "Okay, sure, darling."

There's that fucking word again.

Taking the ice cream cone to a container, the lady pressed down a tap of some kind and out poured the thick, red sauce.

Teddy turned her lips up. "What. Is. That?"

Sighing in frustration, the lady held the cone out. "You wanted strawberry topping, I gave it to you."

It didn't look right. Teddy looked from the cone to the woman, from the cone to the woman. Shook her head. That was not strawberry topping. She didn't care who she had to argue with about it.

"Silly," Teddy said. "Strawberry topping doesn't come out of a container. It comes out of you."

She launched over the counter before the lady could register what was happening, dropping the ice cream cone to the floor with a splat. Her arms around the woman's head, legs wrapped around her midriff, tangled in the woman's arms. She tried to scream, but Teddy ripped into her face,

198

tearing at skin and lip and nose. Spitting cartilage to the floor, Teddy laughed.

"So silly," she said.

The lady scrambled against Teddy, who squeezed her thighs so the lady's arms were immobile. Her legs, like a hysterical chicken, kicked out, thrashing them into the counter top and then into the glass ice cream cabinets.

Teddy needed that strawberry topping, she wanted it. It was the only thing that could satiate her, now that she hadn't killed Patrick. So she pressed her hands hard against the lady's head, squeezing, squeezing.

The lady fell to her knees, and Teddy used the weight of her body to force the lady backward. On the ground now, she flicked the lady's hat away and gripped her hair.

"Don't worry, *darling*," Teddy said through heavy breaths. "This won't take long."

She felt the woman struggle, her eyes boring into Teddy like she was the Devil herself. It was no use. The only eyes that had ever hurt Teddy were her mommy's. Ignoring the lady's silent pleading, she ripped at her chest, digging past the tender flesh of the breasts and reaching, reaching for the muscle beneath.

Hearts were her favorite. They had the best strawberry topping. Tearing the muscle free, the lady went limp with a final gasp. Teddy stood, holding the heart, licking at the blood oozing from its surface. Let it drip across her face and neck.

"Mmm," she mumbled in glee. "Now *that* is good strawberry topping."

Her eyes fell to the fallen ice cream cone, the brown mess melting into the linoleum beneath. Teddy winced at the loss until she remembered there was an entire store of the stuff. Rushing to the Belgian Chocolate Ripple, heart in hand, Teddy dug a handful of the brown sweetness and thrust it into her mouth. Squeezing the heart, blood trickled in after it, and she swirled the brown and red gunk around, tasting the—

"Ew," Teddy said, and spat it out. Looking back to the lady, she continued. "You were right. Chocolate and strawberry don't really go together." With that, she trawled the cabinets for the vanilla, opting for the classic flavor combination instead, and stood there eating, until both the heart and the ice cream had been devoured.

Burping, and wiping at her mouth, Teddy knew it was time to go home. Her daddy would be mad, for sure, because Patrick was alive. And Mommy would be mad, too, because of the ice cream lady. She was dirty, though, and covered in strawberry topping, just like her mommy made it.

So she grabbed some napkins from the counter—somehow unmoved from the scuffle earlier—and wiped at her face as she stepped over the skinnie to the exit.

Chapter 16

Three Days Later

"We normally text every day." Patrick held back tears and reflexively adjusted his bow tie. The line was bad and as the reply came down the phone, Patrick cringed a little. The scratchy voice gave nothing, except the monotone of someone who didn't care.

"Can you hear me?" he asked.

"Yes..." The voice crackled. "Do you...a refere...number?"

"A what?" Patrick shook the phone and swallowed his frustration. "Don't worry, I'll look around myself."

He tapped the red "End call" button on his cell and jammed it into his pocket. Standing outside Sam's house for the third day in a row, knocking until the neighbors had insisted nobody was home, Patrick had phoned the police. Corrigan had tried to get the precinct to look into it, but as usual, they were under-staffed and over-budget. He'd been to look himself, without a warrant, but had come up empty, and told Patrick to keep trying—eventually, they'd given in and sent uniforms around for a welfare check.

A lot of good that did. He'd called them each day after Sam didn't answer the phone, didn't come to the door, and made no sounds inside the house. Patrick being Patrick, he didn't have the gusto to smash a window or try barging through the door. That's what the cops were for.

Each day, he rang from the front door of Sam's house. Each day, the line had been filled with static. Day one had ended with his mother telling him not to panic; a man was entitled to his privacy and allowed to go off-grid every now and then. Especially after a devastating loss. Day three and no change, and Patrick stood once more at Sam's front door.

"Sam." Patrick leaned his forehead against the door. "Please, open up."

The response he'd grown accustomed to—none—lay in wait. Moving back from the house, Patrick saw a stone in the front garden, among the dead and dying flowers. He didn't remember anyone planting those and they hadn't been there when Sam moved in.

He must be here. Who else would have planted these? He swallowed. *Time for that gusto.*

Picking up the stone, Patrick poised to throw it at the front window. He paused, knowing he'd have to pay the repair bill when Sam came storming out. Still, he threw the stone with as much force as he could and watched the glass shatter.

The house groaned. Patrick thought he saw the windowsill dip in reflex. *Impossible.*

The glass dispersed through the front garden and into the house. Patrick climbed through the window, ignoring the groaning that couldn't be there but was, and landed inside the front room. It was empty, save for some moving boxes, and patches of dark, wet carpet in the corners. He felt the squelch of wetness underneath him, too, and lifted his shoes from the shattered glass and the carpet.

"What the hell is this?" he whispered.

A thick, translucent goo.

He turned his attention back to the task at hand—finding Sam—and reminded himself to worry about the weird gooey substance once his friend was safe.

Sam had said this room would be the spare room, maybe the office. Now, as Patrick stood in it, glass crunching under his shoes, it was nothing. It felt strange, though, the way rooms sometimes do. His grandfather's woodworking shed had the same feeling—like he wasn't welcome.

Sam hadn't come rushing to the sound of shattering glass. Sam hadn't appeared with a baseball bat asking who was there or threatening to call the police. Patrick's heart sank.

"Sorry about the window," he called, moving into the hallway. "You're scaring me, Sammy."

He sat on the couch, noticing the boxes that hadn't been touched since moving day. The piles of his beloved *30 Days of Night* and *The Strain* graphic novels gathering dust and collecting too much sunlight.

"Something isn't right," Patrick mumbled, feeling a tug at his chest. "Not right at all."

He grabbed his phone from his pants pocket again and dialed 911. Someone answered—a woman—and delivered the standard 911 introduction, but the static was unbearable. Patrick held the phone away from his ear and as his finger hovered over the red button once more, he heard a faint whisper. The words were incoherent, but the voice sounded different to the person who'd answered the call. It was a man.

"Hello?" Patrick put the phone on loud speaker and cocked his ear to the phone. Listening hard.

"In...base...ment..." the voice whispered. "Base..."

Patrick looked at the phone as the words came again. His eyes darted to the basement door. "Fuck this."

The front door almost hit him on the way out.

"Whose voice?" the receptionist asked.

Patrick shrugged and fidgeted with his bow tie. "I don't know," he said. "It was like...a man's voice. Calling me to the basement."

The police receptionist—Chandra, according to the name tag—raised both eyebrows, her brown eyes staring at him blankly. "Could it be that it was your friend? Maybe he was in the basement and—"

"No!" Patrick landed a fist on the reception desk, surprising himself at the display. Chandra cleared her throat and crossed her arms. "Look, I'm sorry, okay? I'm sorry. I just, I'm worried about my friend. It's been three days."

Chandra released a soft breath and stood to be eye level with Patrick. Hands at her hips, she tightened her lips like she'd just eaten sour candy. "I'm going to be real polite here, sir. Because I can see you're upset and I empathize. But, and I repeat, but, you do not come here—of all places—and speak to me like that. Clear?"

Patrick nodded and averted the woman's gaze.

"Now." Sitting back down, Chandra flicked auburn hair from her face and smiled. Passed a clipboard and a black pen to him. "Fill out the missing persons report and someone will give you a call."

"That's not—"

Chandra glared.

Patrick held his tongue and took the clipboard.

"You can sit over there, sir." She pointed to a row of hard plastic chairs.

He smiled his thanks and sat down. The staticky words rung in his head. The more he thought about it, the more he knew it wasn't Sam. He knew it. In his heart. In everything he was, he *knew* it.

Sam didn't ignore his graphic novels, leaving them in the sun for days at a time to fade.

Sam didn't ignore his calls and texts.

Sam didn't go incognito; he didn't vanish from the face of the Earth. Yet, that's what had happened. His best friend was gone.

The missing persons form was rubbish. He knew that, too. Because Sam wasn't missing. Not in a traditional sense.

It's that house.

Putting the clipboard on the chair next to him, Patrick stood to leave. In that moment, heading to the police station exit, his next actions were clear. Go back to the house. Figure out what happened to Sam.

The glass doors slid open.

"Bub?" a voice called from behind him. The reflection in the glass was a warped version of Detective Corrigan.

"I've been calling and I figured coming here would be better." Patrick feigned a smile.

Corrigan wrapped a meaty arm around Patrick's shoulder and nuzzled into his cheek with a kiss.

Patrick lifted his head. "Something's happened to him, Corry, I know it." He explained the absence, leaving out the whispering voice in the static, and Corrigan nodded along with interest. As if taking mental notes, he scratched at his stubble and leaned forward in his chair. Patrick noticed the beer belly and the way it tugged at the seams of the detective's shirt.

Sam would have liked that. Patrick thought, despite himself. He and Sam both loved bears—thick, hairy gay men—and Danny had been the exception. Patrick found himself wondering if circumstances were different, perhaps Sam and Corrigan might have been a good match. He wondered, not for the first time, what Corrigan saw in him and his red hair.

"Patrick, I have to ask you something." Corrigan leaned close, only continuing in a soft voice when Patrick nodded. "Is Sam…is he… Does he have any history with violence?"

Staring back at the detective, Patrick creased his forehead in confusion.

"It's just that," Corrigan said, "Danny's body went missing. Along with the coroner. I've just received security footage from the area on the night shows Sam's car going to the morgue."

"So?" Patrick raised his voice. "He was upset, he wanted to see Danny again."

Corrigan cleared his throat. "It also shows him leaving the scene—"

"Scene? What do you mean, 'scene?'" Patrick's eyes went wide, but he knew exactly what Corry meant.

"And now he's nowhere to be found." Corrigan made a clicking sound with his tongue and drew in a deep breath. "I'm not suggesting your friend has done anything untoward. I just need to know where he is."

"I don't know where he is." Patrick's voice broke and tears leaked from his eyes. He was conscious of Chandra peering over, ears cocked toward him.

"An APB has been put out on him," Corrigan said, his eyes deep and sad.

In a whisper, Patrick continued. "Corry...it's that house..."

Corrigan scratched at his stubble again and placed a thick hand under his chin, inviting Patrick to keep talking. Patrick saw in the man's eyes that he was willing to believe anything, or at least hear him out without interrupting. While they'd been dating for only a few months, Corrigan had always shown he had an open mind.

So he told Corrigan everything, albeit that wasn't much. He even included the part about smashing a window, eyeing his partner for a reaction. Or a pair of cuffs, to punish him for his crime.

"You think I'm crazy," Patrick said.

"No," Corrigan replied, meeting Patrick's eyes and delving into them. "Not crazy. Maybe a little confused. Maybe a little scared. But not crazy."

"What am I supposed to do?" Patrick asked, wiping at the tears.

"We," Corrigan said, a sad smile shaping among the stubble. "What are *we* going to do?"

Chapter 17

Shelley lay on the mattress, the stench of piss and shit filling her nostrils. She didn't hate those smells. It was part of the thirst. She'd never consumed those things, but the thirst made it seem *almost* palatable. It came from humans, as did blood. It was like tarnished meat, though. You could see what it used to be, but the harsh reality of the rancid stench made it hard to swallow.

Yet, as time drifted through the pitch black and Shelley's urges got the better of her, she contemplated licking the fabric of the mattress. Just to see. Just to taste the excrement. Just once. But she wasn't that desperate.

Not yet.

Her daughter, the fucking demon bitch from Hell, now known as Teddy, hadn't come back. Shelley didn't know how long it had been. She just knew she'd been so hungry and thirsty and hadn't been able to hold on to her bladder. She'd pissed herself, and her clothes were dry again. It had to have been days. In the damp, cold dark, the piss had stayed wet, sticking to her for what felt like eternity. Even now, dry, her clothes were starchy and sweaty, like cardboard. Yes, it had been days.

Teddy, you fucking cunt. When you come back down here, I swear—

Her thought was chopped in half by the sudden presence of a deep, gray glow, emanating from the wall behind her. In her starving daze, Shelley rubbed her eyes. The glow remained; she wasn't seeing things. The chain kept her from moving any closer, all she could do was watch as the cement wall began to shift and change in front of her.

"Of, fuck you." She spat, in a vain attempt to silence the wall.

She knew the truth now. Her memories haunting her gray matter, replaying across her eyelids every time she blinked. She wished for ignorance again, to be in the dark about what those tendrils had done to her. What that house had put inside her.

Thinking over it now, the events that led her to that moment, she traced circles on the mattress. It was something she'd done since she was a girl, a way to focus her thoughts. If Shelley traced enough circles on the mattress, her thoughts led her back to her mom. Her mother had also done it. Her mother. The way she'd died had always struck Shelley as odd. Now that she had time to think, surrounded by nothing but cold, damp, dark concrete—and that fucking glowing wall—the pieces began to make sense.

Tracing another circle, turning her back to the wall to really focus, Shelley took a deep breath, and thought about her dead mother lying on the bathroom floor, chunks of bone and brain smattering the bathroom mirror.

Suicide.

Yet, just an hour prior, they'd chatted on the phone. Her mom had invited her round for tea and cake. She wouldn't have done that if she'd planned on killing herself in the interim. Who does that?

There was also no note. Shelley's limited experienced with suicide meant she believed, with all her heart, that there should have been a note. The single word formed in the blood and brain matter on the mirror didn't count as a note.

What was the word?

She remembered how strange it was to see it, thinking how impossible it was for it to be there. You can't shoot your brains out and then scrawl words in the mess. You take half your head off, you're dead. End of story.

Another circle on the mattress. Shelley's heart beat slow and steady, calm breaths through her nose, but her chest tight with anxiety.

She was close to something. Some answer for some unknown question that, in this moment, felt like the most pressing thing in the world. Her breathing became heavier as she traced another circle, the focus breaking for just a second. She pulled herself together with a short slap on the face, ignoring the ever-increasing glow from over her shoulder.

The wall doesn't want me to remember.

That made it her mission to do just that. She smiled, whispered another, "Fuck you", and pictured the scene again. She had to remember that word. Figuring out how it got there was the next step.

Among her screaming and crying and blurry vision, her hands and knees covered in blood as she kneeled beside her mother's corpse, that word trickled down the mirror. She couldn't see it, she couldn't see past her mother. Past the wreckage of her once-beautiful face, now limp and to the side. Pale. Eyes hollow and blank.

Squeezing her eyes now, Shelley forced her memories to keep going. Forced her to do what happened next. It was the smell. That horrible, putrid, delicious smell. She'd never tried brains, and as the grief and shock and fear overtook her, it was the smell that grounded her. That shook Shelley back to the reality that even though her mother was dead in front of her, all she wanted to do was lick the blood off the floor.

She remembered how she'd wiped the crimson delight from her hands in a bid to stop herself from tasting. How she'd crawled away from her mother, slamming her back against the bathroom wall. Slid up the wall, hands over her mouth in a silent scream. Turned her head from the body.

Glimpsed the mess on the walls.

Cried at the tarnished tiles they'd picked out together the previous year in the renovations.

Her eyes lifted to the mirror.

Shelley couldn't see it. She traced another circle on the mattress, forcing herself to stay the course. The wall glowed brighter, expanded and contracted—faster and faster. It planted words in her brain, tried to confuse her. Tried to stop her from remembering.

Standing, planting both feet firm on the concrete, and facing the mirror, Shelley stared at the wall. Gritting her teeth, she breathed hard, willing herself to force the wall out of her head.

"You're just a motherfucking wall!" she yelled. "You have no power over me!"

Except it did, and she knew it. She screamed again, repeating the words like a mantra, and closed her eyes again.

The body.

The blood.

The brains.

No. The mirror. Look at the mirror.

The glass was spattered with red. With shards of bone.

No. The word. What is the word?

Through the mess and the remains of her mother, letters began to appear. The letters she'd seen and ignored. Just one word. A small thing that on its own meant nothing, but filled her with fear.

DIG.

She opened her eyes, immersed in the present now, and stared at the wall. The word didn't mean anything to her, but the way the wall was carrying on—thumping and beating and glowing that horrible gray—she knew it had to mean something.

The more she thought on it, the more she remembered her mother spending days at a time in this very basement, shovel in hand. Digging.

"Deeper and deeper," her mother had said over and over. "Deeper and deeper."

How could I have forgotten that? It was like she was on a mission. Shelley scratched at her face. *I can't think about that now.*

Stepping toward the wall, the chain around her ankle scraping at her skin, Shelley reached out her arms. The wall was expanding so much that she could just reach it as it imitated breathing in. She felt the concrete, now like a rubber, against her finger tips.

It reminded her of being in that hole all those years earlier. The same cold wetness, the same feeling of touching nothing, even though it was clearly there.

And her suspicions were confirmed.

"How are you in both places?" she asked. "What the fuck are you?"

She didn't expect an answer, and she didn't get one. The wall was fickle like that. Though it was dawning on her that it wasn't the wall at all. It wasn't even the house. It wasn't any of the houses.

"All the houses…" She shook her head, slow but purposeful. "All of them. Are they all…you?"

"Hi, Mommy," Teddy said from behind her. Shelley hadn't even noticed her come in. Hadn't realized the door to upstairs was open.

Moving her gaze away from the wall and to her daughter, Shelley narrowed her eyes. Blinking through the light in the doorway. "What are you doing with that?"

Teddy held up a shovel. "Oh, this? Daddy told me to dig. I *love* to dig, don't you?"

DIG.

"Da—you don't have a…" Shelley looked back to the wall, expanding and contracting like a beating heart.

"You should have loved me," Teddy said, her voice low. "Things didn't have to go this way."

Shelley reached toward Teddy, grabbed at the girl's legs and arms and whatever else she could reach as she moved past her. Teddy kicked at the cement with a foot and tapped at it with the shovel.

216

Another memory surged forward—her mother in that exact spot, telling Shelley it was dangerous down here. "It's the start of something beautiful, honey, but it's dangerous, too. Go back upstairs and play with your dollies," she'd said. "Deeper and deeper."

How did I forget that? What is happening to me? She started to shake at the memories.

Teddy tapped at the concrete again.

"You'll never break through the cement," Shelley said. "Not with that."

Teddy turned to her and smiled. "Daddy has prepared a spot for me. He told me so. See?"

Shelley blinked a few times and strained her eyes, the girl not having turned the lights on. Among the gray glow from the beating wall, she saw it. Someone must have been down here while she slept, the concrete had been eaten away in places, leaving just soil.

"What's going on here?" Shelley asked, as Teddy began to dig.

"It's the start of something beautiful, Mommy." Teddy smiled. Then she heaved the shovel into the cracked cement. "Dig, dig, dig," she said, panting through the strain of shoveling.

The same thing Mom said to me. She was following orders…back then? What does that mean? "What are you digging for?"

Teddy paused and faced her mother again. "It's not for me, silly. It's for you. You're getting a visitor real soon." She turned away and stabbed at the soil again with the shovel, whistling with each heave.

As the dirt scraped away into a pile at Shelley's feet, all she could think of was the word in the mirror, somehow written in her mother's blood.

DIG.

DIG.

DIG.

Chapter 18

Pete was gone. Last Jimmy knew, the old man was heading to see that guy. What was his name? She forced herself out from under Pete's duvet—hers smelled like vomit—and faced the morning sun. She'd slept here again, in Pete's room, hoping he'd wake her up with pancakes or something.

But he wasn't coming back. Day three and no sign of him or his car. If she could only remember that guy's name, she could figure out where Pete had got to. Thinking on it now, on his last words, Jimmy felt the sting of guilt in her stomach. Like a needle stabbing again and again at her insides.

"Okay," she whispered to herself, flipping the duvet to one side and letting the fresh morning air consume her. The sun filtering through the shutters was almost too much, and Jimmy closed her eyes again. "He picked up his keys, blabbing on about…that guy…and that house. That place with the weird history…and all I thought about was chicken fucking korma."

She opened her eyes again with a sigh, letting a picture form on the outskirts of her mind. The windows that looked like angry, sad eyes. The garden full of dead things. In her mind she walked through that rotten wooden front door, looked at the floor like she had the other day. The floorboards had dried bloodstains and she'd thought at the time it was the drugs, but had the walls been breathing?

Why do I have to be so high all the time? Jimmy thought, slapping at her face with tired fingers. She knew full well that her memory of moving that guy into the creepy-ass house was shrouded by shrooms and weed. And, if she were honest, a bit of acid. It was all fun in the end, until someone got hurt. Or went missing.

"Sam!" Jimmy clicked her fingers. The name rushed back inexplicably, along with the features of his face. She smiled at the memory. He seemed like a cool guy, although maybe a little too depressed for her liking. The way his mouth only sort of half moved when he spoke, like it was an effort.

Jimmy crawled from the bed and stumbled to the shower. The scent of Pete's soap and shampoo still clung to the bathroom tiles, even after days of his absence. His towel was still fresh and folded neatly on the rack. As Jimmy twisted the tap for hot and let the water trickle through her fingers as it heated, she thought about Pete. And Sam. And that house.

"What did you do, Pete?" Jimmy muttered.

The water started burning her skin and Jimmy fumbled with the taps until she could stand under the stream, letting the cascade of water fall around her. She shivered at the thought that Pete wasn't coming back. That she'd let him drive into danger and all she'd given an ounce of a fuck about was her stupid chicken korma.

I could always call the cops, Jimmy sneered. Last time she'd trusted a cop... Well, his dick had more to say than his badge. Something about trans- individuals really bothered some people, and Jimmy had found that out the hard way. She had scars on her ass and torso to prove it.

She lived just down the street from the police station, a constant reminder of the targeted hatred she'd experienced. Pete was always saying some shot about how one bad egg didn't make the batch. He was always nattering on about giving the cops a fair go. But that memory just made it impossible.

No. I have to do this myself.

By the time she'd washed and dried, Jimmy had found the resolve to go searching for Pete. Every cell in her body knew he would do the same. Hell, he had already saved her life by getting her off the streets. She had to go look for him.

Dressing in a *Captain Planet* T-shirt she'd found at a yard sale, an old leather jacket and knee-highs, Jimmy wiped hair from her face and stepped out the front door. Without the use of Pete's car, she'd have to walk it. Pulling her jacket tight, Jimmy headed in the direction Pete had disappeared to the other night. She had a habit of watching her feet when she walked, examining the sidewalk and the stray leaves and the ant colonies. None of it interested her today, and Jimmy looked up to the street.

To the police station. A detective escorted a younger man with red hair from the building. The detective—a bearded, full-bellied man with thick bushels of hair sprouting from his chest and exploding through the top of his shirt—had kind eyes. Jimmy hated that. Kind eyes on a fucking liar.

She reminded herself that he wasn't "the one", and took a deep breath. Pete's voice in her head kept her going, until she looked again at the redhead getting into his car.

I know that guy.

He was wiping at his eyes, and the detective planted a meaty hand on his shoulder. The gesture was kind, too.

Okay, Pete. I know, I know. Give them a chance.

Staring at the redhead, some of the shroom-cloud lifted and Jimmy's memories flooded back. He was with Sam at the house the other day.

"Hey!" Before she could stop herself, Jimmy was jogging toward the car. Both the redhead and the detective shifted their focus to her, and the detective smiled. Kind and gentle. Fucker. "Hey, you're Sam's friend, right?"

The redhead narrowed his eyes. "Yeah, Patrick. Why?"

Jimmy caught her breath as she reached the car. "Are you heading to his house? I think my friend is there."

Looking to the road below, Patrick pursed his lips, and nodded. The detective gave a quick glance to him—*Let me handle this*—and he stopped nodding.

"What friend?" the detective asked, reaching into his pocket for something. Jimmy glanced down, taking a reflexive step back, only to see him pull out a notepad. Flicking to a fresh page, the detective grabbed a pen from his shirt pocket, licked the tip, and held it to the paper.

"Uh," Jimmy stuttered, "I, uh,"—cleared her throat—"I don't speak to cops."

The detective nodded, sympathy pouring from him as he took in Jimmy's form. At this stage in her journey, it was clear to most people that she was assigned male at birth. The cock in a frock, as some drunkards had called the other day.

"Listen," the detective said. "I'm not one of those transphobic cops. I'm gay myself, and believe me, I know how hard it can be sometimes."

Jimmy's cheeks flushed. "You don't know shit!" She spat, and took a deep breath. Pete's voice rang in her ears again. "Sorry," she mumbled, "but you don't know what it's like for me, okay?"

The detective nodded again. Patrick looked between them and cleared his throat. "What's this about your friend?"

Pulling her jacket tight again, Jimmy stood straight. "Pete. The guy who helped Sam move in the other day. He thought something was up, I don't know, and he went round there the other night." Looking at Patrick, Jimmy whispered, "He never came back."

"Sam's gone, too." Patrick's eyes welled with tears and the detective leaned on one knee, wrapped a bearish arm around him. More kindness that Jimmy couldn't fathom from a cop. "And I did hear a voice coming from the basement."

"You went inside?" Jimmy asked.

"Yeah," Patrick replied, adjusting his bow tie. "I smashed a window."

Jimmy flashed her teeth in a smile. "Nice, Patty. You're a bad ass." Patrick blushed. "So you heard a voice in the basement?"

"A man, I think," Patrick said.

Jimmy's voice went up an octave. "Was it Pete? Did you look?"

Patrick shook his head and looked at the ground. "Sorry, I got a bit…"—he looked away—"scared."

"*My* friend could be in *your* psycho killer friend's basement and you wussed out?" Jimmy rushed forward, raising a fist.

The detective stepped between them, and Jimmy backed down while Patrick mumbled how sorry he was and that he freaked out.

"Something is definitely going on," the detective said to Jimmy. "We're heading over there now. Come with us."

"Come with you?" Jimmy asked, frowning. "Is that, like, allowed?"

The bear detective gave a half smile. "It's pretty informal, just going to see a friend."

Nervous, Jimmy clicked her tongue and thought about it for a moment. She really did need to find Pete. These two might have been her best chance. With Patrick's friend missing, too, maybe this detective could open a case—*Like he cares about a missing trans-man.*

"I'll come with you," Jimmy said, pushing her negative thoughts to the side. "For Pete." They approached a police car and the detective—Corrigan, his badge read—opened the door her her. "If you think I'm sitting in the back, you've got another thing coming."

Corrigan and Patrick gave a small laugh. "Sure thing," Corrigan said. "But at least let me drive."

Despite herself, Jimmy smiled, and got into the front passenger seat. As Corrigan pulled away from the curb, she held her breath and tried to ignore the swelling sense of fear in her gut.

Chapter 19

Curled in a ball, arms tight around his knees, Sam stared into the clock. The time never changed. The hands didn't move. It was stuck on 10:14. Yet, he heard the comforting, hushed tone of the *tick, tick, tick*. After a while, the sound disappeared—just white noise—but he still felt the ticking inside him. The clock was a part of him now. He knew that. He liked it. But he hated that he liked it.

All sense of time dissipated into the walls, breathing into him as though he was between two lungs. Like he was the heart of the home, just out of place. He'd find his home soon, he could feel that, too. One thing of what he came to think of as "outside" remained. The turning of his stomach. The need to eat. Although, that had changed. He didn't *eat* anymore, not in a traditional sense. Just gulped on crimson death.

Staring into the clock, into the timeless void, Sam ignored the hunger and breathed. Just breathed. Calm and focused. Quiet. As though he'd never breathed before. The clock gave him a gift. An eternity to lie there, between time—outside time—and just breathe. Let his anxieties melt away.

Let his father—falling for eternity in that hole—melt away. Let Danny melt away.

Danny.

Sam caught a glimpse of his hands, and his eyes fought to move from the clock. Shifting to his body, he saw the blood. Remembered Danny and the coroner and what he'd done to them. What the house had done. The way Danny's body had sunk into the floorboards. The way he'd tasted the blood and rejoiced in the flavor as it flowed down his throat.

He remembered it all—the jock still in his trunk, how he'd pushed his father into the void—and his stomach knotted. Intestines pulling tight inside him, begging for blood.

The comfort of the ticking, the steady beat inside him, became a hammering in his chest. A wake up call from the stupor of his timeless dream.

"What have I done?" His voice was small and scared, but it echoed through the chamber back to him.

Sitting up, Sam closed his eyes. To stop himself from being sucked into the clock once more. He looked around for the tiny door, his route through the tunnel back to the real world. The door was there, though just a shimmer.

"How long have I been here?" The question seemed absurd to Sam, even as he asked it. The concept of time held no meaning to him. Yet, he needed to know. He crawled through the tunnel, noticing he fit more easily now. Like the tunnel had adjusted its size for him. He pushed open the door and moved through the gap, every inch feeling closer to something dark and heavy. Closer to food.

As he climbed into the real world, back into a realm bound by minute and second hands, Sam felt the rush of anxiety fill him again. He hated that feeling. The guilt and the fear and depression and—

Ping.

His phone. On the bench. Still charged.

I can't have been in there for too long, then.

Sam stood and raced for the phone. Its battery was down to red. He ran for a charger in his bedroom and plugged in the phone. Sitting on the mattress—he still hadn't even made the bed—Sam stared as the screen lit up.

Another GPS ping.

"Please." Sam begged. Looking to the ceiling, he dropped the phone and clutched his hands under his chin. "Please, I can't do this. Don't make me. Not again."

The phone pinged again, and Sam picked it up with shaky hands. Ignoring the time-stamp of 9:46, he tapped the notification. The coordinates weren't far. His breath caught in his throat and Sam slammed the phone down.

"Do your own dirty work."

Ping. Ping. Ping.

And the ticking started again. A countdown, that's what it was. The clock inside that other realm, counting down to some unknown death. And as Sam blocked his ears in a futile attempt to drown out the ticking that now came from within him, he felt sure that the clock was counting down to something.

Death.

The *tick, tick, tick* counted down to someone's death. That's when he heard it. When Danny died. When he'd attacked the coroner. When he'd pushed his dad. And now, someone else would be dead, too. The clock had known, sitting at 10:14 for however long he'd stayed in there. It knew the time of death of everyone.

It knows when I am going to die.

"I'll do it," Sam shouted into the house, holding both hands to his growling stomach. "Please, stop."

Checking the phone, the battery was back into the healthy green range, so he pulled the charger cable free, and stormed through the house toward the front door. He could smell the blood on his clothes and body, but in that moment he didn't care. Someone was dead, and the house was hungry. He was hungry, too, despite his best efforts.

He had work to do.

According to Apple Maps, his destination was just up ahead, on the right. 66 Sixth Street. The number alone made Sam's stomach lurch. With everything that had happened in the last two days, the 666 inference was just a bit too much. His skin crawled as he pulled up to the house, and his arms began to itch under the skin as he looked upon the exterior.

It was a "nothing" house. Dried patches of grass for a lawn, a few dying plants here and there. Weeds. Lots of weeds, springing up from the cracks in the driveway. A rusted mailbox on an angle and sun-bleached blinds drawn at the front windows. But the thing Sam noticed the most when he looked at it was how it made him feel—nothing. No sadness. No happiness. No sense that the place had created or witnessed any memories. Despite the neglected appearance, Sam didn't feel anything.

And that scared him.

The GPS ping indicating someone was dead—someone was ready for the house—had led him here. With the jock still in the trunk, he thought better of taking out of the garage. Maybe the fresh air would be good for him, for a change.

"This is the last time," he said to himself. He didn't believe it for a second.

He walked to the front door, hearing the scrape of dead grass against his shoes, the pointy blades like tiny knives scratching to get at him. Knocking at the door, Sam felt a gust of wind travel past the house. A crow cawing in the distance.

He swallowed hard.

The door opened.

"You're here. I've been waiting." A little girl greeted him, holding out her hand. "I'm Teddy." Sam shook her hand, fighting the urge to recoil at the utter coldness of her skin.

He looked past Teddy into the house, wondering if he had the right address. Teddy must have been seven or eight, long black hair and dark eyes. *That hair...* Her smile revealed yellowed teeth—too yellow for a girl her age—and she had cigarette burns on her arms.

"Hi, Teddy. I, uh, is your mom or dad home?" Sam asked.

"Mother is waiting for you." The girl stepped aside to let Sam in, scratching at a burn on her forearm. Sam saw she had a bite mark in her arm, too, and despite it looking fresh, it didn't bleed.

"She is?" Sam's heart beat faster as he breached the entrance. "Who's your mom?"

Like the outside, the interior gave Sam nothing. Devoid of emotion and feeling, the house was just a house. But it felt like something else. Something he couldn't describe.

"Shelley," the girl said, and closed the door.

Sam knew that name. The realtor who'd shown him the house. *It can't be a coincidence.* "Is she a realtor, by any chance?"

The girl shrugged. "Probably. She gets around a bit." When Sam raised an eyebrow, she continued. "She's always going into people's houses and putting up 'For Sale' signs."

Nodding, Sam's heart raced faster and faster. He was in the right place, he could feel it. *Shelley's dead? Does this kid know her mother is dead somewhere in this house?*

"She's expecting you," Teddy said and tugged at his hand to lead him through the house.

Not dead then. Although, as he checked his phone once more, the time was only 10:11. Three minutes til death.

Sam let her guide him through the living room, an old television blaring static and a strange gray shadow across the cane furniture.

"Down there." Teddy drew his attention, pointing to a staircase to the basement. Her attention wavered as she noticed a scab forming over a recent encounter with a cigarette, and promptly picked at it. She flicked the scar tissue down toward the basement and Sam followed it, his skin breaking into goosebumps once more.

The creaky stairs feeling like putty under his feet, Sam heard the *tick tick tick* again. He was in the right place, that much he knew. He was also in the very, very worst of places, if the feeling growing inside him was to be believed.

232

That hair. Her size. Is she—

A cold broke across his skin and his spine was on fire with chills. Sweat dripped from his underarms and Sam became aware of his breaths: heavy and jagged. Each step down pushed him further into discomfort, his hands beginning to tremble.

"Don't worry," Teddy said from behind him. "It'll be quick."

Sam stopped at this, his shaking hands just out of reach of the basement door handle. It looked new, as did the locking mechanism.

"What'll be quick?" Sam asked, without turning around.

Teddy giggled. "Silly billy," she said, and nudged Sam in the lower back. "Open the door."

Her words were like an order. Despite the trembles and the uneven breaths and the sweat and the intense desire to run home back to the safety of his chamber, Sam turned the handle. He was outside himself again, watching his body move while his mind could only watch.

He watched himself enter the pitch-black basement. His nostrils burned with the stale air.

He watched himself move through the darkness. A light came on. He was vaguely aware of Teddy behind him.

He saw a hole, dug through the cement and the earth. Smelled the soil and the piss and shit and…

I can't be here.

He walked further.

A woman—*Shelley?*—was lying on a mattress, chained by the ankle.

His legs buckled under him, but he kept walking. His breath caught in his throat as the door shut behind him. He felt Teddy's presence guiding him forward, and she whispered, "You know what to do."

He did know.

His body knew. His mind cried out, begged his legs to stop moving. He couldn't hurt another person. Not like the coroner. His body moved toward a shovel, lying near the freshly dug hole.

No, no, no.

He watched his hands pick up the garden tool. He knew what it was for. The hole would be deep enough.

"Sam?" Shelley's voice broke through his trance. "Is that…is that you?" She sounded weak.

He tried to answer, tried to tell her he was going to get her out of here. Tried to apologize when he kept moving to her.

"Ignore her, Sam." Teddy's voice echoed through the basement.

I need the chamber. The womb. The coffin.

With all his might, he tried to stop his legs from moving. He buckled again and stopped. Teddy appeared at his side, her stare piercing his soul. "She has to die, Sam. We both know it."

"Why?" His voice was dry and cracked, and he knew she was the figure he'd been chasing.

"Because Daddy said so."

He didn't know what she meant, yet somehow it made sense. The GPS pings. Danny. The coroner. The chamber. That hole. It all led him here. To this moment. To Shelley. She'd been prepared for him, laid out like a lamb at the slaughter.

"Please, Sam." Shelley struggled to her elbows and raised an arm up as far as she could. Her weak body couldn't do much else.

I can't do this. "I have to do this."

10:13.

"You don't," Shelley said.

Teddy frowned. "Maybe it'll be easier with the lights off." She moved to the door and flicked the light switch, drowning them in black.

He was at Shelley's side now, her weak grip around his ankle, begging for mercy. Sam raised the shovel, aiming the blade at her neck. One swift motion and—

"Wait." Shelley pleaded through the darkness, a glint in her eyes the only thing keeping Sam from plowing the shovel into her neck. "I know who killed Danny. And I know what happened to his boyfriend."

Sam choked back a laugh. "Bullshit. You'd say anything—"

"No! My...*daughter*...if you can call her that," Shelley said, spitting out the word daughter, "killed them both. She's not human, Sam. She's not... She's evil."

Teddy flicked the light on and rushed to her mother. "You shut your face, you lying bitch!"

Sam lowered the shovel and stepped away from Shelley. Staring into Teddy's face, watching for the smallest of facial movements, he saw it. A slight uptick in the lips.

Hiding a smile.

"Sam." Teddy moved to him, put her hand over his, and smirked. "I'm just a child. How could I do something like that?"

"Listen to me, Sam..." Shelley started.

Her words disappeared into a static white noise as Sam thought it over. Teddy was right. She was just a kid. Abused by her mother, who as far as Sam could see had every reason to lie to him. But that smirk...

"Tell me something, Teddy." Sam lifted the shovel again, this time directing it at the child. "How did you know I was coming?"

Teddy's gaze shifted between the end of the shovel and Sam's eyes. Back and forth. Back and forth. Sam could see the cogs turning in her mind. She took a step back, back toward the door. Her steady movement to the basement steps sent chills up Sam's spine. Everything she did was calculated. And that fucking smirk—

Sam launched at her, swiping the air with the shovel. The blade missed by an inch, Teddy's long black hair flicking against the rusted metal. She raced to the door. Sam swiped again. She was small and nimble and the shovel was heavy in his hands. His rage kept him moving, but Teddy was fast. Reaching the door, she smiled at him and slammed it shut, just as the edge of the shovel connected with the wood.

"Let us out of here!" Sam beat at the door with the shovel, listening to Teddy's heavy breaths on the other side. Dropping the shovel, he beat the wood with closed fists until he started to bleed, screaming again and again to be set free.

"You have thirty seconds, Sam," Teddy called. "Tick. Tick. Tick." A hollow laugh echoed through the door.

The reminder did something to him, and Sam gripped the shovel once more. As he stared back at Shelley, his heart pounding in his ears, a desire for blood washing through him, he remembered what she said. Teddy, the little girl, killed her Danny.

"I really wanted us to be friends." Teddy sighed through the door. Then, "I have somewhere to be…and Daddy wants me to tell you, the next GPS ping is for Patrick."

"Patrick?" Sam banged his fists against the door again. "You leave him alone! You hear me?"

10:14.

"Sam," Shelley said behind him. "It's no use."

He dropped to his knees, punching at the door one last time before hunching over. His forehead, drenched in sweat, smacked against the wood, and he breathed. A shadow under the door told him Teddy was still there. He imagined that smirk and banged again.

Holding back tears, he pleaded in soft whispers to Teddy until the shadow disappeared and footsteps thudded up the stairs and left them in silence. Sam shifted to lean his back against the door, wishing he was back inside his safe place. Wishing he could crawl back through the tunnel and curl up in the room with the clock.

Tick. Tick. Tick.

He smiled as the sound came to him, reminding him he was safe. Somehow, in this basement, locked away, he was safe. Time still ticked away, and that knowledge was like a constant knife to his wrists, slicing away his sense of existence.

"I'm sorry about Danny," Shelley said, bringing him back to the present.

Sam lifted his head to stare at her again. "I'm sorry, Shelley. I have to do this. The house…it needs me to do it…"

Shelley's eyes went wide. "Wait! Check the time."

He did.

10:15.

He frowned. "But, it was supposed to happen at 10:14."

THE COUNT

Shelley smiled. "You beat it, Sam." Her words were fast and desperate. "And you can do it again."

Sam looked at his phone again, the time glaring at him in the dark. "I don't understand."

"You're not a slave. None of us are," Shelley said. "The house chose *you*, but you don't have to choose *it*."

He looked between Shelley and his phone, still processing what this meant. The digital display clicked over to 10:16.

"You said Teddy killed Danny? What did she do to him? Does that mean that it wasn't me?"

"It was Teddy. Her bloodlust is...intense."

"But the morning they found him...I woke up holding a bloody knife."

Shelley thought for a moment, and sighed. "I can't explain that one, I'm sorry."

"Why did she do it?" Sam asked, climbing to his feet and walking to Shelley. "Why did she kill my Danny?"

"She's connected to your house. Maybe to all of them. She sensed your pain and...I think she thought she was doing you a favor."

Sam's eyes welled with tears. Wiping at them, he choked out, "A favor? By killing the only man I've ever loved?"

They remained in silence while Sam processed the information. While he imagined Teddy stabbing and stabbing and stabbing and stabbing and—

"You said you knew what happened to his new boy-friend?" Sam asked, shaking off the images of the knife penetrating Danny again and again.

"Yes," Shelley said. "He's in your house. His body is in the basement, waiting. Unless it's fed on him already. Teddy will be heading over there, I imagine."

Fumbling at Shelley's chained ankle, Sam said, "Why?"

"She thinks the house is her father"—dodging Sam's disbelieving stare, she continued—"it's a long story."

"Look," Sam said, rattling the chain and following it to a metal plate on the wall, "I don't know about any of that. I just know we have to get out of here, and we've got to find her before anything happens to Patrick. I have to find a way to get you free before the ticking comes back. I can't help myself when it enters me."

Shelley gave Sam a knowing stare, then looked away.

Glancing at the shovel, Sam went to it, and raced back to the metal plate. "Maybe I can..." He banged the shovel against the plate again and again.

"Keep going," Shelley said, her eyes wide with excitement. "It's working!"

Part Three

Part Three

Chapter 20

Daddy had said the redheaded man was next. She was supposed to kill him at the library, but he was way too nice for that. He didn't deserve it, not like that other one. Danny. What a cunt. She wasn't supposed to know that word, she didn't think. Mommy had spat it under her breath enough times for Teddy to pick it up, but she knew she wasn't supposed to say it.

She wasn't in trouble for not doing it—*Thank god!*—and Daddy had said he was proud of her for what she'd done to the ice cream skinnie. She deserved it, he'd said, because of the strawberry topping. Still, she owed him a dead Patrick, and even though she wasn't in "trouble" and Daddy wasn't mad at her, she still had to make amends. *That's what you do.* Daddy had told her. *You make amends.*

"How do I do that?" Teddy had asked him.

Next time I tell you kill someone, you do it. That's how.

"Even if they don't deserve it?" Her voice was low, trying to disguise her desire to let Patrick live. To just leave the guy alone. Because, to her, he wasn't a skinnie. He was a human being—a real one, with a heart and a soul, and that was something she'd never encountered before.

They all deserve it.

Now that she was thinking about it, really putting two and two together, Teddy wasn't so sure.

Walking away from the basement door, Sam still banging and pleading, Teddy wasn't so sure the ice cream bitch had deserved it. Sure, she'd betrayed her with that horrible topping, but it was a mistake. No, she didn't deserve to have her heart ripped out, even if it was beyond delicious. By the time she reached the top of the stairs, she wasn't sure any of them deserved it. Patrick certainly didn't, so maybe she'd been wrong about some of the other skinnies, too.

It doesn't matter, she thought. *When Daddy chooses someone, they have to die.*

Taking a deep breath, Teddy pulled on some boots, grabbed a hoodie, and headed out. She flung the hoodie over her head, letting her hair stream out the front.

She hadn't lied to Sam; Patrick really was next on the hit list. She hadn't decided whether she was heading over to the house to save him, or to help him die. Either way, she needed to be there—Daddy had said—and she didn't want to let him down again. She just wanted to be a good girl, and she could never get that right for her mom.

A bus went past her on the street, the driver giving her a foul look as it went by. Skinnies were *always* doing that to her, and it reminded her why she once believed they all deserved whatever was coming. It was either the upturned lip, a scowl with gross teeth showing, or a smile and a whistle. Three options for the male skinnies when they saw her. She thought back to the pedo she'd encountered at the library and decided, unequivocally, that he did deserve to die.

Danny was a real piece of shit, too, just like the bus driver and the pedo. She'd appeared in his backyard to look at him. That was all she wanted, just to look. The way he and his new man were rolling around the sheets looked primal and animalistic. So what if she'd pressed her face against the glass of their bedroom window to get a better look. He didn't have to—

Patrick was nice to me, though.

She wasn't far from the house, kept a watchful eye on the traffic and the skinnies, just to make sure Patrick wasn't around. She knew if he wasn't there already that he was on his way. The knowledge sort of just came to her, like she was a prophet or something. Like she was that psychic woman from Medium. Mommy had caught her watching that one night and sent the remote flying into the side of her head.

"TV is for good girls," she'd said through gritted teeth, almost foaming at the mouth with rage. "Go to your fucking room."

Down to the basement she'd trotted before her mommy did anything else bad to her. Daddy explained she was just scared, because Teddy was powerful and unique—the only one of her kind, actually—and Shelley didn't understand that. Still, she never got to see how that episode ended.

A sensation in her fingertips pulled Teddy back to the present, and she twisted her head to the side to see a police car. Breathing slow and steady, Teddy studied the faces in the car. Two she recognized, and one she didn't. Patrick, the redhead. The fat detective from Danny's house. And someone else in the passenger seat. Teddy squinted to get a better look, to assess the threat level, and frowned. She didn't get anything from that person, except that it looked like a woman.

Who is this, then?

As the car came up the street, she caught a glimpse of the woman's shirt, and gave a grunt of approval.

Captain Planet, fuck yes. I love that show. CatDog, then the planeteers. Wind, water, heart...

She was intrigued and began to wonder if this mystery woman was on the shit list, too. Maybe she could get the shirt off her first and then kill her. Seemed a waste to let such an awesome piece of clothing get destroyed. The fat detective had a kind face, too, though his outfit was a little boring. She hadn't had anything to do with him, but as the car passed her, Daddy spoke.

Kill them all.

"Daddy," Teddy said. "Patrick is sooooo nice, do I really have to?"

Kill. Them. All.

Teddy sighed, thrust her hands into her jacket pockets, and listened to her boots scuff against the sidewalk as she headed to the house. With each step, she considered the different ways a skinnie could die, and which methods were her favorites.

She smiled.

Pete's car was right out front, parked across the street from Sam's place. Jimmy straightened and pointed to the vehicle. Corrigan and Patrick sat up, too, the energy in the car changing from one of uncertainty to one of fear. If Pete's car was here—had been here the whole time—that meant he was inside that fucking weird ass house. It had to, it couldn't mean anything else.

Jimmy's heart hammered in her chest and she clutched at her neck to steady her breathing. Something she'd always done, since she was a kid. She didn't like thinking about those days, didn't want to be the same person she was back then, but some habits really did die hard. This was one of them, and as she rubbed her neckline, Corrigan pulled the car into Sam's driveway.

From the outside, the house looked the way she remembered it—sad, derelict—but something had changed. Her brow furrowed, she leaned forward in the seat as Corrigan shifted the car into park. Biting softly at her lips, Jimmy saw the garage.

"Fuck," she said, and unbuckled her seatbelt. Tearing from the car, she raced to the garage door, inspected the concrete driveway for a second, and then tried to lift the door.

Corrigan and Patrick came after her, the detective shouting that they couldn't just do that, shouting at Jimmy that if they did find something, it would be inadmissible. Useless.

She didn't care.

"Jimmy, what's wrong?" Patrick asked, a soft hand on her shoulder.

"Look!" She pointed to a red spot on the concrete, leaking from under the garage door.

Corrigan pulled Jimmy from the door with a firm, but not aggressive, grip. "Jimmy. This is serious. If Pete is in there, we need to go about this the right way. We can't go messing up a potential crime scene."

"Well what the fuck are we doing here?" Jimmy spat, exasperated. "I thought we were here unofficially?"

Motioning to the blood stain, Corrigan said, "This changes things. You two wait out here. I'm going to go in."

Jimmy started to protest, but she knew in her heart that Corrigan was right. Pete was in there, probably hurt, but if Sam had fucked him up, they needed to do this right. She glared at Patrick, who watched Corrigan head toward the front door, his hand resting on the gun at his hip.

"Your friend better not have hurt Pete." Jimmy seethed.

Patrick adjusted his bow tie and glasses and took a deep breath. "Sam would never do that," he said, but Jimmy could tell he wasn't so sure. "Sam is a good guy."

"Then how do you explain this?" Pointing back to the blood on the concrete.

Shrugging, Patrick said, "There has to be an explanation. One that doesn't say Sam hurt Pete. I hope they're both okay."

With the detective disappearing into the house, Jimmy tugged at the garage door again. It was locked, wouldn't budge. Patrick tried to help her, though she didn't know why. It was a silent effort, but he put his back into it.

"Fuck this." Jimmy panted and smacked at the garage door. "I'm going round the back."

"Wait," Patrick hissed. "We should stay here."

"Did you just hiss at me?" Jimmy scowled. "You can do what you want. Go get a fucking taco for all I care. I'm going to find Pete."

Her mother had always insisted Jimmy was headstrong, and made it sound like a bad thing. The comments would come while she was plastered on boxed wine and singing religious hymns at her, so Jimmy never paid much attention. Now, in this moment, she knew her mother had been right.

For all that woman's faults...

Being headstrong was what was going to find Pete, though. Not standing around like a goose, waiting for Corrigan to do things his way. No fucking way.

Jimmy slipped around the side of the house, the dead grass crunching under her boots, wilted flowers almost watching her as she passed by. It was as though the house itself watched her; she couldn't explain it, but the goosebumps spreading across her arms and neck knew it.

As she moved to the back of the house, Jimmy stopped, and stared. Rubbed at her neckline again, and tried to breathe.

Blood. Lots and lots of blood.

Treading carefully, Jimmy looked around. "Pete?" she whispered. "Fuck, tell me this isn't yours, Pete."

No response came. She hadn't expected one. Hoped, but not expected.

The blood was smattered around the yard, but a thick, dried-out puddle began in the center of the dead grass. A trail extended from that point, and Jimmy saw pieces of blackened flesh scattered among the blood. She followed the trail, holding her breath, hoping Pete wasn't lying dead just around the corner somewhere.

The trail led to the back door, and Jimmy headed straight for it, determined to find her friend.

"Jimmy," Patrick called from behind her. "It's not Pete."

She turned to face him. Saw him crouching by what was once a flower bed, but now only resembled a skeletal, rotting version of one.

Taking a heavy sigh, relief washing over his face, Patrick continued. "Come look at this."

Jimmy raced toward Patrick, crouched beside him, and peered into the garden. "Jesus fuck... You're relieved about this?"

She was staring at a squirrel. Just the head. Entrails and a snapped spinal column jutting from the poor animal's decapitated form. She held back a rush of bile as the stench reached her, and the image of maggots swimming in the decay of the severed head.

"I am relieved. It means the blood isn't Pete's," Patrick said, eyes wide with the hint of a smile. "It's just a squirrel. A neighborhood dog could have done this."

Standing, Jimmy followed the path of the garden, searching for more remains. Rubbing her neckline, she swallowed hard as she saw the squirrel's tail, and a pile of what might have been guts before the birds got to it.

"It's been torn apart," Jimmy whispered, stepping away from the scene.

"Like I said, it was probably a dog." Patrick didn't sound convinced, and he tugged at Jimmy's jacket. "We should go back to the front and wait."

"Yes, you should." Came Corrigan's harsh voice.

They spun to face him, both looking sheepish. Patrick apologized, but Corrigan held up a hand to silence him.

"There's nobody here," he said. "I looked everywhere. This house is really weird, though."

"Did you hear a voice?" Jimmy asked, rushing past Corrigan. "Patrick said it came from the basement."

Corrigan blocked her path with a sad smile. "Nobody is here," he repeated. "I don't think it's safe in there, either. It's, like, leaking."

Patrick nodded. "I saw that, too, when I was here. Like a weird…mucus…or something."

"If Pete is in there," Jimmy persisted, "I *have* to find him. Please." Shaking his head, Corrigan started to speak, but Jimmy cut him off. "He's like a father to me and I was too high to care what he was saying. I let him come here by himself and now he's missing. This is my fault."

"Well, the house was unlocked," Corrigan said, his smile a little less sad this time. "So we technically haven't broken and entered. Plus, Patrick, you had plans to meet Sam here, right?"

Patrick frowned. "What?" Then it dawned on him, and he gave a hollow laugh. "Oh, yeah, we had plans for sure."

"There you go." Corrigan shrugged. "We're tagging along with Patrick, who was invited. The house was unlocked because Sam was waiting for him to arrive."

Smiling herself now, Jimmy raced inside the house, letting the back door creak shut behind her. She looked back to see where the other two were, and saw them embraced in a hug. Corrigan kissed Patrick on the cheek, then their foreheads touched, and they exchanged a few small words.

Get a room, she thought, and searched the house for the entrance to the basement.

As she moved through the living room, moving boxes still full of junk, Jimmy knew something suss was going on. Sam had been in the house for, what, a week? No way he wouldn't have made more progress than this, unless he was busy kill—

Don't go there. Not yet.

Resting a hand on the kitchen bench as she went past it, Jimmy pulled it back. Wet. Patrick was right. It felt like mucus, like the shit you blow out your nose when you're really sick. Thick and sticky and translucent.

Looking around, Jimmy saw the house was bleeding the stuff. From the ceiling, down the walls. Everywhere. Even at her feet, the floor was soaked in the stuff. The house groaned around her and Jimmy got the sense that she was in real trouble.

"Don't worry, Pete," she whispered. "I'm coming."

She found the basement entrance, clicked the door open, and headed inside.

Chapter 21

"I love you," Corrigan whispered, pulling Patrick close.

Patrick rested his head on Corrigan's chest, ignoring Jimmy's prying eyes from inside the house. He always felt weird when people watched them, but in that moment, he couldn't care less. His heart had been on fire since Sam went missing, and now, at his house, they discover a trail of blood and a mutilated squirrel.

"Corry," Patrick replied, "we need to look in the garage. You know we do."

The detective nodded and released Patrick from his grip, kissing him on the neck. "Let's go."

Slipping down the side of the house again, Patrick took Corrigan by the hand. Leading him away from the blood trail and the disemboweled squirrel, back to the garage. The

red stain on the concrete didn't help Patrick's burning heart—
he could feel the edges stinging with each thump. Swallowing down his anxiety, he stood in front of the garage door
and waited.

"How do we get in?" he asked.

Sighing, Corrigan peered up and down the street,
a coy expression covering his face. Reaching into his back
pocket, he pulled out a leather case. Unzipped it. "With
these." Holding out the open case, he showed Patrick thin
metal implements.

Patrick smiled. "Are they what I think they are?"

"Tools of the trade, Patty, tools of the trade." Corrigan
kneeled down by the lock and began working his magic. Patrick stared on, his heart burning a little less, but his bow tie
getting a workout with his thumb and forefinger as the pos-
sibilities of what lay inside the garage ran through his head.

He waited, turning his back on the garage door and
staring over at Pete's car. He remembered when he'd seen
it driving up to the house that first day, the way Sam had
looked nervous and excited and unsure, and how he himself
had thought the move was going to be a fresh new start for
his best friend. Waiting for Corrigan to break into the garage
now, expecting to find who knew what, Patrick realized just
how wrong he'd been.

"I shouldn't have let him move here," he said, as Corrigan tinkered with the lock.

"We don't know what's going on yet, Pat," Corrigan replied, focusing hard, making one final twist with his implements. "And, we're in."

Patrick took a long, deep breath as Corrigan pushed up the garage door. Looking inside the space, it looked like any other garage, though admittedly, less tools that one might expect. Just Sam's car, and some unused fishing poles from that time they thought it might be fun and then realized neither of them actually thought that.

"Patty," Corrigan said, his voice low. "Do you see this?"

Following the direction of Corrigan's pointing finger, Patrick saw the red spots on Sam's trunk. He moved to touch it, but Corrigan pulled his hand away.

"I think this is a crime scene," Corry said. "I don't know what Sam's up to, but something is really wrong here."

Patrick wasn't about to argue with him, to tell him that this could all be explained if they could just find Sam and ask him what was going on and then Corrigan and everyone would realize nothing was what it seemed and it was all just a big mistake—

Thump.

—but he knew in his heart that wasn't the case. He could feel it. Sam wasn't Sam at the moment, something had happened to him. His scar had changed, too. The other day at the café, it was black and—

Thump.

"It's coming from the trunk." Corrigan stashed his lock picks away in his back pocket and fumbled with the trunk of the car. It was sealed, as they both expected, and Corrigan scanned the area for a way to open it.

Thump. Thump.

"Is...someone in there?" Patrick breathed hard. "Why would Sam do that?"

Corrigan ignored him, rushed to a cabinet in the garage and searched. Pulling out a crow bar with an "Aha!", he ran back to the car and pried at the trunk. After a few moments, it popped open, and Corrigan stepped back.

"Fuck," he said, short and sharp.

Standing at the detective's side, Patrick clasped his hands over his mouth, eyes wide with fear as they processed what he was looking at. A man. Covered in red. Bruised. His hand weakly knocking at the inside of the trunk. *Thump. Thump.*

Corrigan reached in, but didn't touch the man. Just sized him up, assessing the damage. He looked back at Patrick, who was stumbling backward. "Stay with me, Patty. We need to get him out of here."

Breathing heavy, Patrick shed a tear. He looked back at the man in the trunk, back at Corrigan, and moved to the car. He tried to steady himself, but his head was foggy. He wasn't built for this kind of thing, he didn't want to be here.

"Come on, help me." Corrigan gripped the man's shoulders and began to heave. "He's really weak, Patrick, he needs help."

As though his body took over, Patrick grabbed the man's legs and hoisted them out of the trunk as Corrigan did the same with the man's upper body. As weak as the stranger was, he mumbled, "Thank you, thank you," over and over, until Corrigan ordered him to save his strength. Placing an arm over his own shoulder, Corrigan managed to get the man in a standing position, though his legs and feet were unmoving and limp. Patrick followed suit, wrapping the man's other arm around his shoulder.

"What are we doing, Corry?" Patrick asked. His head throbbed and his mouth was dry, but he knew he had to keep focused for a while longer. No stumbling, no chickening out. Not now.

"Get him inside. He needs water and bandages."

They hauled the man from the garage, across the front yard, and toward the front door. He was still bleeding and his feet were dragging. He was pale and his head drooped, a line of thick, reddened saliva dangling from his mouth.

Kicking the front door open, Corrigan took the lead as they heaved the stranger down the hallway. "Bathroom?" he asked Patrick.

"Down the hall, to the left," Patrick huffed, and they headed in that direction.

They sat the man down on the tiled bathroom floor, leaning him against the bath. His head still drooped and he no longer mumbled "Thank you", or anything else. His body lay limp before them, and Corrigan searched the bathroom for bandages.

"I need towels. Water. Go."

Patrick raced through the house to the linen cupboard, grabbed a bunch of towels, and threw them at Corrigan in the bathroom. Running to the kitchen, he opened a cupboard, searching for a container—anything—to hold the water. Nothing. Sam hadn't unpacked anything except a bunch of knives and forks.

Boxes.

He scanned the boxes in the living room for any reading "Kitchen". Tipping boxes left and right, he found only "Bedroom", "Memories", and "Office".

"Fuck!"

He heard water running in the bathroom and Corrigan slamming cupboard doors, making his own search. If Sam hadn't unpacked the kitchen, what were the chances he'd unpacked the bathroom? Standing in a mess of cardboard boxes, he saw it. "Bathroom".

Tearing the packing tape and flipping the lid open, Patrick saw what Corrigan needed. Bandages, medicines. He lifted the box and ran to the bathroom, dropping it down on the tiles.

"Here." He kneeled down. "What do I need to do?"

"Call 911."

Patrick watched Corrigan tear open bandage packets and search through the box for anything else he might need. He had that covered, all Patrick could do was get on the phone and call for reinforcements.

Slipping his phone from his pocket, he dialed 911.

No signal.

"My phone isn't working, where's yours?"

"Fuck, it's in the car," he said, wiping at the man's chest with a wet towel.

He heard the front door slam shut. *Jimmy!* Racing back to the hallway, Patrick saw it was empty.

"Jimmy?" he called. "We need your phone!"

No response.

He looked at his phone again. Emergency signal wasn't working, either.

"Get my phone out of the car!" Corrigan called. "Hurry! Or use the radio!"

He moved through the hallway as fast as he could, gripped the door handle and pulled. The door didn't move. He tried again, fumbled with the lock. It wouldn't open. He pulled hard again and again, but the door wouldn't budge.

"The door is jammed!" Patrick called, and he slipped in some mucus as he raced to the front room where he'd smashed the window earlier. "What the hell?"

Corrigan cussed from the bathroom, and Patrick ran back to him, falling to his knees on the tiles. "How is he doing?"

The detective's hands were stained red, a pile of bloodied towels by his side, and a bottle of antiseptic open on the vanity. He'd bandaged the stranger in a few places, but by the look on Corrigan's face, the diagnosis wasn't good.

"I honestly don't know how he's still alive." Corrigan wiped sweat from his brow with his wrist. "If we don't get him to a hospital soon, he's going to die." He stood and left the bathroom, hurrying down the hallway, Patrick hot on his heels. Trying the door himself, he cussed.

"It's jammed," Patrick said, noticing the translucent mucus dripping from the crevices in the ceiling. "It's…"

"I'll smash a fucking window," Corrigan said. "That guy needs help and we can't fuck around with a jammed door." He stormed into the front office, just off the hallway, and slipped on the carpet.

Looking down, they both saw the carpet was covered in the same mucus leaking from the ceiling. Patrick recalled the wet patches when he threw the rock through the window earlier. He peered over at the window, not believing his eyes, sure the panic was making him see things.

The window wasn't smashed. There was no glass on the carpet. Yet, the rock he'd thrown lay in the middle of the room, where it had been earlier.

"It's not going to let us leave," Patrick whispered.

Corrigan stared at him, steadying himself on the wet carpet. Lifting a foot, a trail of thick mucus grabbed at him, like he'd stepped in glue. "Pat," he said. "What the hell is going on here? What is Sam into?"

Shrugging, Patrick walked backward out of the room. The walls were dripping now, and he saw Corrigan's feet sinking into the carpet. The detective heaved with each step until he was back on the floorboards, though both men knew it was a matter of time before the wood, too, began to hunger for them.

"We have to get out of here." Corrigan pulled Patrick by the collar. "I'll get the guy, you head for the back door."

"What about Jimmy? And Pete?"

"There's no time." Corrigan sounded disgusted with himself. "You need to get out of here."

Patrick did as he was told, and headed for the back door. Back to the disemboweled squirrel. Heading through the living room, the rug covering the blood stains, Patrick stopped and frowned. The floorboards were clean—pristine, in fact.

As mucus oozed toward him from the edges of the walls, Patrick flung the rug aside. There were no blood stains. It was possible that Sam had cleaned it away, but it wasn't just the absence of the blood that made Patrick curious. It was how, among the mess of boxes, the floors looked new.

Like they'd been laid only yesterday. The house, he knew, was over a hundred years old, and the floors in the hallway had been scratched and scuffed, just like the rest of the house. Yet, this section was new. As he stared down at the floor, he watched as the shine on the wood grew.

It's restoring itself.

"Corry!" he shouted. "We have to go!"

The mucus seemed to know where he was, moving at him with purpose. With consciousness. Patrick stepped back, bumping into a "Memories" box, knowing he couldn't leave this house with Corrigan. He ran back to the bathroom, his eyes not comprehending what awaited him there.

"Help me!" Corrigan cried.

The stranger was sinking into the tiles, his body melting through the floor like it was a mirage. Corrigan pulled at the man, trying to heave him back from the void. Patrick grabbed one of the man's arms, and tugged hard, using the weight on his back foot as an anchor. He was heavy—dead weight—and Patrick wasn't doing any good.

The man sank further, blood bubbling from his mouth. His eyes opened wide, suddenly awake and terrified, and he stared into Patrick's face. Confused, scared, soundlessly begging for answers to questions he didn't have. He looked down at his body, half gone into the floor, and screamed.

Despite the blood loss and his weakened state, the man screamed like Patrick had never heard anyone scream before. A gush of blood came from his mouth and his body convulsed. Corrigan and Patrick pulled. He shook hard, screaming and bleeding and begging for help.

Corrigan gave a final, forceful pull, and they fell backward to the tiles, the man set free. As Patrick sat up, clawing at the shower screen to stand, and smiled. He wondered why the stranger wasn't moving. His eyes drifted, and he saw the lower half of the stranger's body still in the floor, thin strands of intestines connecting the halves like a thread. The man's lungs and stomach and pancreas were splattered on the tiles in a puddle of muck.

Tearing his eyes from the scene, he looked to Corrigan. For comfort. For safety. For the hope that this was all just a giant fucking nightmare. The detective was frozen in place, staring between the man's two halves. Watching as the floor ate the organs and slurped on the intestines, snapping them free from the upper half of the body with a sound like a cracking twig.

"It's got me," Corrigan whispered. "My leg."

Staring down at Corrigan's leg, Patrick saw it was starting to sink into the ground, too. He pushed the dead stranger away from him and pulled at the detective's limb as hard as he could. He could feel Corrigan straining, trying to get himself free, too.

"Come on!" Patrick yelled. With both men working together, the leg came free, and Corrigan was up.

They tore through the house, slipping and sliding on the mucus that was somehow everywhere now, and headed for the back door. Patrick was sure it would be jammed, too, but they had to try.

"Where do you think you're going?" a small voice came from behind.

Twisting to face it, Patrick saw the little girl from the library. She stood just at the end of the hallway, the front door clicking back into place. She'd just walked right in.

"What are you doing here?" Patrick asked. "It's not safe, we have to go."

The girl giggled, covering her mouth for a moment. "Silly billy," she said. "You can't leave now. Daddy's hungry."

Shelley twisted and writhed, pulling at the chain on her ankle, cursing that fucking kid again and again. Sam smashed the shovel down hard again and again, the metal bond resisting less each time. Still, she pulled and strained until, finally, it fell to the concrete with the thud. Useless.

"Thank you." Shelley got to her feet and hugged Sam, who threw the shovel across the basement in a fit of rage.

"Get off me," he said, and pushed her away.

Shelley eyed Sam with caution and confusion, and then looked toward the basement door. "We have to get out of here. Teddy's going to kill Patrick." She rushed to the door, a slight limp working itself out as she walked.

"Why did you do it?" Sam's voice came as a hollow mumble.

Shelley stopped and turned. Avoided his angry stare. "Do what?"

"Don't fuck around." He spat, and stormed over to her, his face an inch from hers. "You knew that house was haunted—or whatever—and you let me move in there anyway. How many others have you done that to, huh?"

Shelley tried to step back, but Sam grabbed her arms and shook her. "I—"

"Tell me why!"

The two stood in silence for a moment, Shelley wiping Sam's spittle from her face. She shed a tear and muttered an apology. Sam shook her again and she pushed him off. "I'm sorry! I don't have a choice. It...makes me."

"You said we're not slaves."

"The pull is...hard to deny..."

Sam considered her words, understanding what she meant. He'd watched himself do things, vile things. No matter how hard he tried to fight the urges, they always won out. His only salvation since he'd moved into that fucking house was the chamber.

The clock.

He realized now that he hadn't felt it since being in the basement. He hadn't felt the hands ticking away inside his veins, or the rhythm beating with his heart. As he thought about it now, the back wall of the basement began to glow.

Soft. Gray.

"Don't look at it," Shelley warned.

He couldn't look away. It was speaking to him, the words not yet formed, but somehow clear. As he stepped closer, entranced by the gray glow and the shallow expanding and contracting of the concrete wall, his concern over Patrick dwindled. His guilt over Danny vanished. His scar began to bleed, but he didn't care. He just kept walking.

"Sam," Shelley called. "Sam, please."

He heard her mutter a cuss word. Heard her steps behind him. Felt her hands gripping his arms. He walked.

"Sam, what about Patrick?" she said. "We have to go!"

Patrick... He blinked. *Patrick...*

Shelley spun him around.

Sam. Come to me.

He blinked again, the words coming stronger now. Fully formed, a beacon, speaking inside his head.

You belong here.

"Who are you?" Sam asked, placing a hand on the wall. It shuddered under his touch, but expanded and contracted nonetheless.

Come to me. Come to me.

"I'm here," he said. "Who are you?"

Shelley pulled on his arm again, to no avail. She tried again, and stopped as she saw what was happening to Sam.

His scar bled, a thick black liquid dripping to the ground, pooling at his feet. It traveled up the wall—into the wall—and the gray glow began to change. The color deepened, the wall throbbed and shuddered, and Sam's hand, once resting on the surface, began to sink into it.

"Fuck." Shelley gasped. "Sam, get away from it!"

You belong to me.

The *tick tick tick* came back, like a drum in his ears, shutting the world out. His hand sank further into the wall, now up to his elbow, sucking him inside. It was warm and gooey and hugged his skin. Just like the chamber had done that first time.

A womb.

Through the *tick tick tick,* Sam heard Shelley yelling and begging and pleading him to move away, screaming at him that Patrick needed him, that he was going to die unless—

Patrick.

—they got out of this fucking basement.

He turned to face Shelley—standing beside him, her eyes wide and teary—and nodded. "Okay," he said. "Let's go get Patrick."

Sam tried to pull his arm back, but the more he fought, the more he sank. "What's wrong?" Shelley asked.

"It's like quicksand," he said, sinking further. His shoulder was submerged now, and it pulled his body in. "I can't get out!"

You belong to me.

Shelley grabbed his free arm with both hands and tugged hard. He slipped further inside the wall, and as she pulled again, she saw the defeated look in his eyes. Whatever the wall was doing to him, he wasn't fighting it anymore.

She let go of him as his torso disappeared with a small slurping sound.

"It's okay," he said. "You have to save Patrick."

His shoulders disappeared now, and half his head was gone. With the one remaining eye staring at Shelley, and half a mouth, Sam gurgled. "Save him."

As he vanished into the wall, leaving nothing but a ripple, the glow stopped, and it returned to concrete. Shelley stared at the wall, sliding her hand over the surface, but knowing Sam wasn't there anymore.

He was gone.

And Patrick was going to die.

Shelley rushed from the basement, grabbed her car keys, and let the front door swing hard on its hinges as she fled her house.

Chapter 22

The door closed with a soft click, and Jimmy swallowed, breathing in the musty dampness of the basement. She searched for a light switch and couldn't find one, so took her phone out of her pocket and used the flashlight function. The beam of white light illuminated the steps before her, casting odd shadows around the basement. Taking a step, she held her breath, listening hard for any sounds—breathing, crying, anything—to indicate her friend's presence.

She knew Pete was down there, he had to be. Patrick had heard a voice down there, calling for help, and the wimp had run away scared. Didn't matter. Jimmy was here now. She was going to make up for letting Pete come here by himself.

After all that man had done for her. She couldn't let him waste away down in some dark basement. Patrick and the cop had been hugging and being romantic—at the worst possible time, no less—so she'd left them to it and headed straight for the basement.

Now that she was here, the steps creaking beneath her, she was beginning to think maybe Patrick wasn't such a wimp. Maybe she should have waited.

"Hello?" she called.

The light touched the floor now, and Jimmy thought it was strange that it was just dirt. Her boots kicked dust into the air as she walked on it, and she sneezed into her elbow.

"Who..." a voice came from the somewhere beyond the light. Weak and hoarse. "Who's that?"

Spinning to face the voice, Jimmy shone her flashlight into the darkness. Squinted as a face was revealed. A man sat against one of the walls, limp.

"Pete!" Gasping, she raced toward him and kneeled next to the man, whose face was a mixture of relief, happiness, and utter terror. "Petey, what happened?"

She wiped at his face, a thick black goo sticking to her fingers. Setting the phone down so the light was facing up, she hugged her friend. He didn't hug her back, and as Jimmy pulled away, she realized he was barely keeping his eyes open.

"We gotta get you up and out of here, Petey," Jimmy said, and looked around for something to help her lift him. Pete was a hefty man, and Jimmy wasn't all that strong, despite being a professional mover.

"It…didn't…" Pete muttered, shedding a tear.

"What's that?" Jimmy asked.

"It didn't…want me." His eyes were empty, but they cried anyway. A stream of water trailing down his mucky face.

"I don't know what you're saying," Jimmy replied, still searching for something to help get Pete to his feet. The basement was empty, except for a giant hole in the ground.

Jimmy picked up her phone and shone it at the hole.

"It doesn't want me," Pete whispered from behind her.

"What the hell is this?"

No answer.

Jimmy spun back to face Pete, his eyes closed. She crouched beside him and slapped him hard on the cheek. "Wake up, Pete. Don't fall asleep on me, okay?"

He opened his eyes, blinked once, and smiled. "Jimmy," he said. "You came for me."

"Of course," Jimmy said softly, and pressed her forehead against his. "You've got to help me get you up, okay?"

He lifted his arm, just an inch, before it plunged back to the dirt with a thud. He was too weak, Jimmy knew. He'd been down here without food or water for three days, and something had clearly happened to him.

"I'm going to get help," Jimmy said. "There's a cop upstairs, and he's, like, a good one. I think."

She stood to leave, but Pete cleared his throat and said, "Wait."

273

So she did.

"It's not going to let us leave," he said.

Jimmy creased her brow and looked around, noting they were alone. "There's nothing here, Pete. We can go any time we want. Sam isn't here, we're okay for now."

"Sam…" Pete cried again. "Poor Sam." Reading the confusion on Jimmy's face, Pete continued. "It's not Sam. It's…" he trailed off, but looked over at the hole in the ground.

Following his gaze, Jimmy bit her lip. "None of that matters right now. We have to get you up and out of here."

She leaned in to him, wrapped her arms under his armpits, and heaved. Without Pete having the energy to help her, he was dead weight. Jimmy pushed the word "dead" from her mind, and tried again.

"Leave me," Pete said, as she heaved a third time.

"Like hell." She hissed. "Just fucking help me!"

He let out a small, choked laugh. "It swallowed me, Jimmy." He laughed again, in disbelief. "But it let me live."

"That's great," Jimmy said, heaving again. "We can chat about that later, okay?"

Groaning, Pete lifted a hand and pushed Jimmy away. He breathed hard, and in the phone's flashlight, she saw the emptiness in his eyes. Like he didn't want to be saved. Like he didn't want to live.

"What the fuck is going on here, Pete? What happened to you?" Jimmy held back tears, her voice quivering.

"It devours people," he whispered, motioning to the hole again. "It takes everything from you until you're just a shell." Pete's words echoed through the basement, and Jimmy sniffled. Waiting for him to continue. "I don't know what it is, but...it tasted me for days. And then it spat me out."

As his words faded into the nothingness of the basement, Jimmy heard noises from above. It sounded like shouting. She listened close and heard Corrigan calling something. *Bandages.* Someone was hurt. *Fuck.*

"I'll be back," Jimmy said. "With help."

She grabbed her phone and raced for the stairs, avoiding the giant hole in the ground. As she passed it, a darkness seemed to rise, like fog—or something else—and it called to her. She didn't listen, instead gripped the staircase railing and headed for the ground floor.

The door was locked.

She banged hard.

Twisted the knob.

Nothing.

It won't let us leave. That's what Pete had said. His delusional ramblings about being swallowed whole settled into the hairs on her nape. Worked their way into her breaths. She turned around.

The darkness lifting from the hole wasn't a fog. It looked solid, moving with purpose. Not tentacles. More earthy. Like roots. Whatever they were, they came for her.

Jimmy screamed and begged for help, but nobody came. She heard Corrigan and Patrick on the other side of the door, panicked and terrified. Something was happening to them, too. Was it these roots?

"It won't let us leave." Pete's voice repeated in the darkness.

Ignoring her friend, but feeling in her heart that he was right, Jimmy watched the roots rise from the ground like a hand.

One of the roots came for her face and she dodged, ducked, and had no choice but to head back down the stairs. Into the danger. Another root grabbed her ankle and pulled her down, her phone flinging from her hands. Her face smacked hard against one of the steps. She tasted blood. Felt herself being pulled back.

She reminded herself of all the trauma she'd suffered up to this point—abandonment, discrimination, harassment, rape, beatings—and let her rage outweigh her fear. She let it bubble inside her until it seeped from her pores.

"Fuck you!" she screamed, and grabbed at the steps. Clutching onto the wood, she saw it was old and loose. She tugged at it, letting the force of the root pulling her help her loosen the wood further.

It came free with a snap, jagged and sharp. As the root pulled her across the dirt, Jimmy spun onto her back and stabbed the root with all her might.

You belong to me.

Sam knew it was true. He felt it. He hadn't felt like he belonged anywhere since Danny broke up with him. Until he'd found this house. Or the house had found him. The lines were a bit murky around which was which, and Shelley hadn't really answered his question.

Hugging himself tight, Sam took a deep breath, and let the chamber walls envelop him. The journey through the basement wall to the chamber was incomprehensible. He'd slipped from one reality to the other, and sort of emerged, like a newborn—covered in gunk and mucus—in the chamber.

The voice, not male and not female, guided him through a void until he slipped out here. Back in the room with the clock. His clock. *Tick tick ticking* away just like a clock should. He stared at it now, and breathed.

11:58.

He didn't know what the time was now, or if time even mattered in the chamber. It seemed that as long as he was in there, the time was irrelevant. It only became important when he stepped out. People would only die if he was in the real world.

Where am I now, then? If not the real world?

The chamber felt real. It felt more real than anything else in his life. Except Patrick. Their friendship. He had Corrigan now. The detective. Patrick didn't need him.

He hugged himself tighter and shed a tear. Nobody needs me.

I need you.

The voice was soft and gentle. Sam knew he shouldn't trust it, he knew it would make him do something bad again. Kill someone. Eat something alive. Yet, it sent waves of calm through him, just as the clock itself did.

You belong here.

Except that wasn't true. A niggling feeling at the edge of his existence tapped on his consciousness. The chamber was real. The clock was real. The voice was real. Did he belong here, though? No. But he didn't belong out there, either. Not anymore.

Not without Danny.

Patrick was out there, though.

So was Teddy.

Teddy.

She was going to kill Patrick.

Not if I stay here. The time doesn't matter if I stay here. Anxiety surged through him as the thought came out. He wanted to believe that with all his heart. With every tick of the clock. *What if I'm wrong?*

Patrick was going to die at 11:58. That much he knew for certain. Looking toward the tunnel that would lead back to the real world, Sam breathed hard. His fingers and hands trembled at the thought of going back out there. Back into the world where he was a killer. Where he drank blood and felt such hatred.

Despite his fear, Sam moved toward the tunnel. He had time to save his friend.

Stay with me. You belong here.

He shook his head. The voice grew stronger, firmer. He kept going, ignoring the voice and the *tick tick tick* that boomed in his ears. His whole body vibrated as he crawled through the tunnel, the walls collapsing around him, enveloping him. Where once they were warm and inviting, the womb-like walls were cold and tight, forcing him backward. Back to the chamber.

You belong. To me.

"No!" Sam yelled. "I don't belong to anyone!"

The tunnel disagreed, sealing itself up before him, blocking his exit. He pushed forward with all his might, using his fingers as spades to sift through small gaps in the walls. Digging his way through.

You. Belong. To. Me.

Patrick needed him. He needed Patrick. And that's what was becoming clear to him as he continued to force his way through. He *needed* Patrick. Their friendship was what had saved him when his mother died. Their friendship had saved him when his father stopped speaking to him. And again when Danny left. And when Danny died.

He belonged with Patrick.

Pushing harder now, the tunnel walls loosened and stretched. The walls shuddered and contracted, just as the basement wall had done, and he crawled faster. The exit was in sight. The impossible door that had once been so attractive and appealing, was right in front of him. He reached for the handle and twisted.

He was the only one who could save Patrick.

And he had to try.

Chapter 23

The roots recoiled for a moment as Jimmy stabbed and swung and screamed. Her ankle free, she rushed to her feet. She tried to run, but a searing pain shot through her ankle and she rolled it. She almost fell, but refused to let her body fail her. Cussing and screaming again, she limped through the basement toward Pete.

He sat there motionless, eyes unblinking, staring at the roots as they snaked through the air after Jimmy. She crashed by his side, sweating and panting hard, not taking her desperate eyes off him.

"Get the fuck up." She ordered.

Pete shook his head, defeated.

"You think this—*this*—is the worst thing that's happened to you? Is that it?" Jimmy slapped the man to surprise some sense into him. "This is nothing. Some stupid tree roots trying to kill us?"

"You don't understand," he whispered, tears rolling down his cheeks again.

The tree roots grabbed at Jimmy's arms and she stabbed them away with the piece of wood. She knew it was a matter of time before the weapon was futile.

Jimmy slapped him again. "We have been left by our families, Pete. We have had society turn their *fucking* backs on us, treat us like psychos and criminals, and change laws to make us invisible. And we are still here."

Pete looked at her, and smiled, despite the roots wrapping around his legs.

"These weak-ass tree roots don't hold a candle to that." Jimmy continued, pulling at the roots and stabbing again. "So get up, and let's go."

Finally, Jimmy thought, as Pete struggled to his feet. Panting and huffing, and moving in what looked like slow motion. He was up, though, and they were going to get him some help.

Wrapping her arms around his neck, she heaved, and this time, he wasn't dead weight. She smiled, despite their situation, as hope surged through her. But then Pete was up, off the ground, and hanging in mid-air.

The roots had him. She stabbed with her broken piece of wood, but the roots enveloped him, squeezing around his body. He groaned as they tightened around his chest and stomach, and Jimmy threw her piece of wood, instead tearing at the roots with her bare hands.

"Let him go!" she cried, tears flinging from her face.

She tore and pulled, even as the roots moved Pete through the basement, back toward the hole. She broke off one of the roots—snapped it right off—to reveal a powdery black substance, like charcoal. Or dirt.

It didn't slow the roots down.

Pete was at the edge of the hole now, and Jimmy kicked and punched at the roots, scratching at the damn things, and begging for whatever was happening to stop.

"It's okay," Pete said to her.

He hovered above the hole now, the entrance to the void, swaying back and forth in the grip of the roots.

"It chose me, after all." He smiled at her.

"Please let him go," Jimmy said to the roots. "Don't take my Petey."

He hovered for a few seconds more, the roots bringing Pete close to her. Jimmy reached out for him, begging again and again for Pete to be set free. He was in front of her now. She cupped the man's face with her hands and brought her forehead to his, the way they always did.

"Run," Pete whispered. "Don't let it take *you.*"

Stepping back, Jimmy searched his face and realized what he'd done. Jimmy screamed after him as the roots descended into the darkness, her friend and companion vanishing. Thrust down into the gaping abyss, Pete was gone. Sacrificed himself to give her a chance.

Silence engulfed her and she felt the darkness touching her, like it was alive, and clinging to her skin.

Run.

She heeded Pete's advice and headed back for the stairs, taking them one by one—her ankle still pulsing with a shooting pain. She knew the door would be locked, but there had to be a way. There was always a way. As she climbed the stairs, the roots ascended from the hole again.

Five steps to go. The door was right there.

Four.

Three.

The pain in her ankle spiked again. She cried out and looked down. Another fucking root. Before it pulled her back, she lunged at the railing, wrapping her arms around it tight. Just as the root yanked at her, lifting her body into the air. She held firm on the railing, the wood digging into her shoulder and chest.

Her ankle was on fire, the root squeezing hard, and she felt the bone snap.

She resisted another scream, closed her eyes as tight as she could, and let the pain course through her. Screaming again now would sap too much strength. Broken bone or not, she wasn't giving the roots the satisfaction.

Another root spiraled around her legs, another at each arm, pulling her hard. She gripped the railing tighter, even as the bones in her legs crunched and snapped, and the muscles in her arms burned. She couldn't hold on much longer, she knew she couldn't.

Her body was going limp, the pain too much. Her grip loosened. The roots squeezed, splintering her legs into odd angles. She felt herself letting go, her fingers scraping against the wood.

They've won.

Jimmy prepared herself for whatever was in that hole. Tried to convince herself that Pete was still in there, floating around somewhere, happy. They'd be together again, real soon, and nothing else would matter. She tried to believe it, but didn't, a sensation in her guts telling her whatever was down there was worse than Hell.

Her fingers tasted air now, her grip finally gone. The roots squeezed around her, snapping her limbs hard and fast. One arm outstretched, fingers still reaching for something, the last vestiges of hope.

They've won.

A burst of light smashed into the basement.

The door was thrust open.

Someone grabbed her hand.

Chapter 24

Sam spilled from the door, his lungs gasping for oxygen. The tunnel walls folded around him, trying to suck him back inside, and he kicked and kicked until he was free. Slamming the door shut behind him, locking the tunnel and the chamber and the clock in whatever realm was in there, his hands slipped on the floorboards and he crashed to the ground.

He heaved for air, still not quite sure how he'd gotten from Shelley's basement to the chamber. Or how he'd climbed free from the tunnel. His hands were slick and wet and—

"Sam?" It was Patrick.

He got to his feet and found Patrick and Corrigan in the living room, translucent mucus at their feet. It covered the floor and the walls. Patrick's face was drenched in confusion and fear, but he was alive, and Sam was going to make damn sure he stayed that way.

"There you are." Another voice came.

Teddy.

"How's my mommy? She buried?" Teddy asked, that evil smirk wetting her lips.

Sam didn't answer, just fished his phone from his pocket and looked at the time. He noticed a line striking through the reception bars, but focused on the numbers on the screen.

11:37.

Twenty-two minutes. "Pat, you have to get out of here."

Patrick stared between Sam and Teddy, Corrigan by his side. The detective clutched at Patrick's hand, their fingers interlocking. Sam smiled, but his heart clenched at the display.

"Sam, what the hell is going on?" Patrick's voice cracked as he looked around the house. "The floor is, like, *eating* people."

Teddy clapped her hands in glee at that, and they all turned to face her as she moved through the mucus like puddles of rain. Skipping and splashing, and kicking mucus into the air, she wasn't sinking at all. She spun around a few times as it drenched her on its way down.

"None of this has to happen, Teddy," Sam said. "They don't have to be here."

"It's way too late." Looking at Patrick, she frowned. "You're really nice, Patrick, for a skinnie. But Daddy says you have to go…"—shrugging with a sigh—"…I have to kill you."

Patrick stepped back, conscious that his feet were slowly sinking into the mucus.

Moving between Patrick and Teddy, Corrigan held up a hand. "Come on now, kid. Let's all just calm down."

Teddy raised an eyebrow and scoffed. "I'm not a kid. I'm *eight*."

"Okay, sorry." Corrigan lifted his own feet and shifting on the unsteady floors. "Why don't we all go outside and—"

A scream came from the basement. Another one.

"Jimmy! She's down there!" Patrick's voice was desperate, but he didn't move. "We have to help her!"

"Something tells me it's a little late for that one," Teddy said.

"But—"

"You need to stop talking." Teddy pointed at them and scowled. Turning to Sam, she said, "Do you want to take care of them? Or shall I?"

Sam walked to her and grabbed her arm, twisting her away from Patrick and Corrigan. "I'm not doing this. And you don't have to, either. We don't have to let it control us."

Another scream. It sounded like Jimmy was hurt. Really hurt.

"Don't you want to make Daddy happy?" Teddy asked, shrugging out of his grip. "Don't you feel special that he chose you?"

"Chose me?" Sam asked. He had her attention, her eyes firm on him. Low at his side, he flicked his fingers at Sam and Corrigan. A message: *Get out of here!*

They started inching backward, toward the rear door. Quiet and slow, the mucus making a low swishing sound as their feet waded through. They moved past the dining room, pulling hard as their shoes clung to the mucus.

"Yes," Teddy replied. "When Mommy showed you the house, He chose you. You're like me, you have the bloodlust."

She was right. Sam knew she was right. Even before he'd moved here, he had wondered about the taste of blood. Had enjoyed the smell of it. He'd never indulged, though. Never taken a life to satisfy his curiosities. The house had done that to him. The clock.

And now it wanted Patrick.

"So your dad chose?" Sam asked, noticing Patrick and Corrigan edging closer to the door. He just had to keep Teddy busy for a few seconds and they'd be free. "Who is your dad?"

Teddy put her index finger to her bottom lip and considered the question. "I don't really know," she admitted. "But he loves me. And he loves you. So we have to do what he wants."

"Not if he's asking you to do bad things," Sam replied.

"Sam, they're just skinnies… Skin suits. They're like the people on TV. They aren't real."

"Did your dad tell you that?" Sam asked. "Because that's a lie."

Corrigan and Patrick fiddled with the back door, swearing under their breath as it refused to budge, sinking, sinking. Teddy turned to face them, and sighed. "Really? You can't leave, I thought that much was obvious." Then to Sam, "Skinnies, am I right? Pfft."

Jimmy screamed again. It sounded closer now, like she was right behind the basement door. She was so close.

"Fuck, I wish that bitch would *shut up!*" Teddy moaned, agitation rolling off the tongue.

Sam was about to tell Teddy that she had it all wrong. That these were people and that what she was doing—what he'd done, too—was wrong. That they'd been manipulated, that whoever her daddy was, he was a bad, bad man. Or thing. He opened his mouth, forming the first word, when Teddy tore across the room, sending mucus flying through the air.

Chasing after her, Sam dove to tackle the girl to the ground. Missed. She was too fast, and was now out of reach. Corrigan was between her and Patrick, the sizable man blocking her path. She launched herself onto the detective, landing on his chest. He fell back, onto the dining table. Slipped, and was pushed to the floor. She swiped at his neck and face with nails none of them knew she had.

Corrigan fought her off, shouting at Patrick to smash a window or something. "GET THE FUCK OUT OF HERE!"

Teddy's teeth were sharp now, and she bit down into Corrigan's neck. Before she could rip his flesh free, Sam was behind her. His hands around her neck, squeezing. This time he wasn't watching from outside himself. This time he was right there, doing this on purpose. To a little girl. And he hated himself for it.

She recoiled at the lack of oxygen, and elbowed Sam in the guts. He loosened his grip just long enough for Teddy to slip free. She shot him an evil eye, but then ran to Patrick, who was still pulling at the back door and punching at the glass to no avail.

He saw her coming for him and dodged, threw a dining chair at her, but the girl was fast. So incredibly fast. Her hands clung to him, swiped at him—he didn't stand a chance.

Sam pulled her off, but she kicked him in the groin and went back to her rampage. He tried again, the pain in his groin swelling in his guts, and grabbed her arms. Holding them behind her back, he shouted at Patrick, "Run! Hide!"

He did, without a word. Pausing at Corrigan, who was recovering on the floor, the detective told him to go. "Sam's right. You have to go hide somewhere, until this is over."

He disappeared somewhere into the house. Corrigan was on his knees, reaching for his holster. It was clear Teddy was no ordinary girl; pulling his gun might have been the only option. As he pointed it at Teddy, she just laughed.

And laughed.

"Go ahead." She teased. "Do it."

Corrigan wavered, as they all knew he would. Pointing a gun at a kid was not in his genetic make up. It went against everything he believed in, and both Teddy and Sam could see it. She struggled against Sam's grip, goading the detective to shoot her in the face.

"What do we do, Sam?" he asked, one hand pressing hard against Corrigan's neck. "Tell me what to do!"

"Go get Jimmy. I've got this." A lie that nobody believed.

He left anyway, and Sam was glad. It was for the best. Teddy had almost ravaged his neck, destroyed him. One more attempt at him and the detective would be dead. He watched Corrigan head straight for the basement door—slipping and sliding on the mucus-laced floor—the distraction enough for Teddy to slam her foot down into Sam's shin.

She slipped free again and faced Sam, folding her arms. "Why are you doing this, Sam?"

"Doing what?"

"Look around." She motioned to the floor and the walls and the ceiling. "The house is starving. *Daddy* is starving. Do you really think you can fight those urges long enough to save them?"

"I have to try," Sam said, curling his hands into fists. "Whatever it takes."

Teddy rolled her eyes, and then smirked again.

That set Sam on edge. Every time that smirk appeared, something bad was about to happen. He tensed his shoulders, and scanned the house. The walls leaked mucus, covering every inch of the house, and he saw the liquid start to bubble on the floorboards.

"What are you doing?" Sam asked.

"It's not me." Teddy giggled. "I told you, Daddy chose you."

The mucus inched up his legs, sucking him toward the floor. He remembered Danny and the coroner, the way the house had feasted on them. There hadn't been any mucus that time, they'd just sunk into the wooden floor. This was something different. He clawed at the liquid climbing his legs, tried to move, tried to run.

Teddy watched with wide eyes, clapping and dancing as the mucus traveled to his midriff and his chest. It was fast and wet and warm, sticking to him the way the tunnel walls had that first time. He fought the sensation growing inside him, the warmth and feeling of home that had manipulated him since he moved in. The emotions coursing through him—it loved him, it needed him, and he needed it—made the mucus enveloping him feel almost like a skin. Like it belonged there.

Until it entered his mouth, sliding down his throat. Drowning him.

Sam fell to his knees, Teddy kneeling in front of him, whispering to let it happen. To let Daddy inside, because it was the only way forward. It was the only choice now, and it was best for everyone.

You belong to me.

The voice echoed in his head, and Sam could only convulse as the mucus filled him. As quickly as it started, it ended, letting his body fall to the floor with a splash. His eyes closed, his body still convulsing, the translucent gooey mucus leaking from his mouth.

"Come out, come out." Teddy shook Sam's body until his eyes opened. "Come play, Daddy."

"Indeed," Sam's voice said. He heard the words, felt his muscles moving as he stood. It wasn't him. He was locked inside himself, banging at the edges of his mind. "Let's play hide and seek."

"Patty, Patty, Patrick! Where are you?" Teddy clutched Sam's hand and they began to walk through the house, while the furniture and boxes sank into the gooey muck.

Into nothingness.

Chapter 25

Jimmy felt the thick fingers grabbing at her, heard the detective's gruff voice—*Hold on!*—as he scrambled to save her. She was grateful for the effort, but it was too late. Almost every bone in her body was broken, she felt the jagged, exposed things tearing at her skin. The air was squeezed from her lungs. She was being pulled through the air, dragged toward the hole. Toward Pete. Toward nothingness.

Her body was wrecked, the bones in her legs and arms crushed. Her ribs cracking under the pressure of the roots. Corrigan's grip around her one free hand was tight, but he wasn't strong enough to stop what was happening.

She closed her eyes.

Felt Corrigan let go.

They always let go.

She thought about her mother. Her father. Those cunts who hated her for being who she was, and whom she still loved so much. Her mom's hugs were the best, the way she'd held Jimmy as a kid after a bad dream. Playing ball with her dad in the yard. A tear squeezed from her, and she resigned to death, knowing those moments would never come again. Those people would never see her again.

They had let go. Just as Corrigan was doing now.

BANG!

Her eyes sprang open. Focused. Corrigan, gun in hand.

BANG! BANG! BANG!

He fired into the roots.

She felt the grip loosen.

"Keep...going." She managed.

He fired again. Again. Again.

The roots loosened further. He grabbed her hand once more and yanked as hard as he could. Jimmy spilled free, and Corrigan shot once more, for good measure, as the roots recovered and came back for them.

Hugging Jimmy tight—warm, comfortable, nurturing—he heaved her into the main house, and slammed the basement door shut.

"Can you walk?" he asked, his voice desperate and dripping in fear.

Jimmy shook her head.

He holstered his weapon, and lifted her with both arms to carry her. She fell limp in his hold, comforted by the swell of his belly as he pulled her close, and watched as the detective moved through the house. He was slow—too slow—and her eyes darted around to search for an answer. He was injured, but it was more than that.

The house was wet.

The walls and the floor and even the kitchen bench as they moved past it.

"What..."

"Save your strength," Corrigan said to her, blood drizzling down his neck.

She must have been dreaming—the furniture was sinking into the floor. The severe damage her body was suffering must have sent her into a weird fever dream. Sam's couch, the dining table, his untouched moving boxes. It all sank into the floor.

"Where's Sam?" Jimmy murmured, the effort sending ripples of pain through her ribs and chest.

Corrigan ignored her, searching for a way out of the house. She could tell he was getting weak, his footsteps growing slower and slower. She looked down to the wet floor. His feet were stuck, enveloped by the liquid.

"Let me go," she said. "Save yourself."

"Fuck that," Corrigan replied. "Either we both get out of here, or neither of us do."

He strained hard and pulled his left foot free from the floor with a groan. The liquid sloshed at his feet, trying to recapture him. He pulled his right foot free, somehow steady for a few seconds, and ran.

Jimmy rocked in Corrigan's arms as they raced down the hallway. The front door in sight. Her heart fluttered and her blood pumped hard, the adrenaline surging through her wasted body. She looked up at Corrigan, his face steadfast and full of determination.

Pulling his foot free again, he kept going, despite the heavy breathing and the panting, and the visible signs of strain from carrying her this long.

Halfway down the hall now, the front door covered in translucent muck, but never looking so goddamned perfect. They were going to make it.

The door burst open, swinging on its hinges, revealing a woman. She held something small in one hand, but Jimmy was drawn to the woman's face. Confusion, fear, sorrow. Corrigan stopped, shouted at the stranger to get the fuck away from the house.

She raced in, despite the command, and held the front door open. "Hurry," she called, and Jimmy saw the door shifting closed. The woman held it, pushing with all her might. "I can't hold it much longer."

Corrigan stomped through the hall, the muck grabbing at his feet with greed. They passed the threshold and

Corrigan called to the lady—*Whoever you are, fucking run!*—but Jimmy didn't hear another set of footsteps.

Just the detective's, as he raced to his car. She had never felt so safe, so glad, to be heading toward a police car.

Shelley kept a few things in her car, like most people did. However, where most people kept tissues or wet wipes for their kids, and maybe some tic tacs or breath mints, she kept a survival kit.

She had the obligatory rape whistle, but more important was the holy water. She'd never actually used it, but it always made her feel much safer than the whistle did. It wasn't *men* that were her problem. It was…she didn't really have a name for it, and she had never seen its face. Or even a form. Just the terrible darkness swirling inside her. Holy water was the largest item in her kit, but it wasn't all that easy to store.

Razor blades, though, they were easy to stash. They were the easiest item in the whole kit—they could be bought in bulk, didn't take much space, and they were deadly as hell. One slice to someone's face, and they were pretty much out of the game. She remembered Kathy spying them one day, a bunch in a plastic container in her glove box, and smirking.

"What are they for?" she'd asked.

"For the inevitable," Shelley had replied. She didn't explain, and Kathy hadn't asked. Just sort of given an appreciative nod, like it made perfect sense.

Thinking back on it now, as she reached for one and held it firmly in her hand, she wondered if that was how Kathy had gotten the razor blade. Taken it from her stash. So many deaths had been because of her, or at least preventable by her. She could have warned Kathy. Should have warned her. *Should* have warned Sam or refused to show him the house.

She'd parked right behind the cop car, and hoped like hell that it meant the house had already been evacuated. But the street was quiet—empty—and something in her gut told her to get ready.

Shit was about to go down.

Shit was about to get real bad.

Taking a breath and squeezing a razor blade in her palm until her skin almost broke, Shelley got out of the car and jogged to the house. As she approached, she heard groaning and something else. Weird sounds, like water splashing around a sink.

Oh no.

She knew what that meant, and hoped she wasn't too late. If someone was still making sound in there, she might have been just in time.

She tried the front door. Rolled her eyes when it refused to open. These houses were all the same, with a mind of their own. Except she knew the houses had nothing to do with it, they were just a symptom of something much larger.

Standing back a little, Shelley gathered her strength and kicked at the door. Right by the lock, like she'd seen in so many cop shows. The door budged, just a little, and groaned as if it were laughing at her.

"Fucking thing." She spat, and tried again.

Harder.

The door swung open and Shelley flashed a quick smile before dropping her face into something else. A large man carried a limp woman down the hallway. His face was red and sweaty, his neck pulsing with red, he was pulling his feet from the floor as it tried to eat him.

She'd never seen them before and assumed they were the cops. Hesitating for a moment, she thought about explaining, but realized there was no time. The male cop could make it, but she had to help.

Noticing the door swinging back, she stepped inside the house, conscious that she was now on the menu, and held the door open. *Better me than them.* They took their sweet time, but she could tell the guy was trying hard to not be swallowed, and held the door with all her might. It pushed hard against her, wanting to shut, wanting to seal everyone inside.

As they slipped out the threshold, into the safety of the world outside, Shelley released her grip and let the door slam, landing somewhere in the hallway. Teddy was in there—

in the house she was suddenly terrified of—and she had to assume Patrick and Sam were, too.

Gripping the razor hard again, this time breaking the skin, Shelley winced. Not from the pain, though. She winced from the knowledge of what she had to do.

She had to find her daughter.

She had to kill the fucking bitch.

"Teddy?" Shelley called. "Are you in here, pumpkin?"

No response came, just the mucus at her feet shuddering and rippling as she stepped through. Her feet didn't sink, and she hated that she knew why. She hated what she'd become, even though it wasn't her choice.

"Teddy!" Shelley called as she reached the end of the hallway.

The house was revealed now, it's wide open plan layout. Shelley scanned from the kitchen to the living room and the dining areas. Boxes of unpacked crap were scattered around everywhere. The house appeared empty, but with the mucus still streaming down the walls, waiting for food, she knew her daughter was around somewhere. Doing god knew what.

"Teddy, where are you?" she called louder this time. "Mommy is here."

"Psst." A harsh whisper came from behind her.

The front room. The office, Sam had said.

She spun around to see half a face peeking at her from the door to the office. Red hair, freckles, a crooked bow tie. "You must be Patrick."

"You shouldn't be here. It's not safe," he whispered. "I saw you open the door. Can you do it again?"

Shelley shook her head. "Probably not. Why didn't you run for the exit when it was open?"

"The mucus...it had my foot."

She looked at his shoes, covered in muck, the leather rotting from the mucus' hunger. Back to his face. He was looking at the razor in her hands, and held up his arms in a defensive posture.

"Relax, I'm not here for you," Shelley said, looking back down the hall. "I'm here for Teddy."

Patrick gulped, and strained to unstick his foot again. Stepping toward her, he asked, "Who are you?"

"I'm her mother." She scowled, and held up the razor. "We don't get along."

"Right..." Patrick creased his brow. "Well, I haven't seen them for a little while. Teddy or Sam."

Shelley nodded and ushered the man behind her back. "Stay with me. Better to have someone protecting you than be on your own."

They walked down the hallway, Patrick fighting the mucus with each step. Shelley could tell the house was desperate for food, which meant Sam was in even more danger than ever. If she knew this place as well as she thought, her bet was on Sam being inhabited by now.

Inhabited by the clock.

Inhabited by the *tick tick tick* that had slowly been working its way inside him. Into his blood. Into the rhythm of his body. Into his soul.

Teddy and Sam emerged from the bathroom, their mouths soaked in red. Sam threw a wet towel to the floor and Shelley saw it was drenched in blood.

"Hungry, Sam?" she asked, testing his reaction.

He looked at her, but his eyes weren't his own. They were the same as when he'd almost killed her with the shovel. Empty, cold. His scar...

His body belonged to something else now, just as hers had for the nine months she carried Teddy. And every day since she scratched her way out of the womb.

"Famished," he replied, and stepped forward.

Not toward her, though.

Toward Patrick.

Sam licked his lips, Teddy by his side, smirking. From the small of his back, she pushed Sam forward, his unblinking eyes sizing up Patrick.

The redhead stepped away, sliding backward a little through the mucus. "Sam," he said, extending an arm out in front of him. "Whatever is happening to you, we can stop it."

Ignoring him, Sam took slow, deliberate steps.

"Sam, please." Patrick begged. "You're my best friend."

Shelley saw Sam's hesitation. It was the briefest pause, but she saw it. Sam—*the real Sam*—was in there. Fighting. Patrick's words were getting through.

"Keep talking, Patrick," she said. Teddy moved toward her mother, a disapproving glare in her eyes, and Shelley smiled. "Keep going!"

"Remember when we were twelve and we watched *Stand by Me* for the first time? And you cried because you felt just like Gordie? Remember that, Sam?"

Sam paused again, an angry tear rolling down his face.

"Remember, Sam? It was the day after your mom died and you said you didn't know what you'd do without her. I told you I'd always be here, Sam, and I am. I'm here—"

"Patrick"—Teddy's voice was dry—"Sam is gone. Daddy is inside him now."

"No, Patrick, Sam is in there!" Shelley said.

"Mother, you need to shut up." Teddy pointed to Shelley and walked toward her.

Shelley stepped back, the razor between her thumb and forefinger. It was the smallest of weapons, but the most powerful. Even though Teddy didn't bleed, slicing her skin would keep her at bay.

As Teddy and Sam descended on Shelley and Patrick, the mucus reached up to Patrick's knees. He fell backward, unsteady, and plunged into the mucus with a splash. Shelley reached for him, but Teddy grabbed at her, throwing her against the kitchen island. A sharp pain spiked in her back and she collapsed to the ground, falling into a stack of boxes. Watched as Sam leaped onto Patrick's chest, pushing his face under the mucus.

She crawled over, swiping at Sam with her razor. She knew, just like Kath had, that the evil could seep out. Drip back to the ground, back into the house.

Teddy grabbed the back of her hair and pulled hard, thrusting her to her back. The girl climbed on top of her, nails out like claws, and scratched her mother's face.

"Why didn't you just love me?" she spat. "How hard is that?"

Shelley fought her daughter off, thinking, *It's fucking impossible*, but unable to get the words out. Instead, she eyed Patrick as he was drowned in the mucus. She grabbed at Teddy's hands and swiped with the razor. She aimed for the eyes this time. It caught her on the face, a long cut from her lip to the cheekbone.

"Fuck you!" Teddy screamed. "I fucking hate you!"

"Likewise, bitch." Shelley swiped again, and even though Teddy didn't feel physical pain, the cuts on her face made her recoil. She pushed Teddy aside, careening into a box labelled "Danny's Stuff".

Shelley stood—dripping with mucus and sweat—rushed to Sam and kicked him off Patrick, who raised his head with a sharp intake of air. Coughing and spluttering, he rolled to his side, and spat mucus back to the floor.

He tried to say something, whisper a word of thanks, but Shelley told him to save it. She pulled him up, and despite the mucus gripping his arms and body, they were on their feet. Searching for an option—an exit—Shelley realized there was no way out. The doors wouldn't budge, and she didn't have the strength to pry them open. Patrick was no help, still recovering.

As she scanned the house, the tunnel door appeared. *Fuck.*

It shimmered into existence with a hollow *tick tick tick*. It was almost midnight. 11:55.

Teddy came for her again, kicking the back of her knee. Shelley fell, taking Patrick with her, toppling over a stack of boxes. Instead of coming at her, Teddy ripped at Patrick's back. He screamed and screamed, and begged, but she kept going.

"11:55, Patty! It's almost time!" she cried in glee.

Sam recovered, too, and joined Teddy, tearing at Patrick's back with gnashing teeth and claws. His face sank into the floor again.

Shelley tried to pull them off, but Teddy knocked her away again and again. Even with the razor slinging at Teddy's arms, face, legs, the girl was in a frenzy. Eating and chewing and sucking at the blood spewing from Patrick's back.

A loud bang rang through the house, and Teddy flew backward, landing on the floorboards with a splash. Shelley twisted to the sound and saw Corrigan, a smoking shotgun aimed at Sam. He squeezed the trigger, but missed. The shell hit a wall somewhere and the house groaned.

Teddy sat up slowly with an annoyed groan. "Fucking skinnie," she muttered, inspecting her wound. The shot had gone straight through her shoulder, her arm slinking and holding on by a thread of skin.

"Get away from my Patrick!" Corrigan boomed, reloading his weapon. His neck was bandaged, but he was still weak.

Sam didn't stop, instead dug deeper into Patrick's back, the spinal column now exposed.

Corrigan shot again, missing Sam by an inch, and firing once more. Sam fell back, a spray of blood shooting through the air behind him, and he splashed into the mucus. Ignoring Shelley, whose fingers were pressed in her ears, Corrigan raced to Patrick—the shotgun by his side—and pulled the silent redhead into his arms.

"Patrick." He gently tapped at the man's cheeks.

His eyes fluttered, but the pain was too much, and he closed his eyes again. Corrigan looked at Sam, rising from the mucus, and reached for the shotgun again. But Sam didn't come for Patrick, he didn't do anything. Just stood there, looking down at his friend, limp in his partner's arms.

"What have I done?" Sam gasped.

"You did what you had to do." Teddy stood by his side, clutched at his hand, and looked at the drizzling wound in his arm. "Daddy, are you still in there?"

Sam looked at Teddy, shrugged his hand out of her grip, and felt the *tick tick tick* coursing through him. He pushed her away, staring down at Patrick. Without looking at a clock, his body felt the time.

"Is he..." Sam asked Corrigan.

The man hugged Patrick hard, rocking back and forth, crying and begging for Patrick to wake up.

11:58.

Just as the clock had predicted.

Chapter 26

As Patrick stopped moving and Teddy was thrust backward by the shotgun blast, Shelley pressed her fingers into her ears. Shock took over for a few seconds and all she could do was watch Corrigan reload and blast Sam, who fell backward.

He hit the floor, mucus clinging to him and wrapping around him, and Teddy sat up. She was saying something about skinnies—she *hated* that fucking word. Corrigan cradled Patrick, and Teddy was over at their side, and Shelley started to breathe again. Her daughter's arm had almost been blown clean off, hanging on by a shred of skin. The girl held it in place, but didn't seem bothered.

The shock ringing through her ears dissipated—only a little, but enough—and she emerged on the other side with renewed intent. While the others were distracted, Sam begging for Patrick to be okay, Shelley jumped to her feet. A razor wouldn't cut it, she needed something bigger. Racing to the knife block in the kitchen, she grabbed one, ran a finger over the blade, and smiled.

This'll do.

While Teddy had her back turned, asking Sam if Daddy was still in his body, she crept up behind her. Careful to move slow so the mucus didn't slosh at her feet, and give her away.

"Is he…" Sam asked Corrigan.

Shelley ignored the detective as he cradled Patrick, limp in his arms, crying and begging. He was a perfect distraction, and as she looked from Corrigan to Teddy, she saw her daughter smiling. It was a real smile. Like she was happy at the violence and the death and the grief.

She couldn't wait to stab that little bitch.

"Teddy," Shelley said, with the knife poised.

The girl spun around, the smile shifting into confusion. "What do you think you're going to do with that?"

"What I should have done while I was pregnant with you." Shelley spat, and launched forward.

Teddy moved back in surprise, and Shelley tackled her to the ground, sawing at the shred of skin holding Teddy's shoulder to her body. The arm came loose, Teddy scrambling to keep hold of it in some asinine attempt to stay whole.

Shelley pushed the arm away and turned the knife to her daughter's chest.

"Fuck. You," she hissed, and plunged the knife down.

The sound of metal splicing through skin sent chills through Shelley's body, and she put her weight behind the blade to dig it as deep as it could go. Teddy looked more annoyed than anything, and clawed at Shelley with her remaining hand.

Tick tick tick.

The shimmering door was more solid now and the booming of the clock made the house walls quiver. The house shook and Shelley stumbled as Teddy continued clawing.

Teddy was strong. It wasn't normal, it wasn't human. Even with the missing arm, her strength was too much, and the impossible door and that ticking made her stronger. She twisted and writhed underneath Shelley, but only to reposition herself. Clawing again at Shelley's face, a stream of blood leaking from a gash in her cheek, Teddy made a fist and punched her mother in the nose.

Falling back into a stack of boxes, she blinked through the pain. Scrambling against the cardboard, she got back to her feet as Teddy rushed at her. She swung the knife at the kid's face and it scraped away her pale skin. Teddy laughed—actually laughed—like this was the most fun she'd ever had, and Shelley felt the wet cardboard under her back again. Teddy grabbed at the knife in her mother's hand, still surprisingly strong. The blade began to twist toward her now, and Shelley grabbed her wrist with her free hand, to push the blade away.

Fuck.

She was too strong. Searching for an alternative, Shelley looked around at the boxes. Something heavy had to be lying around.

Fucking comic books, really?

Piles and piles of plastic-wrapped comics spilled to the floor. Pushing against Teddy's strength, but feeling herself caving in, Shelley looked again. A figurine of some kind. It looked heavy. It would do.

Tick tick tick.

She let go of her wrist and reached, crying out when the blade sank into her shoulder. She grabbed the figurine, lifted it and smashed it against the side of Teddy's head. She fell off her mother, tearing the knife free as she did.

Sitting up and pressing against her wound, Shelley saw Teddy coming for her again, her eyes wild with rage and hatred and hunger. She crawled away, as fast as she could, stopping on the rug, untouched by the mucus.

This fucking thing.

She knew the faces would call for her, their silent screams vibrating through the fabric of existence. The impossible rug, a graveyard of all the souls stolen by the house. She elbowed one of the faces, the expression one of torture and terror. "I'm sorry," Shelley murmured through a heavy breath, thankful the rug—*The house's trophy*—was a safe space in this chaos.

She tried to stand, but felt hands on her feet.

Teddy.

"Shelley!" Sam called, finally pulling himself out of his stupor and his grief. He reached for Teddy's waist to restrain her, but the effort was half-hearted. The darkness still moved in him, and his actions were slow.

"Get out of here, Sam. While you can!" Shelley demanded, tightening her hand around the figurine and finally getting to her feet. The *tick tick tick* would soon be inside Sam again if he didn't get out of the house. Maybe even then, she didn't know.

"I can't just leave you…"

"This is between me and her now," Shelley said, and ordered them to leave once more.

Tick tick tick.

She saw Sam helping Corrigan to his feet, and the detective grabbing him by the collar with one hand while Patrick hung from his other arm. The guilt she felt for those men burned in her soul, and fed her desire to murder her offspring. Whatever fight the men had been having seemed over, and they carried Patrick through the house.

Good. Save yourselves.

Teddy lunged at her mother, and she dodged, swiping the knife away before it stabbed her again. She spun on the rug, conscious of the eternally damned she was stepping all over, but thankful for a reprieve from the mucus.

She pushed a box over and Teddy stumbled on it. Shelley seized the moment and grabbed the knife from the girl's hand.

"Why are you doing this, Teddy?" Shelley asked, her breaths coming thick and heavy. "Because a voice from the wall told you to?"

Shaking her head, Teddy looked between her mother and the knife, and back again. Her own chest heaved and she stood at an awkward angle, the missing arm affecting her balance.

"Or is it just because I'm a shitty mother?" Shelley continued.

Teddy began to look weak, but shifted her eyes toward Sam and the others. Scowling at her mother, she turned to follow them. Her footsteps were weak and unsteady, her strength waning. Even without blood, she was being hurt. The girl tried to act like she was fine, missing arm and all. But Shelley knew better; the expression on her face gave her away.

"Let them go," Shelley said, following her gaze, and throwing the figurine to get her daughter's attention.

Tick. Tick. Tick.

"Do you hear that?" Teddy asked, lifting her chin at the sound, and letting the rhythm sink into her. "That's Daddy. And he's saying he doesn't want me to let them go."

315

She stepped after them, and Shelley saw they were stopped. Realizing they might have been trapped by the mucus, she thought fast for a distraction. If Teddy reached them, even as weak as she was, she could kill them all.

The basement.

Shelley stormed to her daughter, the mucus still not sticking to her. She didn't think about why she was immune. Or why it didn't want her. Grabbing Teddy's arm, she spun her around and pushed her toward the basement door.

The girl steadied herself, moved to follow Sam again.

Shelley lifted the knife to Teddy's eyeline. "You want to kill someone, kill me."

Teddy giggled—a hollow sound. "I can't kill you."

Stepping closer, Shelley said, "What the fuck not?"

"Silly billy," she said. "You're my mom."

Shelley smiled, and Teddy paused for a moment. Even though she hated her daughter—wanted her to die in the pit she was conceived in—she felt a lightness in that moment. As the house quivered again and the *tick tick tick* traveled through her bones, Shelley felt a closeness to Teddy she'd never felt.

The girl hobbled to her, and Shelley closed the gap. "I am your mom, aren't I," she said.

Teddy's smile was different. She smiled with her eyes.

"Can we just put this all behind us, and go home?" Shelley asked. "So I can look after you?"

"You won't chain me up anymore?" Teddy asked.

Wrapping her arms around her daughter, Shelley kissed the top of her head. "No, sweetie. I won't."

They embraced for a moment, even as the *tick tick tick* boomed again and the mucus lapped at their feet.

"Just one more thing," Shelley said softly. Teddy met her gaze, still smiling, and Shelley plunged the knife into Teddy's stomach. "There's gotta be blood in there somewhere," she said. "And I'm gonna find it!"

Smiling, Shelley squeezed Teddy tight and dragged her, kicking and screaming, toward the basement door.

To where this all started.

Flinging her daughter inside, she crashed down the stairs into the darkness.

"You lied to me, Mommy!" Teddy screamed from the basement floor. "Silly. BILLY!"

"Yeah well," Shelley said with a shrug, "it got you where I wanted you."

At the top of the stairs, Shelley stamped at the creaky steps. Testing them. A few of them were broken already. She was sure with the right amount of pressure she could finish the job. Then neither of them would leave this place.

Teddy watched her stamp again and again. "What are you doing?"

Ignoring her, Shelley continued, until she heard the top step splinter and crack. Jumping on it now, she felt her foot crash through the wood. The step was gone.

Next one.

"What are you doing?" Teddy asked again. "How will we get out?"

"We aren't leaving this place," Shelley said as she crashed through the next step. "Silly billy."

"Daddy won't let you do this." Teddy was desperate now, and Shelley smiled.

She loved Teddy's scared voice.

Third step, gone. Fourth. Fifth. There was no way up now. Shelley turned back to the door, a crack of light seeping into the basement. Mucus dripped over the threshold, spilling into the basement, and Shelley saw the walls around her begin to glow.

The gray glow, like at her own house.

Through the darkness, tendrils rose from the giant hole. The entrance to the abyss, where Teddy was conceived. Her skin crawled at the sight, but she moved down the remaining steps anyway.

Toward her daughter.

Toward the darkness.

Toward the void.

Chapter 27

The tendrils, now that she could see them in the light, were roots. Thick, woody, covered in layers of dirt and grime from inside the Earth.

Teddy was by her side, and clutched at her mother's hand, smiling. The violence between them hushed for the moment as they watched the roots ascend from the depths of the planet. From somewhere unknown—untouched—by humankind.

"Hi Daddy," Teddy whispered, and shed a tear.

Shelley let the girl hold her hand, stilled by the vision before her. They snaked through the air, the way seaweed does during the ebb and flow of the tide. Tickling at the basement ceiling, feeling their way around the edges and crevices.

Exploring.

"He wants to be here," Teddy said. "He wants to be like me."

"What does that mean?" Shelley whispered, her breath catching.

Teddy glanced at her mother, then back at the roots. "He wants to walk among the skinnies."

"Why doesn't he?"

Teddy shrugged, and they fell into silence.

In the gray glow and the silence—the *tick tick tick* a quiet thrumming in her head—Shelley thought back to the moment those roots had taken her. What they did to her in the darkness. What the *darkness* had done to her.

She trembled at the memory, and clutched the knife tight in her hand. Whatever it was doing, searching the walls and the ceiling for something, Shelley didn't like it. She stared, unblinking, at the roots, watching them taste the air and snake their way through the basement.

Tick.

Her time was coming to an end, one way or another.

Tick.

She could sense the darkness tasting for her. Getting her scent.

Tick.

And she wouldn't let it take her again.

Shoving Teddy's hand away, she stormed to the roots, knife poised, and swiped. The roots reacted to her presence, to her violence, and the tips of the roots turned to face her. Like snakeheads without eyes. Pointed and sharp.

Swallowing hard, Shelley swiped again.

"Don't hurt him!" Teddy said, and pulled at Shelley's shoulder.

"I won't let it take me again," Shelley replied, and turned the knife on Teddy once more. "Do you know you come from inside there?"

Teddy looked into the void.

"Do you know what you are?" Shelley spat.

She raised the knife, and the roots shot toward her, wrapping around her arms and waist and neck. Tight, but not harming her—not yet.

"Mommy," Teddy said. "It doesn't have to be this way. We can be a family."

Shelley laughed, the sound broken and hoarse with the root tight around her neck. "We've never been a family."

Tick.

"Well, it's never too late." Teddy walked to the edge of the hole and peered in.

Tick.

"It's time to go home," she said. "Time to rest."

Tick.

And vanished into the void.

As Teddy disappeared into the darkness, Shelley gasped, tears dripping from her eyes despite herself. She hated that kid so much, hated what she stood for, hated how she'd been conceived. Yet, as she was consumed by the abyss, Shelley fell into a deep sadness.

The roots around her body tightened and squeezed, the *tick tick tick* coming louder and faster now. Covering her face and eyes, enveloping Shelley into nothingness, she felt herself pulled down into the hole after her daughter.

Time to rest.

Chapter 28

"Get away from him!" Corrigan grabbed Sam by the scruff of his collar, spit flinging from his angry mouth as he yelled.

"I'm sorry." Sam wept. "I'm so sorry."

"Fuck you and fuck your sorries." Corrigan shook Sam hard. "Patrick is dead!"

Just then, Patrick coughed. It was weak and soft—a choked whisper—but the sound meant he was alive.

Sam and Corrigan exchanged glances and the detective let go of his collar to focus on Patrick. "Hey." His voice was low and sweet. "Patty, you with me?"

Patrick suddenly breathed in short, gurgled bursts.

Sam looked back to see Shelley and Teddy in the throes of their fight, Shelley attacking the inhuman child with a knife. She'd yelled at them to get out of there, and instead they had been arguing as the mucus rose to their knees.

"Come on," Sam said, and guided Corrigan to the hallway.

As they waded through the mucus, Sam heard the *tick tick tick*. He stopped. Turned.

The door.

It was shimmering, like a beacon, telling Sam to go inside. It would be dry and warm and he'd be safe in there. They'd all be safe in there.

No. We have to go.

The chamber was home. It was the only home he'd ever truly had. It kept him safe and—

NO!

He knew it was a lie. Even if time stopped in there and his worries and cares melted into nothing. Even if the *tick tick tick* felt like home, felt like it belonged to him.

This is what Shelley warned me about.

She'd said the ticking would get inside him. He knew she was right, but as he stepped through the mucus again, realizing he wasn't sinking like Corrigan and Patrick, something else came to him.

Knowledge, from somewhere deep in his veins.

I belong here.

The voice had said that before. The voice had lied to him.

Had it?

Patrick wheezed again, spluttering blood and choking. He was running out of time. Corrigan waded him through the mucus—now at their thighs—and Sam looked at his friend. The only thing he had left in the whole world.

His mom was gone.

Danny was gone.

His dad—*Oh god, what did I do?*—was gone.

Patrick was all that was left. Their friendship had saved him so many times, and he'd let the darkness in. He'd let the darkness tear skin and bone from his best friend, the only person he loved.

And now he was dying.

Gurgling his last breaths.

What if...

With the ticking rushing through his body, but somehow feeling in control of it, Sam put a hand on the detective's shoulder. "Wait."

"There's no time," Corrigan dismissed him and kept going, the mucus sucking at his upper thighs.

"I know you don't trust me," Sam said, forcing the detective to stop, "especially after...this." He motioned to Patrick's wounds and his wheezing breaths. "But we both love Patrick. And I can save him."

"Sam, we'll deal with what you've done later." Corrigan kept forging ahead, even though they all knew the front door wouldn't budge, and his feet were sinking further and further into the nothingness beyond the floorboards. "Right now, I have to get Patrick to a hospital."

Tick tick tick.

Tick tick tick.

Time was running out. Sam felt it. He saw it. The mucus was rising, the floorboards were all but soggy cardboard now. He wished circumstances were different, that he and Patrick and Corrigan could have been meeting for the first time at a café. Laughing and eating and talking about their futures.

Watching Corrigan fight until the end, he wished he and Patrick could live a long life together.

Tick tick tick.

Moving to an unpacked box—"Laundry"—Sam opened the lid. He pulled out his iron, and paused for a moment. He had to save his friend. He had to try and undo what he'd done.

Behind Corrigan now, he whispered, "I'm sorry," and brought the metal of the iron down on the detective's head. "I have to do this."

He was down, splashing around the mucus, desperate to keep hold of Patrick. His grip loosened as Sam attacked again—*I'm sorry, I'm sorry, I'm sorry!*—and the detective stopped moving.

Floating face down in the mucus.

Sam's heart ached at what he'd done, just one more crime for the list. He raced to Patrick, lifted him from the mucus, now waist high. He cradled Patrick in both arms, carried him back through the house.

Tick. Tick. Tick.

The door would be there, Sam knew it. It would be there, and it would lead to the chamber as it always did. Reaching the door, he kicked it open, a gush of mucus spilling into the space. He dropped to his knees, pushed Patrick inside the tunnel, and followed, shutting the door behind him. The mucus had soaked into the tunnel walls, the fleshy pinkish hue began to collapse around him. Folding in on him and Patrick as Sam pushed them through the tunnel.

A womb.

He could feel the warmth of the wall as it hugged him, pushing him through the canal towards the chamber.

Tick.

The closer he got, the more at home he felt, and the greater the sense that Patrick was going to be okay. He heard the faint sounds of the banging at the door—Corrigan yelling to let him in—and kept going. He couldn't stop to think about the detective now. Patrick needed him. Patrick was alive and the only way he could stay that way was in the chamber.

Pushing into the chamber, Sam heaved Patrick in his arms and sat by the nearest wall, facing the clock. Cradling his friend, rocking back and forth, he gave a soft, "Ssshhh-

327

hh," and shed a tear. The banging was overlayed with the *tick, tick, tick*. Gentle now. Like a hum, vibrating through his veins with a comforting buzz.

"You're going to be okay, Patrick," Sam whispered, and the banging faded underneath the *tick tick tick* until that was all he could hear. "You're going to live."

And he rocked and rocked, knowing that time was irrelevant in this place, but staring into the clock face anyway. He breathed a sigh of relief as Patrick choked out another breath.

"It's just us now," he said, and let the time on the clock sink into him. "Just the three of us."

Chapter 29

"You were in a coma for three days," the nurse said, as he fiddled with some buttons on the EKG machine.

Jimmy stared at the nurse, unable to do much else. Her body was wrapped in bandages, limbs plastered in place to set and heal. A doctor had delivered the news to her upon her first waking—save for one hand, her neck, and her spine, everything was broken. Ribs. Arms. Legs. Even some bones she didn't know she had were splintered. Had been jutting from her skin when she'd arrived.

She didn't remember how she got the hospital, only that Corrigan had carried her out of that house.

That house.

It had tried to kill them both. The roots in the basement, whatever they had been attached to. Jimmy led a tear slide down her cheek as they considered the monstrosity that had taken Pete. Considered the mucus leaking from the walls and the ceiling.

"It might not seem it at the moment"—the nurse continued—"but you are really lucky."

"Where—"

"You'll be drifting in and out for a while," the nurse said. "Save your questions for later."

"How did I get here?" Jimmy managed a defiant smile, despite her scratchy and dry throat.

The nurse took a seat next to the bed and yawned. Rubbing his eyes, and checking the time, he said, "Ambulance, I think. I wasn't working when you came in, sorry, hon."

Jimmy fell into silence, her mind fuzzy and fading. Her eyelids began to flutter, and she felt the world vanish around her. Felt the mucus around her, pushing inside her mouth and pores, the roots ripping her apart—

She jolted awake, breathing hard, expecting to be back in that basement. The *beep beep beep* of the EKG comforted her, told her she was out of that nightmare. That even with her entire body smashed and crippled—*You'll need a lot, and I mean a lot, of physio*, the doctor had said—she was safe.

Alive.

That was more than she could say for Pete.

"We tried to contact your next of kin." The nurse broke her train of thought, and her foggy mind landed in the present once more. "Nobody could get through, unfortunately."

"Pete died," Jimmy whispered, the words sounded foreign and made up.

"Oh, hon, I'm so sorry," the nurse said. He fiddled with her EKG again, and then retreated, pulling her privacy curtain around and mumbling that she needed rest.

Amazed at how little privacy the curtain afforded, Jimmy resisted the urge to sleep. Every time she closed her eyes, she was back in that house. She was back in that basement, watching Pete disappear into nothingness. Even blinking gave flashes of her friend, who she'd never get to hug again, and never get to make fun of or play video games with. Who would never be able to console her when another girlfriend split. Who she'd never protect and defend.

"I'm sorry, Pete," she muttered, and wished she could wipe at her own tears.

"Who's Pete?" a familiar female voice asked.

Flicking her eyes across the small, cordoned hospital space, Jimmy frowned. "What are you doing here?"

"I..." The woman cleared her throat. "The hospital rang, they still had my number on file. I didn't know if you'd want to see me."

Jimmy choked out a hollow, joyless laugh. "Well, you've been now. You did the 'parent' thing, so"—she sighed long and hard—"you're off the hook."

The woman walked slowly around the bed, taking in Jimmy's injuries and the pain written on her face. Sat on the seat next to the bed. "I'd like to stay…if you want…"

"Mom," Jimmy said, shedding a tear, "you haven't tried to see me in years. I don't need pity."

"Your father and I…" she trailed off as a man pushed the curtain aside to slip into the small space.

"Oh," he said with a shy smile, "you're awake."

Jimmy looked between her mother and father, never feeling so vulnerable in her life. After years of abandonment and hurt and unanswered questions, they showed up now, at the worst moment in her life, and expected—

"Why are you here?" Jimmy asked, holding back tears with as much strength as she had. *Don't let them see you cry. Not again.*

Her father came around the side of the bed and stood next to where her mother sat. He rested a gentle hand on her cheek, caressing it, and Jimmy recoiled.

"Jimmy," he said softly. "We've been trying to get in touch with you. We didn't know where you were."

"Bullshit." She spat. "When I came out as trans you fucking threw me out!"

332

He nodded, and her mother clasped a hand over her own face, ashamed.

"We did," her father said. "And we can never make up for that. It was…vile. It was… We didn't understand."

"We love you, sweet girl," her mother whispered, and rubbed at a tiny spot on Jimmy's body not covered in bandages and plaster.

Jimmy stared at them. Read their faces. She opened her mouth to tell them to fuck off and never come back, but then Pete's voice started in her head again.

Forgiveness starts with you.

He was right, she knew he was right. Whether they were here out of pity or some sense of responsibility—or something else entirely—Pete would have said it didn't matter. He would have said, "Hey, they're here. It's a start."

Taking a long, steady breath, and thinking her decision-making skills were impaired by the heavy drugs, she said, "Pete would want me to say you can stay. He'd want me to make an effort."

Her mother looked at her and gave a sad smile. "Who's Pete, honey?"

Jimmy gave a sad smile. "Pete was my friend. Pete was the best…"

The sound of her own beating heart woke her, and Shelley sat up, holding her head. She felt like she was spinning, unsteady, and groggy. Blinking through the sensation, she felt the pain in her shoulder throb, and remembered where she'd been before. Remembered how the darkness had stolen her again, how Teddy had willingly jumped into the void, calling it home.

As the pounding in her head stabilized and settled, Shelley looked around. Wherever she was, it was dark. But she felt something underneath here, which meant she wasn't floating in an endless void. No roots coming for her in the darkness.

Breathing a sigh of relief, she squinted through the dark. Stood, and tried to walk.

"What the hell?" She looked down at her ankle.

Shackled. Again.

You belong to me.

The silence of the room—*No, I'm home. I'm in my own basement*—was disrupted by the glow of the walls. That dull, gray glow that Shelley had come to hate so much. It was never just the glow. It came with that voice.

You belong to me.

The chain around her ankle was tighter than before. Had less leeway. She could walk three steps in any direction before the chain pulled at her. At her feet, the mattress. The same one she'd made Teddy live on for months at a time, and never cleaned or washed or bothered to care for.

The teddy bear sat on the mattress, staring at her through its glass eyes. Shelley wondered if she could pry the glass out and use it as a weapon in some way. Maybe smash the small glass beads and use the shards to—

Don't even try it.

Shelley looked up from the shit-stained mattress, gazed at the glowing concrete wall.

"Why am I here?" Shelley asked, her body trembling and her mind racing. She pulled at the chain again, even though she knew it was useless.

No answer came.

"Come on, you fucking asshole," Shelley cried. "Why am I here? What do you want?"

The wall glowed brighter, a pinkish hue growing in the center. A shadow moved behind it, and Shelley stepped back—three steps, the maximum of her new world.

"What is that?" she asked.

Look closer.

She focused on the pink center as it glowed brighter, the shadow shifting into a fetal position.

Not a shadow.

The voice was right. It was solid. Something captured inside the basement wall. The walls began to expand and contract, slow and steady with a *thump thump*. The

335

figure inside the wall moved again, a hand pressing against the pink. The wall moved around the hand like putty, and Shelley understood.

"Teddy?"

Your daughter.

"It's...a womb."

The wall thumped and thumped and the gray glow was so bright that Shelley covered her eyes. Slowly taking her hands away from her face, Shelley stared through the light, at her daughter swimming in an unnatural womb in the wall.

"What do you want from me?"

She is your daughter.

"I know that," she said, "but what do you want from me?"

You will love her.

Shelley laughed. "You can't *order* someone into love."

The wall thumped again—expand, contract—and Shelley felt the air in the basement begin to thin out, and disappear. A warning. A reminder. She was in His domain. Whoever *He* was. Still, what was being asked was impossible.

"I can't just start to love something because you tell me to." Shelley insisted.

Love her. Or stay here.

"Just kill me," she said.

Love her. Or stay here.

"I can't—"

You. Are. Her. Mother.

Shelley paused at that. There was no talking her way out of this. If she didn't want to stay chained up forever, with a walking distance of three steps, she'd have to phone it in.

"Okay." She nodded. "I'll do it. But I have a question for you."

Expand. Contract. *Go ahead.*

"Who are you?"

The walls glowed brighter, an intense gray light drowning Shelley's vision until she saw nothing but black. She held her head as the *thump thump thump* of the wall moved through her brain. Giving her the knowledge she sought.

"No." Shelley wept, wishing she could forget. Wishing she had never asked, for the truth was too horrible. "No!"

She fell to the mattress, hugged her knees.

And she wept.

Chapter 30

One Year Later

Patrick had once shown him a film about two lovers separated by eons of time. They had fought to be together through centuries of displacement—never sharing the same space or time—until one day, inexplicably, time had shattered.

The lovers had destroyed time.

The lovers were together.

Corrigan watched that film every day as he waited. One eye on the television, the other on the space where the door would shimmer into existence.

After Sam stole Patrick into that room, he'd banged and banged and shot at the door. It would never open for him. He'd begged and pleaded with the house, with whatever was inside the house, to let Patrick go. To let him live. He'd promised he would do anything if Patrick could just live.

As the words had left his mouth, the mucus dissipated into the floorboards. The walls stopped leaking, and he'd been thrust into silence. Pulling at the door handle one more time, Corrigan had thought it might open.

Instead, it disappeared.

Patrick was gone.

He'd stayed in that spot for hours, staring and crying, until he realized there was nobody else in the house. The basement stairs were destroyed. He'd called for Shelley but had received no answer. Shelley and that kid were gone.

Nothing in that house made sense.

In the months that followed, Corrigan had Sam's things moved into storage, and his own things brought in. The house was his now, at least until Patrick emerged from that shimmering door. And he would.

Patrick would come back. He had to come back. Sam was his best friend, there was no way he'd keep him in that room for long. Just until Patrick was healed up. He waited, day and night, one eye always on the spot where the door should be. He stopped going to work, in case he missed its return. In case it showed up only for a second or two. He had to be there when it did.

Even without ever seeing it, Corrigan believed it would return. He had to believe that, for the alternative was unbearable. After living in the house for a few months, he'd started getting the GPS pings.

UNKNOWN.

At first he ignored the notifications.

They came again. The same coordinates.

The first time he'd plugged the coordinates into his car, Corrigan was led to a park in the dead of night. Searching the grounds, he'd found a woman lying on her side by the swing set. He'd lifted her up to make sure she was okay, but the tracks in her arms and the empty needles strewn around her told him she was never going to be okay again.

"Why am I here?" he'd asked into the night.

His phone pinged again. The coordinates were his home, and the message was clear. Bring her back. He remembered the way they'd all been sinking into the floors, the way the mucus was like saliva, hungry to devour them.

And that's what it had done with the woman.

Corrigan lost count of how many people he'd fed to the house, and each time he watched them sink into the floor, he lost a bit of himself. Yet, he kept going. Because somewhere inside, he thought it was the only way he'd see Patrick again.

Now, a year later, he was still waiting.

Sinking into the couch and pulling out his laptop, he searched once more the person he'd been researching since the day Patrick was stolen from him. The name that had been ringing in his head. The name Patrick had given him that day at the police station.

Morris Hart.

The man who built the house he now lived in, and who'd had one daughter before he died. The records he could find were among the strangest things he'd ever seen, including one scanned copy of a letter Hart had written after being retrieved from the Kola Well in 1979. It had been posted in a subreddit years earlier—Corrigan only found it by chance, doom scrolling through the internet for months on end.

The person who'd posted it was convinced Hart had unlocked a gateway, or awoken something deep in the Earth. Their post had links to all sorts of websites on the dark web, a community of people talking about the Kola Well and the Earth itself as a being, with a consciousness.

They'd posted the links, and the letter, in the hopes that someone would know who it was intended for. That they might have some answers. Corrigan read the letter again, studying each word.

Dearest Michelle,

I was in the darkness for the longest time. It devoured me, ripped me apart, and put me back together again. But I am something else now. I can't explain it. I just feel different. I was in there for an eternity, I watched you grow. I watched you and your mother.
And I saw her die.

*I wish I knew that telling you this would do
any good. I wish I could stop what is going to
happen to you. But I know in my heart that it's
happened already. Time is a…strange mistress.
I learned that down there, in that giant hole in
the ground.*

*There are many of these around the world. I
built a house on top of one to hide the evil. I fear
it didn't work. But I will return there, anyway, and make sure nobody else suffers the way
I have.*

*You will suffer, too. Have suffered. Will
suffer again.*

*I've seen what the void will do to you. And I
know that it's my fault.*

It's all my fault, and I'm sorry.

*Much love,
Grandpa*

Corrigan picked up the phone and pressed on one of
his contacts. It rang.

And rang.

"You have reached the voicemail—"

He hung up. Tried again.

On the fourth ring, he heard the line connect.

"Hi…" The voice was low.

"Is your name Michelle?" Corrigan asked.

Silence.

"You there?"

"I'm here," the voice replied.

"Well?" Corrigan pushed.

A pause. "Yeah. It is. I haven't heard that name for a long time, though. Not since my mom…"

"Did you know?" he asked.

Another pause.

"Shelley," Corrigan said. "Did you know you were related to the guy who built this house?"

"I…have to go."

The line went dead and Corrigan rubbed at his beard. Remembered the way Patrick would run his hands through it, the way he'd smile and nuzzle their noses together. Looking back to the space by the kitchen, where the shimmering door should be, Corrigan took a deep breath.

He moved to the kitchen island and pulled out a bar stool. "I'm here, Patrick," he said. "I'll always be here."

Planting himself on the stool, he faced the wall.

And waited.

Epilogue

"It's got really good bones," Shelley said, flashing a smile. She wondered what trophy this house kept. It was something different in each one. Maybe another rug. *Nah.*

The couple exchanged a glance as they walked through the house, the husband wiping an index finger through the thick layer of grime.

"That'll all be cleaned up before you move in." Shelley waved a dismissive hand. "Have a look at the bathrooms, though."

She led them up a set of stairs, commenting how the creaking was "old charm" and "character", and showed them the renovated main bathroom.

"Oh, honey." The wife gasped. "This is nice."

"Hmmm," he replied, unconvinced.

Shelley looked them up and down, ignoring the now-constant voice in her head saying, *I want them*, and asked, "Do you have kids?"

The wife smiled and nodded. "Two. Rob and Arnold. Five and seven."

"Awww, what a fun age," Shelley said. "My daughter—Teddy—she's almost nine. And already so grown up." *I love her, I love her, I love her.*

She made sure to smile when she mentioned Teddy. She was being watched. Even if the sight of her crawling out of the basement wall, fully formed and healed, made her wretch. Even if her "daughter" had been reborn with her own mother's mission. To dig. Teddy hadn't said what for, but Shelley's new role as "loving mother" meant she was tasked with driving her around town.

"I'll be fine," Teddy had said. "I just need my shovel. You should leave."

Shelley had obliged then, and would again in the future. Since that day, Shelley had sensed a shift in the ground beneath her feet. A shift that told her something was coming.

I want them.

The voice nagged at her, breaking her concentration, and she thought hard about her next move. She could tell the wife was keen, and even though the husband wasn't, Shelley was sure she could seal the deal. Get the voice out of her head for a few seconds.

"The backyard is nice," Shelley said. "Lots of room for the kids. And the old tree would make for an amazing treehouse."

"Old tree?" The husband raised an eyebrow.

Shelley smiled, pointed out the bathroom window.

"How long has it been there? Is it safe?" the husband asked, craning his neck to get a better view. "I'd hate for a branch to fall on the house."

"Oh, I wouldn't worry about that," Shelley said. "The tree is as old as the Earth itself, I think. It's always been there. We had it inspected recently, actually, before putting the house on the market. It's very sturdy."

Give them to me.

"Can we think about it?" the wife asked, scrunching her nose in a "gee, this is a big decision" kind of way. It was all an act, part of the game. Shelley was better at it.

Shelley nodded. "Sure. I can't promise it'll be here when you've decided, though. I have another couple very interested." *Maybe it's the old chest I found in the attic. That'd make a nice trophy.* She shuddered, and then smiled again.

The husband and wife exchanged glances, and the husband bowed his head. The wife clapped her hands and squealed. They began the paperwork for the rental, and started talking about where the furniture would go.

Internally, Shelley was picturing them hanging from that tree. Them, and their kids. A pet dog, too, if they had one. The knowledge annoyed her, but mostly because she'd be back in a week or so to collect their bodies.

"You'll be really happy here," she said, and watched them sign their lives away.

Sam listened to the chokes and the wheezes, and rocked Patrick back and forth. He'd get better soon. He just needed time. Looking at the clock, he knew they had as much time as they wanted. As long as it took for Patrick's wounds to heal.

As long as it takes.

Sam had a sense of time passing, but it was more an instinctual knowing than an experience. He knew time was passing outside, in the real world. Just as he *knew* Corrigan was out there, waiting for them. But he didn't feel time passing anymore. It didn't matter.

"Sam?" Patrick looked up at him. "How long have we been here?"

Smiling down at his friend, Sam said, "How you feeling, buddy?"

"How long, Sam?" His friend's voice was shallow.

Sam took his phone from his pocket. He tapped the screen and the phone lit up. It still had battery, but no signal.

He didn't need a signal, the only person he wanted to talk to was right here with him.

The screen gave Sam the information Patrick wanted. July 14, 2024.

A whole year. "Not long," he said, and put his phone away. It was then he understood time didn't stop here. It simply didn't exist.

"I can't stay here anymore." Patrick wheezed. "I'm in so much pain."

Sam tightened his grip around his friend. "You'll get better. And we'll stay right here, together, until you do."

The wounds on Patrick's back still bled. His spinal column still jutted from his back from where he and Teddy had torn into him. His face was still pale. Sam looked at his friend, pressed a gentle hand to the wounds to ease the bleeding, and rocked back and forth again.

"It'll be okay, Pat," he whispered. "We can stay here forever if we need to."

"Why are you doing this to me?" Patrick gurgled.

"Because I love you, Patrick."

"Then let me die."

Sam shook his head. "I can't do that. I can't lose anyone else."

He hugged Patrick tight, and stared at the clock. It had predicted when everyone he loved would die. It had been wrong once. He could cheat it again. He could stay here with

Patrick forever, and Patrick would live. They'd be frozen in time, just the two of them, and Patrick's death of 11:58 would never have to happen.

Now, as he stared at the clock, it showed a different time. Sam smiled, knowing there was nobody else to take from him, nobody else he cared about. That could only mean one thing. The time it read now—12:00—was for one person.

It was for him.

The End

About the Author

David-Jack Fletcher is an award-winning Australian horror author, specializing in LGBTQI+ fiction. He dabbles in comedy-horror and dark fiction, but his true love is body horror. He is the author of the #1 International Amazon best-seller, *The Haunting of Harry Peck*, and has appeared in several anthologies across the US, Canada, and the UK.

His most recent novel, *Raven's Creek*, won the 2023 Bookstagram Award in the category of LGBTQ+ Novel of the Year. It was also a #1 Amazon bestseller, and was nominated for a 2023 Splatterpunk Award.

David-Jack is working on his next novel, *Wires in the Gut*, which centers on a family in the Southern Tasmania who realize their house is host to an ancient evil. He will also be releasing a short story collection in 2024.

He is the co-founder of Slashic Horror Press, which began as a way to increase the diverse, queer voices in horror. David-Jack is also a qualified editor, operating a small online business, Chainsaw Editing, where he specializes in copyediting and developmental editing for horror/thriller, dark fiction, mystery/suspense, and the occasional YA, or historical romance.

When not writing and editing, David-Jack can be found on the couch with a book, cuddling his dogs and his husbear.

Acknowledgments

As with all my work, I have some people to thank. My husband, Paul, is always by my side, urging me along when I think I've written a pile of utter crap. His unfaltering belief in me, and what I'm doing—with my writing and with Slashic Horror Press—literally gets me up in the morning.

My business partner and dear friend, Lee, has a lot to do with why I still write, and his enthusiasm for the grotesque and disgusting in my work makes me so happy! His eagerness to read my work is unmatched, and for that I am forever grateful.

A massive thank you to the beta readers—particularly Alexa K Moon—and my ARC readers and reviewers, for taking the time to provide honest, critical, and generous feedback. I workshopped an early version of this—when it was going to be a short story, and then again when it was going to be a novella—and received such incredible feedback that it propelled me to continue when I wanted to give up.

Without the advice and encouragement of so many people, none of my work would exist, and it certainly wouldn't be what it is today.

I am, indeed, a lucky man.